MER

Tome 1

JADE M. PHILLIPS

Kith Books

MER

A Kith Book
Published by
Kith Books
Tucson, AZ

www.jademphillips.com
MER on facebook
www.facebook.com/merbook1
Follow Jade on twitter here
https://twitter.com/JadeMPhillips
Cover art by Paul Beeley
http://www.create-imaginations.com
Map by Juan C. Heinrich
http://www.facebook.com/JuanCHeinrih
Author photo by Lance Lundy
http://www.facebook.com/lance.lundy.9
Formatting by Jason G. Anderson
http://www.jasonga.com

This book is for Abigail and Brandon. May you have the greatest gifts bestowed upon you; a mother's love, and a lifetime full of magical adventures.

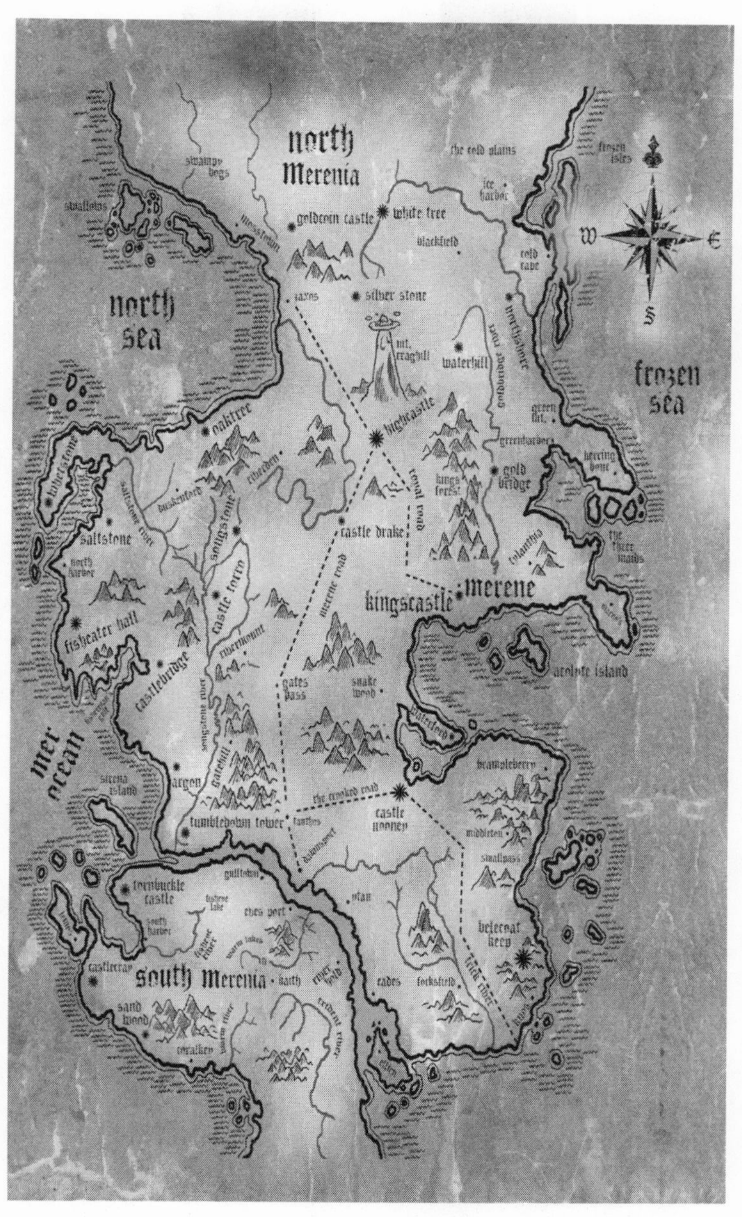
north Merenia
the cold plains
frozen isles
swampy bogs
swallows
goldcoin castle
white tree
ice harbor
blackfield
cold cape
W
E
S
saxos
silver stone
north sea
mt. craghill
waterhill
goldbridge river
frozen sea
green hill
oaktree
highcastle
greenharbor
herring house
gold bridge
kings forest
royal road
saltstone
saltstone river
songstone
castle drake
north harbor
the three maids
castle torro
merene road
kingscastle
merene
fisheater hall
castlebridge
rivermount
acolyte island
gates pass
snake wood
mer ocean
songstone river
waterford
bramble berry
sirena island
argon
the crooked road
tumbledown tower
castle hooney
middleton
smallpass
gulltown
tornbuckle castle
ches port
south harbor
warm lakes
castlecray
south Merenia
cades
forksfield
sand wood
trident river

"When need is great and balance in peril, a celestial being will be brought forth from sleep. The true born savior far from birth will rise from the shadows, waves they will keep."

—The Prophecy

FISHERMAN

The fisherman inhaled deeply, breathing in the fresh pre-dawn air. “Haaaaahhhmm,” he yawned loudly as he exhaled and reached his arms out to his sides, stretching the sore and tight muscles caused by the cramped night’s sleep. He had shared a room below deck with the other five crew members, and as his back agreed, it hadn’t been the most pleasant of experiences.

It was their third day out in the deep water, a short ways out from the lively fishing village of North Harbor. Their catch had not been as abundant as it should have been, due to the early and unexpected summer storms, and if they were to get back to the village before the Beltane Festivities, they’d have to make up for their lack of fishing today.

The sun was just cresting over the horizon making the thick morning fog glow luminously with subtle pinks and oranges. The air was crisp and cool, and the mist touched the crewmens' faces like the cold fingers of a tavern girl. Even in the near darkness the outline of the land mass, which was the large town of North Harbor, could be seen off in the distance, nestled cozily in the Bay. The fishing cog rocked softly as the fisherman heard the approach of another boat, sounds of sails flapping, and looked to see tiny dots of light through the dark muddled fog up ahead. After a few moments, the hazy outline of the large boat became clearer and the tiny dots of light sharpened into hanging lanterns, swinging merrily and warmly lighting the large figure of the boat's captain.

"Mornin'!" yelled the captain as the vessel came in close proximity.

One of the crew members wrinkled his thin face and whispered, "Here comes that crazy Captain Longship."

The fisherman yelled back, "And what a fine one it is at that!" The other vessel passed swiftly as though floating across the mist.

The large captain shouted in return, "Keep yer eyes peeled for Giganta! Wouldn't want her sneaking up on ye now."

Captain Longship gave a warm and hearty laugh that echoed over the water. His voice faded as the sound of the sails grew quiet and the merchent vessel disappeared into the mist.

Giganta was an old legend passed down from father to son through many generations past. It was said that Giganta was the greatest fish ever to be seen, as long as a horse cart and as wide as an ox, with golden scales that glittered in the sun. As it was told, whoever might catch the fish would be granted life's greatest treasure; as to what that treasure might be, the fishermen didn't know. But many a man was frightened of the stories that told of the great fish swallowing humans and boats whole.

"Wouldn't that just be our luck. Giganta would capture us before we could capture her," the fisherman murmured under his breath as he stared into the fog.

"Aye, that she would, Higgins," spoke the oldest crew member. Higgins snapped out of his trance and began to grab the lines.

As the fishermen worked, they commenced to talk of the strange Captain Longship, the taller one saying, "I've heard tell that he used to be the most vicious pirate of Mer Ocean, lashing and torturing any poor sod he came across."

The oldest crew member chimed in, "Nah, he's no pirate. He's a sorcerer, me old mum used to say. He can conjure up all sorts of magic that'll turn this ship upside down."

All of the men started talking at once, putting out their own opinion of the mysterious Captain Longship.

"That's enough bantering, ladies," said Higgins, the unspoken leader of the cog, "You all sound like washerwomen on laundry day!" The crew looked sheepish, hanging their heads.

Brushing off the childish behavior, Higgins proceeded, "I think we should set sail a bit more south. The sea hasn't given us a bit of luck here. Pull in the nets and hoist the main mast." Higgins scratched his scruffy black beard as he gazed south toward the open sea.

Just then the fishing cog lurched forward abruptly. The men stumbled to catch their footing. They all stood stock still, and searched each other's faces questioningly for a hint of explanation. Again the boat suddenly jumped, causing the men to lose their balance.

"The net!" yelled the thin man as he looked over into the water. The group rushed to where he was, peering over the edge.

"We've caught something! It's a big one!" cried the crew members as the boat began to move slowly and steadily across the sunrise-colored water.

"Whatever it is," shouted Higgins, "It's mighty strong. It's actually pulling us!"

"Jefferson! Duncy! Get the spears!" Higgins grabbed the net to try to steady the sea creature. A streak of shiny scales could be seen, as their catch struggled to free itself. A loud ripping and popping sound could be heard. "It's ripping the net!"

In a flash, the creature emerged from the water, free of the net, and in a blur, a large fish tail smacked the water as it dove back in, creating a large splash that hit the men square in the face.

Higgins was caught off guard by the splash and wiped his eyes with the back of his sleeve. He was suddenly aware that the boat was swiftly moving again, faster than before. *The damned thing is pulling us again,* the fisherman thought.

"The tip of its fin is caught in the net!" cried Duncy as he ran to the front deck with his spear. The whole group was now at the head of the boat, gripping and pulling at the net, while the large fish swam desperately, tugging the small cog behind it. Faster and faster they went, almost as if the boat itself was alive and swimming.

Higgins pulled with all of his might at the wavering fish net and yelled, "Duncy! Spear the beast!"

Duncy wobbled and wavered, his arm propped in preparation. "I can't get a clear view of it. It keeps swerving back and forth like a crazed dolphin!"

"*Just do it!*" spouted Higgins over the chaotic noise of shouting fishermen and rushing water. Duncy stretched back his hand and steadied the weapon as much as was possible, and threw the spear straight and true directly at the fish net. The boat slowed and the net loosened its slack in the men's grip. For a moment they dared not breathe in the tension-filled silence.

Suddenly with a splash, the broken spear came shooting up out of the water, followed by a second piece; the splintered shaft launched through the air. *What the bloody heck kinda' fish is this?*

The little fishing cog began to build up speed again.

"What in the…?" The thin man's words were cut off by Jefferson bursting through with another spear.

"Out of the way!" The young and strong fisherman thrust the spear so hard into the water that he almost toppled over with it until another crew member caught him by the back of his shirt. The speed of the boat slowed, and again the net slackened in the crew's hands. They all stopped to catch their breath.

Gasping for air, Jefferson said, "Look!"

The great fish floated up sideways towards the surface of the water, golden scales glittering in the now vibrant sunlight. The men finally got a good look at it and stared in awe. The huge fish was a bit longer than the tallest man and half as wide.

Higgins wiped the perspiration off of his forehead with the back of his hand and let out a big sigh of relief. "Whew! Now that's what I call fishin'! Everyone to the net, let's pull this monster in."

The men gathered and grabbed a part of the fish net and hooted and hollered, laughing about their triumph, as they worked to hoist their catch over the edge of the boat and on deck. They spoke of how everyone would applaud them at the Beltane Festival when they presented their prize.

"That is the biggest fish I ever seen," the old fisherman said as he struggled with the net.

Jefferson had a look of pride on his broad face while he pulled on the net with all of his strength, "I can't wait to see the young maiden's faces when they hear we've caught the Legendary Giganta."

All of the other crew members exchanged glances and then burst out into laughter. The old man, half laughing and half coughing, said, "Oh, you're just a… gr… green boy, Jefferson. That's no Giganta. The Great Fish would be four times the size of this one here."

Jefferson looked disappointed but asked, "Well, what kinda' fish do you s'pose it is?"

Higgins smiled. "I don't know, but one thing's for sure, this will be the biggest catch on record in all of North Harbor. Heck, in all of Merenia."

The crew finally pulled the enormous fish on deck with a loud wet *thud* as Jefferson leaned over and ripped his spear from the beast's side. The men stood back to admire their catch, red blood surged and oozed from the wound and ran across the wet planks of the boat.

"We set sail immediately. We won't want to be late for Beltane," the boat leader said. The crew quickly went to work hoisting the sails and making ready for their trip back.

The sun was well past halfway through the sky and beating down warmly on their backs once they turned and set forth onto North Harbor. The men sang a song of maids and whiskey, as Higgins looked to see that the fog had lifted and the waters were clear and sparkling. He whistled a happy tune, scratching at his scruffy beard while manning the helm.

The sweaty and water-sodden men went about their work in the liveliest of moods with the image of North Harbor coming closer and closer.

"Come quick! Something's happening!" Duncy called to the crew. The men jumped and ran to Duncy's urgent cry.

As the fishermen gathered around their catch, they stared in amazement, for what they saw was something they've only heard about in stories.

"What is it doing?"

"This can't be real."

"Something's wrong." All of the men talked on top of each other.

"Son of a goat! Look at that!" the old man said in shock while he stared down at the huge fish, his knees shaking.

Crackling noises were coming from the giant creature, noises that stood the hair up on the backs of their necks. The glittering golden scales of the fish began to bend and shift, flowing long ways down its back.

The men blinked their eyes in disbelief, yet the fish body went on fluidly moving and varying its shape back and forth. The fish head, which was just covered in the golden scales and a large bulging eye, was now bare meat underneath, changing from yellow to green to orange and finally settling on pink. The fish's thick lower half began to narrow and grow thinner, and its rough and stubby fin began to enlarge into a wide, yet thin and flowing dorsal, showing the colors of a fiery iridescent rainbow in the sunlight.

Higgins stood awestruck while a powerful sucking sound emanated from the morphing creature. With a loud *pop*, the so-called fish sprouted two appendages below the pale head, the color of pink skin. *Bloody deep blue sea, I must be dreaming.*

Higgins searched the others' faces, theirs reflecting the mix of emotions he felt creeping along his insides, goose pimples running along his arms.

The creature that was now more shapely than before and a bit smaller but still very large, began to grow a nose, mouth, and fingers; looking more like a man with every passing moment. The screeching and crackling sounds went on while the half-man grew long wavy hair and its features turned solid and its muscles strong.

Then all was silent, except for the groaning and creaking of the wooden boat swaying gently in the water. The creature lay still with a gaping wound in its flesh-colored chest, blood running down onto, what seemed to be, its fish tail.

"Well, I'll be damned to the deep blue sea..." Higgins words were carried away on the ocean breeze.

AARIC

Aaric gripped his cloak tightly in suspense and could feel himself gritting his teeth. He had heard this story a hundred times, though it still made his heart pound yet. The fire crackled, and the warm light made shadows dance back and forth on Nunny Ana's thin face.

Nunny was a small-framed woman, with a tight grey bun atop her head, and very old. Aaric didn't know exactly how old she was, but he was quite certain that she had been alive during the time when man had discovered fire. She had worked at House Castlecray for many years, even before Aaric was born, running the domestic affairs of the house. Nunny Ana was a lot of things, but lacking in personality wasn't one of them. She was like the loving but stern grandmother he'd never had. She was a nursemaid and healer, a teacher, and a nanny of sorts for all of the children at the castle. Nunny's voice, like sand scraping rich wood, continued her account of the story of *Meri and Ithock*.

"Just then, in the dead of night, Ithock the Giant heard a branch snap behind him, and whirled around to find a gleaming sword coming right towards his face." Aaric's younger sister, Aleena, squeaked like a frightened mouse and Noam, the young kitchen boy, shifted uncomfortably in his seat.

Nunny continued, "Being the only thing he could do, he grabbed the sharp sword end, pulling the guard right off of his feet, while slicing through the palm of his large hand. In a whirlwind, the giant was surrounded, dozens of blades coming at him from all directions."

Nunny Ana picked up her mug of ale shakily from the small side table near the hearth and drank deeply, her lined face relaxing. Lightning flashed through the window, illuminating all of the children's faces, giving them an unreal and dreamy look.

"It was said that Ithock's eyes became actual flames of anger," Nunny said in a frightening voice, "and that he bared his sharp teeth, dripping with saliva like a savage wolf." Quinlan, Aaric's youngest sister, was now hiding behind a blanket, her long brown hair hanging over and only her eyes peering out.

"The giant was in an enraged trance, only thinking of protecting his beloved princess. He swung the bloody sword, and the man still attached to it, sideways, using him as a battering ram, knocking down not one but six guards with his mighty strength. They toppled like dominoes, armor clanging one into the next."

Nunny's face was intense as the storm cast her face into flickering shadows.

"The man on the end of the blade was flung so hard that he landed a stone's throw away from the fight, and Ithock tossed the sword into the air and caught it properly with the other hand. In one swift movement, he sliced through the bellies of three approaching guards, and their bodies slumped to the ground in a bloody heap."

"Eeeeeww!" All of the girls in the room let be known their disgusted and noisy opinions of the violence.

Nunny continued without notice. "And as quick as thought, Ithock felt a blinding pain cut through his calf muscle. As he fell toward the damp and muddy ground, the remainders of the King's Guard were on top of him like flies on honey."

Aaric felt his pulse rise.

"Oh, no!" cried Duncan, the small page boy. The other boys laughed at him and mockingly called out "Oh, no!" in high-pitched voices.

"The giant's neck, which was as big as a tree stump, showed great blue veins bulging with his angry effort. He struggled, trying to repel his assailants with his huge rock arms, but had become weak from his injury and eventually he gave up. Laying his head back, the smell of musty earth filled his cavernous nostrils. The last thought Ithock the giant ever had was the memory of his true love's smiling face: the beautiful Princess Meri."

Aaric unclenched his fists, and took in a big breath and slowly let it out, feeling silly for getting so worked up over a story. He looked over to see a tear running down Aleena's cheek, as she twirled her long brown hair around her finger. His sister was always sort of a mush. Most of the younger boys were cheering, saying things like, "Yay, they got the nasty monster!" and, "Slaughtered him!"

Aleena stood, looking very much like their dead mother and said firmly, "He was *not* a nasty monster! He was *in love!*" She angrily stormed across the room to the window, her long curling brown hair flowing out behind her.

Nunny Ana stood and smoothed out her shirts with her hands, "Aleena is quite right. Though they are twice the size of a human man, and as strong as a dragon, giants are gentle creatures, really, only becoming dangerous if provoked." Nunny picked up her tarnished mug, and started towards the door, "Now, off to bed with you; it will be an early rise in the morning."

"Oh, Nunny!" Quin ran after the old woman, tugging her skirts, "One more story please?" Some of the younger children mimicked her saying, "Please, please, please," like little birds chirping for more breadcrumbs.

Nunny stopped and turned, a look of over-exaggerated contemplation on her face. "Well... I *guess* one more short story wouldn't hurt." She went back to her chair by the fireplace. "This is the last one." The kids happily agreed and went back to their places, leaning forward in hunger for more.

Nunny began with her dramatic storytelling voice, "Centuries ago, in a far off place... a place in the depths of the deep blue sea... "

"Ooooh, mermaids!" Quin squealed, her blue eyes wide and bright, excitedly drumming her feet on her chair.

"Yes, Quinlan," Nunny said, "but don't ever call a merman a 'mermaid' or you'll likely become fish bait as quick as you can say 'deep blue sea.'"

The children giggled.

Nunny continued, "The *merpeople*, as they are properly called, lived in the depths of the ocean where the light begins to vanish and the sun does not shine. It is an endless dusk, and an endless dawn.

"They dwell in castles made of seashells and stone and dine by the light of jellyfish. They are a mysterious and powerful people, who have abilities beyond your imagination, each one unique to his own sea-born magic. Time for the merpeople is very different than it is for you or me, as they can live to be almost a thousand name days old."

The children made oohing sounds. "They have many years to perfect their skills in life and are said to be great sorcerers, healers, and warriors."

"Nunny," Aleena asked, her graceful features showing bright white as a flash of lightning bounced off the walls from the rain-streaked window, "are there still merpeople alive today?"

The old nursemaid cleared her throat. "No, m'lady, they perished years ago during The Great Hunt. Humans were scared of their magic, and believed that the merfolk were causing storms to sink their ships, and droughts to kill their crops. It was said that these sea creatures could control nature's elements, and that they used them to their advantage.

"Great armies of people were created to hunt down the merpeople and brutally kill and spear them. This went on for many years until the merpeople were all wiped out, and all was forgotten." The story was interrupted by the sound of the heavy wooden door creaking open.

"There's no need to go filling these children's heads with nonsense," a deep and commanding voice said firmly, "and it's time you all were in your bedchambers."

Aaric looked up to see his lord father's face frowning, his large jaw and sharp features highlighted by the dying light of the fire. Emrys Castlecray was father to Aaric, Aleena, and Quin, and lord of Castlecray Keep. He was a stern man, and ever since the death of their mother years ago, he kept things running strictly throughout the house.

The children timidly gazed upon his disapproving look in silence. Lord Emrys resembled a chiseled statue, his muscular shoulders tense with his hands on his hips, his brown hair hung curling at his neck.

Lord Emrys' scowl cracked into a small smile, and at that, Aleena and Quinlan jumped up and ran laughing into his arms.

"Oh, Father, we love the stories." Aleena said dreamily.

"Look at all of you together!" Lord Emrys's shocking blue eyes scanned the young page, squire, kitchen help, and serving girls. He turned to Aleena. "If your lady mother saw little lords and ladies in the company of servants, she would split her bloomers." The serving girls exchanged wary glances, and Noam, the kitchen boy, eased his way towards the door.

"She's not our mother," Quin mumbled under her breath, Aaric being the only one who heard.

Lady Odelyn was their father's new wife and the marriage had been a strange one, very abrupt and business-like. Aaric didn't think much of Lady Odelyn; she laughed like a jackal, and was always in everyone's personal matters, but Father must have had his reasons for the marriage, the least of all being fondness, Aaric suspected.

"Now off to bed, all of you. We have an extremely full day on the 'morrow; Prince Banon and Prince Tolan Thunderdyn will be arriving in the morning." Hearing that, the serving girls blushed and giggled at the mention of royalty.

"One more thing." Aaric watched his father's eyes lock on his youngest sister. "Quin, I expect you to be on your best behavior tomorrow."

Quin looked downwards, her long dark lashes resting upon her full cheeks, and their father smiled.

"No teasing the stable boys by tying their boot laces together and causing them to fall in the horse muck."

The room rocked with laughter.

Aaric snickered at the thought of his littlest sister's pranks, always being the talk of the castle and the highlighted events of the week.

Nunny Ana began to shoo the children out the door when their lord father stopped Aaric and Aleena with a large hand on each of their shoulders. "Aaric, I trust you will see that the Princes of Thunderdyn feel at home. Show them the castle and anything they might like to see."

"Yes, Father." Aaric said a bit nervously at the thought of it. Aaric, being sixteen name days old now, was given more responsibilities, but he'd never been given the task of escorting royalty.

"And Aleena," Emrys said while lovingly touching her cheek, "Tomorrow is your day, my sweet. Fourteen name days old, you will be! I know you will act the nice young lady that you are and be a good host at your coming-of-age feast." Aaric could see a shift on Aleena's face and knew what she must be thinking.

Emrys continued, "I will be announcing your betrothal to Prince Tolan tomorrow night." Aleena rolled her grey blue eyes. Their father, at seeing Aleena's apprehension said, "Tolan is a good and bright young man. To marry a prince is a privilege that many a young lady could only wish for."

"Yes, Father." Aleena spoke quietly.

"Now off to bed with you both."

AARIC

Aaric tucked himself into his bed, and dim beams of light from the clouded moon lay across his blanketed legs. He tossed and turned, having trouble falling asleep, thinking about the next day's activities and excitement. He could hardly wait to show off his new sword fighting techniques that the captain of the house guard had taught him to the Prince Thunderdyn brothers. Aaric pictured himself whirling and swinging his sword at some great giant, immersed in the fighting dance of combat. Just when he felt the warm pull of sleep taking him into a dream, a voice spoke his name, shooting tingles down his spine.

"Aaric?" Aaric shifted under the covers. "Aaric, are you asleep?" A soft voice came from the doorway of his bedchamber.

"Well, not now!" Aaric sat up to look at the intruder through fuzzy sleep-filled eyes.

Quin, in her white night shift, tiptoed as quietly as a mouse across the room, only visible by the small glowing circle of light that her candle gave off. Aaric ran a hand through his knotted golden hair as his littlest sister set the candle on the bedside table and climbed on to the foot of his bed. Quin peered up at him from her large innocent blue eyes, rimmed with dark long lashes, and Aaric looked at her inquisitively.

"What is it, Quinnie?" he asked in an irritated tone.

"Sssshhhhh!" Quin hissed. "We must whisper. There could be someone listening!" She had a small bundle in her hand and glanced around the room hesitantly.

"Well, alright then, come here," Aaric said appeasingly. "What is this all about?"

Quin scooted her way closer and laid the small parcel in his hand and then grabbed both his wrists, looking deeply in his light grey eyes.

"Can you keep a secret?" She examined his face intently.

Aaric hesitated. "Why... why sure, but..."

"I *need* to know if you can keep a secret... *on your honor*." Quin put a dramatic emphasis on the "on your honor" part. His sister could sure be persistent for a young girl of only ten name days old.

"Yes."

Quinlan began to explain that she had been playing in the tunnels under the castle, where their father had forbidden them to go, and found a strange room with an old locked chest inside. She jiggled it and jiggled it but could not break the lock. Finally she had given up and decided to make her way back up to the castle.

"When I turned the corner and was halfway down the long tunnel, I heard a loud clanging *snap!*" Quin's face was lively with expression. "I nearly swallowed my own heart." The sound she had heard echoed its way from the room that held the old chest.

"I was as scared as a horse in a thunderstorm, but I just *had* to go back and see what the noise was," she continued, saying that she cautiously looked into the dungeon-like room and saw that the trunk was now cracked open. She just about bolted out of there, but felt drawn to the intricately carved wooden chest.

"When I saw that no one was around, I went to the chest and opened it."

"Well, what was inside?" Aaric was now awake with curiosity.

"Nothing but an old rock," Quin pointed to the bundle in Aaric's hand. "And a cloud of dust that put me into a coughing fit." Quin swished her arm back and forth as though fanning away the imaginary cloud.

"Quinnie, you came in here and woke me for a stupid rock." Aaric thrust the dirty cloth covered lump back at Quin and in one motion plopped himself back down with the covers over his head.

"But you don't understand," Quin pleaded. "I don't think it's just any old rock. Why would someone go to the trouble of locking it up and hiding it away?" Aaric made a grumpy growling sound.

"Aaric, look."

He could see a blue glimmer shining through his blanket and he slowly lowered the covers from his eyes. He lay still, looking at the uncovered lump that was casting an eerie blue-grey light over his sister's face. It looked like just an ordinary rock but was black like a piece of coal. It was unlike anything he'd ever seen. The glow pulsed like a heartbeat through his sister's small fingers and the cool ambiance of the room mimicked the rock, rising and falling luminously.

"Here. You try." Quin handed him the glittering object. As they transferred it from her hands to his, the throbbing light grew weak and the room dark. But just as quickly, when Aaric held it firmly in his palm, the frosty blue pulse began again, shining through the inky black surface.

It was like a bright blue sky trying to break through the darkest of boiling thunderheads. Aaric stared at the lumpy piece with his eyes wide in amazement. The only artificial light Aaric had ever seen, or as far as he was concerned, existed, was firelight from the hearth or a tallow candle. He started to say something, but couldn't find the words.

"It fell out of my pocket during my lessons today, and rolled right under Master Dunley's feet!"

Quin said the old master gave her a lecture about being a lady and not carrying rocks in her pockets. "But before he handed it back to me, I noticed that in *his* hands it *did not glow!*" Quin bounced on the bed and whispered, "I wonder what it means?"

Aaric gazed at the wafting light and pondered for what seemed to be forever. "What in the devil is it?" He asked no one in particular. "And *whose* is it?"

"Aaric." Quin said and he looked up at her.

"There's one more thing." Quin looked a small bit frightened.

"What is it, Quinnie?"

"I think someone was following me. How could the chest have been so tightly locked up and then suddenly sprang open?" His sister was biting her lower lip, staring at her hands.

"Maybe you almost had it opened and didn't realize it." Aaric tried to reason.

"No, I don't think so," Quin said matter of factly. "There's more. I felt eyes on me, someone watching. Even as I walked down the tunnels and corridors, it felt as if someone was just right behind me, around the turn."

"This just doesn't make any sense. Why would someone want you to find this…thing, and why would they be following you? We should ask Father…"

"No!" Quin yelled and then cupped her own hands over her mouth. Lowering her voice she said, "No. He mustn't know I was in the tunnels, *please*."

Aaric looked at Quin's pleading face. "Alright, but we should test it on someone else to see if it glows again. Someone we can trust. We have to be careful. If what you say is true, someone either wanted you to have this…rock, or they want it for themselves."

Quin sat quietly while Aaric mumbled to himself the different prospects. Aleena would make a huge to do about it and she couldn't keep her mouth from flapping, Master Dunley would surely tell father and Nunny would too.

"Noam!" Quin whispered loudly. "He wouldn't tell anybody. He'd be too scared I'd pummel him if he did."

Noam the kitchen boy was Quinnie's best friend. They were like two peas in a pod, and got into more trouble than a wolf in a chicken coop…but she just might have it right. Aaric had a notion that Noam fancied his sister as more than a friend, and he would do absolutely anything Quin told him to.

"You got it. Noam it will be." Aaric agreed and Quin got a big smile.

"Not until in the morning, though. We will do it after we break our fast when everyone is too busy preparing for Aleena's coming of age feast to notice the three of us missing." The two siblings shook hands as if agreeing to a pact but stopped suddenly.

There was a very subtle shuffling sound outside of the door that Quin had left cracked when she first came in. It sounded like soft footsteps. They heard it again, but this time it was growing softer as though someone was leaving the door.

Aaric jumped from the bed and raced to open the door and stick his head out. “Who’s there?” He looked from left to right down the empty corridor. “Hello?” he said again, his voice echoing off the cold stone walls. There was no sound, and no one.

Aaric jumped at the touch on his back and looked to see Quin standing right behind him peering out of the door. She looked up at him with the frightened eyes of a doe, “Can I sleep in your room… just for tonight?”

QUIN

Quin sat at the window seat of her bedchamber observing the scene below in the green grassy yard. Wagons and horses were clogging the entryway to the inner wall of the castle with supplies and pack mules, and people darted every which way like little ants in preparation for tonight's festivities. The children were all on the lawn playing what looked to be *Come to my Castle*, one of Quin's favorite games. She pressed her nose flat against the glass wishing she were down there amidst the commotion.

Nunny Ana had banished her to her bedchamber for making Duncan Eadmore cry at breakfast. Well, he *had* asked where bacon came from... while having a mouth full of it. The young page was quite sensitive as it was, but the oinking sounds had probably put him over the top. There was nothing to be done about it now, she supposed.

But everything was all messed up. She wouldn't be able to meet Aaric and put their plan into action. She couldn't very well sneak out, for Nunny had told all of the handmaidens to make sure Quin stayed put. She was stuck, and not the least bit happy about it either. Quin walked to her bed, huffed in frustration, and slumped down onto the soft feather mattress.

Maybe Aaric would still follow through and steal away with Noam to perform the test, she thought hopefully. Quin couldn't stand not knowing what was going on. She gave in, figuring she would just have to wait until the feast tonight.

There came a knock at her door and she popped up, but then came to an abrupt halt. Quin was reluctant to answer, still wary from her mysterious follower from the night before. The knock came again, louder this time. She went to the door, figuring it safe now that it was light out and there were castle occupants and staff fluttering about the halls.

Quin grabbed the iron handle and swung the heavy door open to see a large dark figure looming over her.

"Grandfather!" She flung herself at the big hairy man, with a mane of dark salt and pepper hair and a full beard that touched his chest.

Swinging Quin in a circle high above the ground, her grandfather gave in to roaring laughter, his hazel eyes sparkling. He set her back down on the ground and, with a swoop of his arm and hat in his hand, gave a theatrical bow.

"Captain Gaderian Longship at your service, m'lady." He bent down and Quin giggled as she sat on his knee, encircling his neck with her arms.

Captain Gaderian Longship was a very big man, by anyone's standards. He stood almost an arm's length taller than most men and was quite wide in the middle, but was built with sturdy muscles. He had soft kind eyes, rimmed with laugh lines and round merry cheeks. His dark brows were furry and unkempt, and he wore a long dark, heavy cloak that fell to his sea-tattered boots.

The captain's smile faded and he looked sternly into Quin's eyes. "Now, I heard from a little bird that ye make a very good mockery of a pig." He spoke with his deep Northerland accent, his mouth cracking back into a wide smile.

Her grandfather stood up with Quin still in tow and sat on the solitary tufted chair by the hearth, while she sheepishly told him of the events that had taken place in the Great Hall that morning at breakfast.

With a guttural laugh, the captain said, "Aye, for such a little thing you've got a ball of fire in ye. Your mother was the same way when she was your age, always stirrin' up trouble." He looked at Quin thoughtfully. "She also used to do what yer doin' right now." Quin glanced up, biting her lip, and then with realization, smiled.

"Will you tell me about my mother? I do wish I could remember her."

Captain Gaderian gazed out the large arched window, as if in remembrance. "Ah, Llewylynn. She was quite a handful, I'll tell ye. She had that Nanny of hers runnin' tailspins tryin' to keep up wi' her, ye know." His thoughts were far away as he pulled at his blackish wirey beard.

"I remember a time during Yule Tide. We were all sittin' down for supper and yer mother, a lassie o' nine or ten, couldna' sit still. Gretta, yer mother's Nanny at the time, kept a'scoldin her to sit still and proper like a wee lassie should. But Llewylynn just kept a'wigglin and a'squirmin.

"So Gretta goes and asks the lass if she's needin' a moment to use the privy. Yer mother says no, but again the wee girl is a'gigglin and a'movin as though she's got the ticklers.

Just then, two field mice come a'scurryin outta' that girl's dress. One ran across the table, through the pease porridge, an' the other... right up Gretta's sleeve." Gaderian chuckled and then continued the story in his rough and tumble accent. "I had to employ me a new nanny after that."

Quin burst out with laughter at the thought of bringing rodents to dinner. She tucked that story away in her memory for later use.

Quin had always dreamed what it would be like to have known her mother. There was a portrait that had been painted of Llewylynn before she died, that hung in the library. Quin would often go gaze upon it longingly.

She didn't think she looked anything like her mother, as her brother and sister did; Aaric, with his golden hair and light grey eyes, and Aleena, who took their mother's delicate features and curly locks. The two sisters had their dad's brown hair, but Aleena's always seemed deeper and more beautiful.

Quin didn't like her own hair; it was a mousey brown color and tangled in gnarls most of the time. Her mother's face was long and graceful, as Quin's was round with big lips and a button nose in the center. Some of the boys in the yard would tease her and call her fish face, but Aleena always reassured her that when she grew into her features the boys would be chasing her in a different way. She didn't care about the comments though; she'd just kick those boys in the shin and give em what they deserved.

Quin's thoughts shifted to the magical stone that glowed like frozen sapphires, and debated about telling her grandfather about it. He might tell her father and she'd have to fess up to where she found it. No, she thought, best to wait and see what Aaric might come up with. Quin had left the rock with Aaric anyways, and without proof, the captain probably wouldn't believe her.

"Grandfather," Quin said, coming back from her thoughts, "How long might you be able to stay this time?"

"Well, wee Quinnie-fish, I'll be stayin' for the feast tonight in honor o' your sister, and I'll be off before sunrise in the mornin'. I've got important matters in North Harbor that must be tended to."

"I want to be the captain of a merchant vessel just like you when I grow up. It must be so very exciting, having an adventure every day, and seeing far off lands and strange people. Out on the open sea… " Quin's words trailed off as she fantasized.

"Yes lassie. When the seas are agreeable and the weather accommodating, it is quite lovely." Gaderian said in his deep scruffy voice. "Keep in mind, though, this is no a position for just anyone. It is dangerous even for the strongest lad, and there are many men who leave and never return from the deep blue sea."

"Can I come with you on your next adventure?" Quin became excited and spoke her words quickly. "You're only going to North Harbor this time, and with Father's permission I could… "

"No Quinnie. You've no trainin' on a ship, and wi' the unpredictable weather o' late… "

"Pleeeaaase?" Quin begged, pressing her hands to her heart.

"I'm sorry, lass. No, I canno allow it. It's too dangerous and I'd never forgive m'self if anything were to happen to ye." Quin's lowered her head in disappointment. Her grandfather looked at her compassionately.

"Oh!" The captain blurted out. "I almost forgot! I got ye something on me last trip." He patted around inside of his tunic, under all of his layers, and with a satisfied expression found what he was looking for.

"Here," he said, handing her the item. "It's a rabbit foot. Got it in Nikaydia. The Nikaydians believe it to be good luck and that it wards off any bad doings." Quin gripped the furry little foot, attached to a loop of twine and hugged the captain.

"I *love* it!" she cried. Her smile turned sober. "Grandfather?"

"Yes, m'love?"

"People talk about you."

"Oh, is that so?" Gaderian looked amused with one eyebrow cocked. "And what do these people say?"

"They say you're a pirate, or a smuggler. They say you have a secret, a very big secret that you hide from everyone." Quin watched her grandfather's face as he erupted in laughter.

"Everyone has secrets, lassie. It's the ones you choose to keep and the ones you choose to tell is what's important."

EMRYS

The great hall was as lively and bustling as Quin had ever seen it. Lords and ladies had journeyed from all of the nearby lands and castles, to come for a most joyful celebration, dressed in their finest clothes. Everywhere she looked there were swooping shiny silk dresses, draped with lace, pearls, and glittering gems, slashed with every vibrant color of the rainbow. Noblemen wore surcoats with their house crest on the front, with fur-trimmed cloaks draped across their chests and pinned luxuriously at their shoulders with fancy broaches.

Quin sat at the head table overlooking the whole room from the elevated dais. To her immediate right was her sister Aleena, and next to her, Prince Tolan, who kept stuttering small talk at her disinterested sister. Emrys sat in the direct middle with a prince on either side, looking very much like complete opposites, with Banon's charming white smile and Tolan's toothy and awkward grin. Quin strained her neck to see Prince Banon and her brother, Aaric, next to him chatting away cheerily. To her left sat her stepmother, loudly piping away niceties to the noblemen and women nearby, and then down the line was Odelyn's father, Aurous Goldcoin, with his pumpkin head sweating as much as a criminal in the gallows.

Quin was excited by all of the sound and movement, colors and smells. The humming drone of voices and the ambient noise of layered conversations was a nice change for the regularly quiet and lonely great hall.

Serving men and women buzzed back and forth bringing the first course of dinner and drinks out on a myriad of beautiful silver platters and plates, bowls and goblets. There were delicate honey cakes, and chunks of goat cheese, platters spilling over with colorful fruit, and big golden loaves of crusty bread with sides of honey butter. Men drank deeply from their cups of ale, and ladies sipped elegantly from goblets of fine spiced wine, encouraging the conversations to a livelier mood.

Quin could overhear a couple of different conversations and chose to listen in on her father's. "We are so pleased to soon have you as a new member of our family, Prince Tolan," Emrys spoke to the prince, holding his goblet up in honor of Aleena's soon-to-be husband.

"Y... Y... Yes, m'lord. It is a great p... p... pleasure to b... be here." The prince stuttered and put his hand tentatively on top of Aleena's, his soon-to-be wife rolling her eyes. Prince Tolan was a tall, lanky and awkward young man, with the face of a donkey and teeth to match, Quin thought. He looked nothing like his handsome older brother, Banon.

"Emrys!" Lady Odelyn burst into the conversation with her high-pitched sing-song voice, "We're practically royalty now!" Quin's stepmother pushed her way through Prince Tolan to get to Lord Emrys and, all but choking him, hastily straightened the broach that held his cloak.

Emrys, as gently as he could, pried his smothering wife off of him, "The wedding is not for a small while yet, Odelyn, and even then we will *not* be royalty, only related."

Lady Odelyn wore a tall wig of enormous bushy blonde curls that made her look twice as big as she really was. Though she was short and wide, she made herself known with her boisterous personality.

She airily waved away his remark. "Oh, hahaha!" Odelyn went on laughing hysterically like a yipping dog. "You're so silly, my noble Emrys." Emrys gestured her back towards her seat with remarkable patience.

Quin wondered why her father had married Odelyn; she knew her father very well and could tell that he didn't much care for the terrible woman. Quin watched her father stand and hold up a hand to silence the crowd. Slow like thick honey, the room grew to a hush, with the occasional muffled cough usually heard at such events.

The court herald, standing right behind her father, stepped forward and barked out, "Lord Emrys Castlecray!" Emrys jumped with a start at the shock to his ears.

"Yes." Emrys said befuddled, "Uh um. Yes, thank you." The herald melted back into the wall and Lord Castlecray cleared his throat.

"Lords and ladies of Merenia, I would personally like to thank you all for being here tonight for my daughter, Aleena's, coming of age feast." Emrys gestured for Aleena to stand. As she curtsied the crowd broke out in applause.

As Quin scanned the room while various lords and ladies rose to say a congratulatory response, she discovered a strange man entering the hall through one of the back doors that was hardly ever used. It actually could have been a woman, because the figure was keeping out of the light and she couldn't get a good look. She became nervous, as the dark figure moved in a suspicious manner, cloaked in the shadows. *Could it be my creepy follower from last night?*

Trying to get Aaric's attention and to no avail, Quin snapped her head back when she heard her father's projected voice.

"It is with great pleasure that I, Emrys Castlecray, announce the betrothal of my beautiful daughter Aleena Castlecray, to the…" Emrys paused and Quin followed his eyes to see Prince Tolan grinning widely with a long stringy piece of spinach hanging from a gap in his buck teeth. Emrys finished his sentence, "to the... charming Prince Tolan Thunderdyn." The crowd cheered enthusiastically, the noise bouncing off the vaulted ceiling.

Quin looked towards the back of the room, eyes darting back and forth, searching for the mysterious person, but he or she had vanished.

Lord Emrys held his cup up high towards the room crammed with people. "Then let the celebration begin! Haza!"

In unison, the feasting people followed suit, saying loudly, "Haza!"

The crowd erupted in conversation, and the bard began to play his lute, merrily accompanied by a flutist and fiddlers. People began to slap their knees and stomp their feet to the beat of the lively music.

"Oh, Emrys," Lady Odelyn's shrill voice pierced through the festivities, "Must you leave tomorrow? You're taking the children along, aren't you? Surely you don't mean to leave them here with me." Quin's ears perked up.

Emrys looked at Odelyn like she was out of her mind. "No Odelyn, I will *not* be taking the children away from the castle at a time like this, what with all of the dangers about."

"But..."

"You will all be safe here. I am leaving Captain Swordsby in charge of the House Guard and Garrison, and you will have help from Master Dunley and Nunny Ana running the domestic affairs." Lady

Odelyn took her seat, looking terrified at the fact of being left with *his* children.

Quin slowly stood and wove her way around the chairs to her father's side. She whispered in his ear, "Don't go Father. *Please* don't leave me here with Odelyn. She's wretched."

"Quinnie, my girl, I cannot take you with me. This journey is dangerous business. Besides, your mother…"

Quin cut him off. "She is *not* my mother!" Quin could feel her face start to burn with heat and her eyebrows drew close.

Emrys grabbed her arm and spoke firmly. "She is your mother by marriage and you *will* obey her. I will not be gone but a few weeks at most, and in the meantime you, your brother and sister *will* behave."

Emrys lightened his grip and his voice, "Anyway, I don't think Aaric and Aleena would know what to do with themselves if you weren't around to stir up trouble." He smiled and Quin giggled a bit. "Now, go enjoy yourself, Quinnie. Go dance!" And with that, Lord Emrys was called upon by a very short, balding man with curled lips, garbed in plain grey robes that fell past his feet.

Again, Quin tried to get Aaric's attention by pulling on his tunic. She wanted to warn him about the dark stranger and she just *had* to know if he had tested the magic stone on Noam to see if it would glow for the boy as well. But he was deep in conversation with Prince Banon and waved her away like she was a pesky fly.

Again, Quin searched the crowd for the strange person she'd seen lurking about earlier and saw no one of the sort. But she did spot Noam, sitting at the servant's table, shoveling large scoops of food into his mouth and occasionally laughing, food and all, at what the boy next to him was saying. She decided Noam looked like he was having a lot more fun than she was and inconspicuously slid out from behind the head table. Besides, he might know something about the mystery rock.

As Quin made her way to the back of the hall where the servant's table was placed, she noticed the bard singing a familiar tune.

Hey there goes Stink Bottom Meri
She's got crooked toes and they're hairy
She woke up with the sun and started to run
We say "Hey there goes Stink Bottom Meri!"
Hey there goes Stink Bottom Meri
I know she appears a wee scary
Used her knife on the king and started to sing
We say, "Hey the king's dead by Queen Meri!"
So if you come face to face with Queen Meri
Make sure that she don't try to bury
Her knife in your gut, your body in a rut
We Say "Hey there goes Stink Bottom Meri!"

An obvious favorite, the whole hall swayed and sang together as one, making it troublesome for Quin to move through the hordes of people. Quin just realized the catchy tune she had heard numerous times was about Meri and Ithock, or at least Princess Meri from the stories Nunny would tell at bedtime.

Coming to the servant's table, Quin plopped herself down right next to Noam, nudging the other boy aside and asked him if he'd spoken with Aaric that day while she was cooped up in her chambers.

"No. Why?" Noam said with a face full of mashed potatoes, gravy running down his chin. Quin grunted in frustration. She was just about to tell him about the magic stone, and the sneaky unknown person *or thing* that had been following her, when she felt a rough pull at the back of her dress. She looked up to see her stepmother glaring down at her.

"A lady does not sit with filth," Odelyn said angrily, jerking Quin out of her chair by her dress. "If indeed you *are* a lady. You sure seem to act like servant scum."

Quin, becoming enraged, yelled at the top of her lungs, "He's not scum, he's my friend! You're the one who's scum!"

The music stopped abruptly, and everyone's attention was drawn towards the argument.

Through gritted teeth that oddly resembled a smile, Odelyn's voice became even higher-pitched than usual, "Now that's not the way a lady speaks."

"Quin!" Lord Emrys shouted from the front of the hall, his voice level with reprimanding.

Noam whispered what sounded like a rude comment under his breath.

"What was that?" Lady Odelyn looked to him, her face turning all shades of purple, though she seemed to be trying to keep her composure in front of the sea of watching guests.

Noam was silent.

"What did you say, *boy*?" Odelyn repeated the question, a bit louder this time.

Noam stood and with all of his might shouted, "I *said* you're a pig-snouted nanny nagger!"

The crowd drew in their breaths in a large gasp, sounding as if a whistling wind flew through the hall, although some chuckling was heard sporadically amidst the shock.

Quin felt that if her poufy-haired, pig-snouted stepmother got any angrier, her purple head just might explode. Odelyn dropped Quin from her grip and went for Noam, plates and goblets crashing to the floor as Noam ducked down and just missed the meaty hands coming for his throat. Lady Odelyn tripped over her own feet, and in a *wham*, fell on the table, her head landing in a pile of sticky honey cakes.

When she stood straight, her hand went to her head feeling the dark prickly patches of hair that were now sticking up every which way, her wig staying on the table, stuck in the gooey honey.

The room's shock had worn off, and was now rolling with laughter, as though this was a staged part of the entertainment.

Aurous Goldcoin, Lady Odelyn's father, stood. "Enough of this insubordination! Guards!" Lord Goldcoin pointed at Noam with his sweaty little hands, "Put that filthy kitchen rat in the dungeons where he belongs!"

Lord Emrys's commanding voice echoed through the vast room as he glared at his father-by-marriage.

"HALT! This is *my* castle, *my* guards, and *my* dirty kitchen rat! I will take care of the matter."

Emrys turned and addressed the man behind him. "Sir Captain Swordsby, please escort young Noam here to his bedchamber until further notice."

Quin thought if Aurous Goldcoin ever looked like an angry orange pumpkin head, now was that time.

"A heathen like that deserves the dungeon and a good lashing." The little treasurer shook his finger. "Emrys, this is completely unacceptable. You need to start keeping control of your servants or they will do and say what they please."

Emrys was looking daggers at Lord Goldcoin, "You want to know what *is* unacceptable, Aurous? A guest in *my* house making orders beyond his station." Emrys's voice had turned into that of a roaring lion. "Now if you all will please excuse me, I must make preparations for the journey. We leave early in the morning." Emrys slammed his chair down and stormed from the Great Hall, silent stares watching him go.

Captain Brently Swordsby, a strong and robust man with a kind face, came to the servant's table. "Come, young Noam. You'd best do what Lord Castlecray says and follow me." Noam, like a wounded pup, got up and strung along after the captain, his blonde hair hanging in his eyes.

Quin's head was swimming from all of the commotion. She couldn't believe that her father was leaving the next day for the King's Castle and she would be stuck here with that nasty woman! She wouldn't even have the comfort of her Grandfather Longship, as he was also leaving for North Harbor. She just wanted to hide, or run away.

Finally, Quin decided it would be best to go on up to her bedchamber and stay out of the way. But before she had the chance, a cold hand tightly pinched her ear.

Quin could feel warm stale breath on the side of her face as Lady Odelyn drew close and whispered, "You just wait until your father leaves, I will then teach you and that heathen friend of yours some manners."

NOAM

Noam's stomach rumbled loudly with lack of food, and the swaying motion he felt wasn't helping. It was still dark out, but he was up before the sun every day anyway, as that was normal for the kitchen help who had to bake fresh bread and make preparations for the morning breakfast.

But today would not be a normal day, quite the opposite actually. Noam would never make it to the kitchen to help with the fetching of water and flour, nor would he get the chance to steal a bite of sizzling bacon to eat while working, getting his hand slapped by Olga the grumpy cook. Today would turn out very different indeed, from anything Noam had ever experienced.

The young kitchen boy, no longer hearing the bantering of the grizzly men, decided it was a safe and a good time to sneak a peek out of his secret hiding spot to have a look.

He nuzzled his head out of the rough fabric enough to where only his eyes peered out and was blasted with a shock of cold salty air. He blinked repetitively from the spray of the sea and the breeze that whipped his hair about. The sky was almost black with a silver line in the east, forecasting a not-yet-risen sun and the sails of the boat made light clapping sounds as it whipped in the tender breeze.

Most of the crew men, now done with their preparations and with the boat set to sail, were sitting down at a rickety old table eating eggs and steaming bread that he assumed they had pilfered at the last minute from Olga. The mens' faces, barely visible by the yellow glow of the lanterns, were smiling and cheerful, a common reaction to the open sea air.

It was a frigid morning and Noam nestled down cozily in the burlap sack of goose feathers he had chosen to hide in. He glanced at the barrel of leathers that he had seen Quin get into earlier, and saw one blue eye peering out of one of the holes, studying the hungry men.

"Pssst." He called quietly to her. "Pssst!"

The blue eye darted his way and then disappeared.

Slowly the barrel lid began to lift, with Quin's head pushing up from underneath. She looked like a turtle coming out of its shell; a very angry turtle for that matter. She was fuming actually, her cheeks red with anger. Noam hadn't realized that his heroic gesture would have had that sort of effect on her.

"What in blazes are you doing here?" Quin forced the yell out as a whisper, still trying to stay concealed. They were in the cargo area, and stood a good chance of staying hidden if they were careful.

A booming voice yelled, "Aye, the weather's clear. The sea will be good to us today, she will!" It was Captain Gaderian Longship's voice that grew near. Quinnie's strangely curious grandfather was exchanging words with a crew hand.

The children darted their heads back into their barrel and bag, like two little ground hogs taking cover, as the captain's boots made heavy clomping sounds on the creaky deck. Noam could hear him grunt as he apparently had picked up a heavy crate of cargo and hauled it back to the front quarter deck, footsteps trailing away.

Popping their heads out again, Quin shot Noam a foreboding look.

"Whaaaaaat?" Noam drew out the word in a whine. "I thought you'd appreciate a guard, seeing as you're trying to get yourself *killed*, or far worse, taken back to Lady Odelyn."

"Why... how... did you...?" Quin asked, her eyes blinking.

"I saw you sneaking away from the castle in the dark as I was on my way to the kitchens. So I followed you."

Quin bit her full lower lip in thought. "Well, there's nothing to be done about it now, is there?"

Quin's scowl turned upside down into a mocking grin. "Oh, gallant protector?"

"Yes, m'lady?"

"You look like a silly bird," she giggled.

Noam curiously put his hand to his head and felt fluffy feathers sticking up out of his unkempt hair. Embarrassed, he began slowly plucking them out, feeling his cheeks flush with heat.

Noam carefully observed the scene up at the front of the boat, masked by darkness. He saw that Captain Longship and his crew were also accompanied by a few other people that he recognized from last night's feast. One of them was a very short grey-robed man with curled lips, who was telling a story with exaggerated hand motions as the bald spot on his head caught the gleam of one of the swinging lanterns.

"Hey!" Quin's face was all bunched up and confused-looking. "We're going the wrong way!" Noam looked to see the boat making a sharp but slow turn, due south around a large island of jagged rocks.

"Didn't the captain say he was headed to North Harbor?" Noam asked and Quin nodded.

"Well, we sure aren't headed north." They had literally made an about-face turn and were sailing in the exact opposite direction than they were before.

The sea was very calm and quiet with the occasional splashing sounds of the water lapping up against the hull of the boat and the sky was pitch black, with only a faint glimmer of the rising sun on the horizon, painting low clouds in faint orange and pink brushstrokes.

Noam wondered about what his father must be thinking, and Olga, now that he hadn't shown up for his duties. He didn't even want to think what his punishment might be when he got back, especially after the "pig-snouted nanny nagger" comment from the night before. Probably the belt, he thought and shuddered, his father's belt.

Best not think about that now, anyway. There seem to be more important matters ahead of us; like where are we?

Noam had recognized some of the bigger and important landmarks as they had first made way, but now he recognized nothing, for he had never been south of Castlecray. He didn't think many people *had* been south of Castlecray, as there was not any land except for jagged cliffs and dangerous rocky areas.

"So what were you planning on doing, Quin?" Noam asked her. "Just popping out and saying, 'Hello Grandfather! Nice boat. When's breakfast?'"

"Shush!" Quin hushed her friend. They watched as a looming cliff edge came closer and closer. Quin covered her face with her hands, for it seemed they would crash into it head on, but the boat made a last minute turn just a finger's-width from the jutting rock. The cliff opened up into some sort of natural bridge, with a hollow hole through the center, where the boat tightly squeezed through. The stowaways let out a long breath as they cleared the sharp rocks, not realizing they had been holding it in.

"What is that?" Quin murmured, gazing off to the inky black ocean.

Noam followed her stare to a hazy glowing cloud hovering over the water a distance off to the south. It looked alive, moving weightlessly back and forth, in and out into different forms, sluggish and dreamlike. The ever-changing glow was in the shape of a dome filled with tiny twinkling stars, blinking in and out, zipping back and forth. A luminous light fell across the deck of the ship as the boat neared the strange mass. The little stars took on an individual warm glow, each to its own, golden and shimmering against the dark sky.

The children stood up straight in awe, forgetting their hiding spots for a moment. Noam arched his neck and looked straight up as they sailed right under the domed cloud and the canopy of sparkles parted for them like a curtain being drawn back for a theatre production.

One of the twinkling stars, which was not a star at all, whizzed up to Noam's face and hovered right before his nose, making him cross-eyed to look at it. It was like the thing was actually studying him before it buzzed off.

Bugs! They're lightning bugs! But quite a curious species, grouping together like that and moving as one. They were a bit different from the regular lightning bugs Noam had seen, for these not only glowed, but they seemed to have some sort of a sparkling fairy dust trailing behind them, like from one of Nunny's bed-time stories.

Quin's eyes, which looked like large pools of liquid, had reflections of the golden twinkling lights in them, as she reached her hand out to touch one of the glowing starry insects.

Just then, almost as if on cue, the sun burst from the horizon, thrusting its dusky morning light on a large bulging land mass that had been hidden behind the sheet of diamond-like stars.

Noam ducked back inside the sack of feathers just in time, heart beating excitedly. The band of scruffy deck hands began running about wildly, loosening the rig, furling the sails, and going about other duties as Captain Longship yelled out orders.

"Ready about! Land ahoy!"

Noam kept undercover, wondering what he had gotten himself into. He could hear a large splash as the anchor plunked into the water and the boat slowed to a stop, gently rocking back and forth. He could see dim light of the rising sun now being filtered through the burlap sack, and could hear the captain shouting for a row boat to be lowered.

Again the children's heads appeared out of hiding to inspect their new surroundings. The shimmering lightning bugs were gone, and were now replaced with a monstrous rock island bathed in the sunrise, jutting out from the crystal clear water. The massive earth giant loomed large overhead, casting the boat in a cool gray shadow and Noam shivered at the sight. A small sandy cove dipped into one side, leading to a rigid steep cliff climbing up high in the air.

Noam stood up further seeing that no one was near, and watched Captain Gaderian Longship, the short and tubby grey-robed man, and a couple of other unrecognizable people being lowered into the water from a small row boat that was flanking the larger ship. The small group quickly rowed to shore and pulled the small boat up on the beach. All of the men aboard went below deck one by one, probably to get a nap or play a game of cards while they waited on the others.

Quin picked her way out of the barrel full of leather hides and clumped both feet on the solid deck.

Noam climbed out of his lumpy bag. "Where in the world are they going?" The island seemed to be deserted, not a manmade structure in sight, nothing but lush vegetation and plants covered the immense rock.

"I don't know, but I'm going to find out." Noam noticed that Quin had a rabbit foot strung to her skirt that swayed as she walked, all the more adding to her usually unkempt appearance. Quin stopped at the rail of the boat, and swung a leg over the top, the hem of her skirt rimmed brown with dirt.

Noam gaped at her. "Are you crazy!?"

"I'm not going to just sit here and do nothing." Quin had gotten herself up and was sitting on the edge, both legs hanging over the side. She looked back at Noam. "Well? Are you coming?"

"Ugggghhh, Yes." Grunting, Noam drug his feet across the planks and looked up just in time to see

Quin shove off the side. A few heartbeats later he heard a big splash in the water below and looked over the edge. Quin cracked the surface with a *whoosh* of water, hair wet and slicked back, smiling up at him.

"Here we go," Noam muttered apprehensively and hurtled himself overboard in one fluid motion. The cold water was a shock to his body, and breaking through the top of the waves, he gasped for air. He could feel himself shivering as he paddled, but it was a quick swim to shore.

Hungry, wet, and now cranky, Noam followed Quin, trudging throught the shallow water and out onto dry land. "Where did they go?" he grumbled.

Quin pointed down at the footprints pressed deep into the sand that were filled with water from the receding tide. The trail of prints led them across the sandy cove to a rift in the cliff wall, just wide enough for a large man to fit through, and not comfortably at that. Giving each other a knowing look, they squeezed inside.

The crevice went straight back, getting smaller and darker along the way. They gripped the rugged rock walls, following a long tunnel, twisting and turning blindly, going up and down and then up again. Some parts of the tunnel became so narrow that they had to get down and crawl through, scraping elbows and knees in the dark.

After a while, Noam began to see a glowing light up ahead and could hear a mad rush of hissing water.

Noam, the first to hit the opening to a large clearing, stepped out onto a rock edge only as wide as the length of the plank on a ship. The cliff edge, wrapping around the huge round cavern, disappeared behind a breathtaking waterfall which came crashing down into a shimmering lake that filled the cavern below. The drop off was sharp, and Noam hugged the rough walls as Quin followed, their bodies flat against the stone and their feet barely wedged onto the narrow path. Noam watched her eyes grow wide in appreciation of the powerful cascading water that shimmered like opals, iridescent and colorful.

"Beautiful!" Quin gasped.

"It looks like there's a cave opening behind the waterfall. I don't see anywhere else they could've gone," Noam observed.

Step by step, they inched their way around the circular cavern, arms stretched out flat against the sloping cliffs. The sound of the rushing water was deafening as they came near to the fall. Noam let go and jumped into the passage, curtains of gleaming water showering his body as he went through. Only a heartbeat later, Quin burst through knocking him to the ground, and her going with him.

Breathlessly laughing, the two rose and saw that they were at the entrance of yet another vast cavern, the waterfall acting as a gateway separating the two. Quin followed behind Noam on a short stone path and peering around a rock corner, he stopped in his tracks.

Noam's mouth hung open. Blinking his eyes in disbelief of what he was seeing. *I must be dreaming*, he thought.

"Noam, what is…" Quin's words ended abruptly as Noam felt a large hand wrap around his mouth, pressing hard. He tried to move but was bound to a tall strong body. As Noam struggled, he could hear Quin's muffled cries behind him and figuring she'd been captured too. His heart began to race as he felt a rough cloth sack being placed over his head and then the world went black.

BANON

"This one was unlucky and didn't escape," Jack Piper said, considering the long thin bone he held in his hand.

Banon felt nauseous as he scanned the littered landscape. He nodded at Jack Piper's hand. "Is that a... *human* bone?"

The bard stood up next to the prince shaking the extremity. "It *does* look to be that of a human arm bone. Yes, the one right here." Piper pointed with a dirt-smudged finger and ran it up his forearm.

"Captain," Sheply interjected, "We found more. All of them in their homes, or what *used* to be their homes."

Sir Captain Leof, knight and captain of the Royal Goldenshields, took Banon by the arm, a worried Lord Emrys in tow, and led him to a fallen structure, charred and splintered timbers laid on top of each other all helter skelter. He pointed at a watery red splotch running down some boards that had managed to stay intact with a pile of bones and torn cartilage lying below. “The rain’s washing it away now,” Sheply continued, “but there was quite a lot of blood when we first saw it. It looks pretty fresh, maybe only a day or so old.”

The Captain’s voice was serious as he spoke. “It looks like they got ambushed at night while they were sleeping, completely unaware.” Leof shook his head. “I doubt there were any survivors.”

The band of men had come upon the small village of Snakewood earlier that day on their travels up the Merenese Road, headed towards the King’s castle in Merene. The group had stopped in a line, looking up at the little hillside village, silhouettes of man and horse drawn black against the overcast evening sky, smoke puffs billowing from the town. They had had no idea of what they were getting themselves into, Banon had thought.

Among the group was Lord Emrys Castlecray, the rugged and rigid type, sharpening his knife, a man of not so many words, and Lord Aurous Goldcoin, quite a stuffy little person, with a laced handkerchief, blotting his round orange face, dotted with perspiration, his horse dancing nervously at the smoke.

Jack Piper, the traveling bard who had been the entertainment at Aleena’s feast, also accompanied the band. The tall lanky singer had asked to accompany the group to the King’s Castle, as he had been travelling for months and wanted to settle down somewhere for a while; somewhere that was lucrative. Jack Piper was a positively quirky man, as most bards, storytellers, and keepers of the past were, guzzling away at his tankard of what could only be presumed of as whiskey, while he watched the plumes of smoke rising above the trees.

There were at least a dozen Goldenshield Guards wearing their plum surcoats of House Thunderdyn, led by the grizzly Sir Captain Leof Brawnmont, who at the sight of the town scratched his armpit and had said, "Well, I'll be the son of a motherless goat! The whole place seems to have been burnt to the ground!"

And then there was Banon, the young prince and heir to the Royal Crown with crystal blue eyes and a smile to melt the ladies' hearts, though he thought naught of himself.

He had cringed at the sight of the smoldering village and felt like a silly boy trying to lead a regime of matured men. Banon had only just passed his seventeenth name day, and was *considered* a man almost grown, though he felt no older than twelve at the moment. Uncertain and frightened at best, he was still determined to be brave. His father, the king, would always say, "Courage is not the lack of fear. Courage is facing fear... like a mad man." Banon wished he could find the mad man inside of him, like his father, and be brave.

Without a word, Lord Emrys had heeled his horse and trotted up the sloped earth and into the village, followed by Leof and the Goldenshields. Banon had shaken off his astonishment and hurried to catch up, preceded by Jack Piper, who was having trouble staying in the saddle and Lord Aurous Goldcoin, looking terribly frightened.

The men had all murmured about the supposed “black rebellion” while scanning the place. The small smoking town had been completely abandoned, by the look of it, with the exception of a stray dog munching at something behind a smoking wagon wheel. Almost every single building had been burnt to the ground, smoldering, with only a few supporting beams, splintered, left alone to stand against the sky. The streets were littered with broken cooking pots, crushed wooden chicken coops, shattered glass bottles, the shards glittering in the sunset, linens of all sorts strewn about, and smashed rotten food covered in flies and maggots. From a small piece of wall that had somehow escaped the brutality hung a single shutter, swinging by one hinge and clacking loudly in the wind.

But there was something else very strange that they had noticed that day upon their arrival in Snakewood: the trees. There were great trees thrown haphazardly about the village. The large saplings looked to have been thrust through some of the homes before the structures had been burnt, being mixed in with fractured timbers and planks. Broken branches and limbs were scattered about looking like a hurricane had come through the small town.

The men had coughed profusely as ashes whirled throughout the village on the breeze, covering them in layers of dust like a blanket of sad grey snow.

After orders from the prince, the men had split into groups and searched the place for any signs of life or usable provisions.

And now, here they stood, slouched and weary from travel, in the middle of what seemed to be a morbid graveyard nightmare. Snakewood village had been torn limb from limb, bleeding red blood and crying raindrops. The men stood, somberly, at the vicious destruction.

What had been a drizzle was now a steady downpour, and Banon could hear the hissing sounds of the water mixing with the scorched hot wood structures.

The young prince, wiping rain water from his face, began pacing, his mind spinning. *What in blazes happened here? Who could've done this?* He couldn't imagine what the people of the village must have been thinking and feeling, or how terrified they must have been during this occurrence. Amidst his aimless walk, he looked down at one of the fallen trees.

"Roots!" Banon barked out. "These trees were not *cut* down, nor were they fallen from the storm; they were actually *torn* from the ground!" he said excitedly of his discovery.

Bending over, the prince rubbed the crumbling clumps of dirt that still hung from the tree roots between his fingers. Emrys, appearing behind him, knelt down. "You're right, my boy! This is not the work of man, nor is it the work of nature."

Jack Piper chimed in, "Even a storm, powerful as it may be, could not tear a mature tree as this one out by its roots, or even this *many* trees, for that matter." The bard swept his arm across the many scattered trees on the village ground.

Banon could not imagine what would be strong enough to actually pull out one of these large saps, as wide around as a thick man, from the hardened earth. And then he remembered the rumors. Men clad in all black, with black armor of the rebellion, accompanied by great beasts. He then thought about the human arm bone and shuddered.

"Do you think it's possible for there to be a beast this strong? Or a creature that might...desecrate a human in that fashion?" he said, gesturing to the piles of timbers holding their family's remains. Banon wrinkled his nose, the air thick with the stench of death. "This has the makings of a terrifying bedtime story." He looked hazily around, expecting a horrible monster to jump out at any time.

"Aye, Your Majesty," The large captain of the Goldenshields replied frankly, "This doesn't make a lick o' sense."

"Over here, Your Majesty!" A group of Guardsmen were gathered near the edge of the village clearing that led into the forest and Banon and the rest of the crew made their way to the other men.

"Dear deep blue, look at that!" cried the bard.

What the group found, leading out of the village, were footprints. Not just any footprints, although there were some of those too, but great gigantic footprints stamped into the soil that were now filling with rain.

"Those are twice the size of a man's foot!" Lord Emrys exclaimed as Banon put his boot inside one of the prints, making his own foot seem dwarfed.

Jack Piper, sopping locks of dark matted hair hanging in his face, regarded the large impressions in the muddy ground. He got down on all fours, acting quite peculiar, and traced the inside of the large foot with his finger, scooping up mud in the process and tasting it. Banon grimaced.

"Mmmhmm. Yes, just as I thought." He grunted knowingly.

"What? What is it?" Banon questioned impatiently.

"Three toes."

"Three toes?" The prince asked as he wondered how the bard could tell anything from licking dirt.

Piper scratched his head in wonder. "There's only one thing that could make a track like this. But it just couldn't be… "

"For goodness sake, bard, tell us!" Captain Leof was growing anxious as well.

"Crag Trolls," the bard said bluntly.

"Trolls… " Banon mused.

"Yes," Jack Piper confirmed. "They have enormous feet with only three toes as big as sausages and sharp thick claws on each one. They have the look of a reptile, with razor sharp spikes running down their backs and pale grey slimy skin covered with bone like bumps, an armor of sort, making them very resilient."

The group looked at each other dubiously, wondering what the other person might be thinking.

"And the trolls look like they're smiling at you, thin lips curled around a mouth full of sharp teeth and fangs dripping with saliva."

Aurous Goldcoin was the color of a white sheet, sweating more profusely than usual. The men were pondering what the bard had said when Sir Captain Leof burst into a growling guttural laugh.

"Aye, Crag Trolls it is! Haha! Now you'll have us believin' in fairies and hobgoblins too!"

"There's really no other explanation I can gather from it." The bard said defensively, standing up and puffing out his thin chest, cloak covered in an array of brightly colored patches.

"Tell me, bard," Leof said mockingly, "Do ye think that the black rebellion employs giants and elves too, as well as Crag Trolls?"

Opening his mouth to speak, Jack Piper was interrupted by the prince, "Sir Captain! Let the man explain himself. Go on bard." Banon motioned for Jack to continue.

As the bard began to explain the history of the Crag Troll, the men, growing more and more interested, took seats among the fallen logs under the cover of a large umbrella tree, looking like anxious children listening to a storybook.

The keeper of the past, as Jack Piper was often called, told how centuries ago the supposedly mythical creatures roamed the land in the time of the Great Freeze. Merenia, which was at that time under the rule of the Redbearded king, was covered in snow and ice, looking like a winter wonderland, and stayed that way for many years. Though the crystalized land was beautiful and seemed peaceful, it was far from that. King Redbeard created a curfew such that no man would be outside after the sunset, for that was when the Trolls would come to towns and villages in great numbers and hunt viciously, their favorite treat being the tender meat of young children.

Banon flinched at the bard's gruesome words.

Merenia was in extreme peril during The Great Freeze, and because travel was seen as a death warrant, the trade exchange decreased greatly, and when the trolls became thwarted by the curfew, they turned to the peoples' livestock. Illness and famine spread quickly from lack of food and nutrition, and even the king and his Army would not travel very far, for fear of an attack by the bloodthirsty Trolls.

Though travel was slow, rumors spread fast of safe havens near the shorelines of Merenia, where people were comfortable and happy. It was said that the trolls would not venture near the ocean on either side of the country for whatever reason. Was it a fear of water? The people did not know, but they began abandoning their homes and everything they knew, only taking with them what they could carry on their backs and horses, relying on safety in numbers, in search of the beaches of Merenia.

"Not only were the Crag Trolls wicked and violent, they were cunning and brilliantly smart." Piper said in his mysterious storytelling voice.

The bard continued telling how the Crag Trolls had caught on to what the humans were doing and began to ambush the groups of refugees, and kill many. Just when it was thought that all hope was lost, a great change swept over the lands.

The earth began to crack and a great mountain erupted from the ground in South Merenia, shaking the earth to its core. The colossal mountain exploded with hot liquid fire that ran down the land in gushing rivers, pushing the Trolls north to colder climates. The snows began to melt and the ice began to break, while green vegetation burst from the thawing ground and plants and flowers pushed through in astounding reds, pinks, and yellows.

As the earth grew warmer, the Trolls grew weaker, and the humans became more confident and started to fight back.

Piper's face was wet and gleaming in the twilight as he finished the story. "It is said that the surviving Trolls retreated to the icy tops of Mount Craghill never to be seen again—hence giving the tallest mountain in Merenia its name, "Mount Craghill."

Whether it was from being wet and cold, or from the effects of the story, the men shivered, bundling themselves in their cloaks. Even the big and scruffy Leof looked chilled to the bone.

Lord Emrys stood, rubbing his chin thoughtfully, and said, "What I don't understand is, if these truly are the Crag Trolls from the story, why would they be appearing now, and down on lower and warmer elevations for that matter."

"Have ye not noticed the weather, m'lord? Mother nature's actin' as if she's gotten it all backwards, cold rains in the summer, fall weather in the spring?" Captain Leof spoke as if he'd had a change of opinion.

The prince nodded his head. "It sure would make sense that if there were still trolls living in this time, they might be stirring because of the weather change. But the weather itself is not cold enough yet to be the only thing driving them out. I wonder what else it could be."

Just then, with a gust of wind, Banon felt the air grow even more frigid than before and he blinked at a small frozen chip that landed on the tip of his nose.

The men, walking out into to the open, looked up overhead to see what had been a fast falling torrent of rain turn into a lazy flurry of sparkling white snowflakes floating on the air. The band of men watched the drifting snow fall in astonishment, creating an eerie white scene in the dark and destroyed village.

Lord Emry's words came out as a cold fine mist, "We'd best send a word to the king. And fast."

QUIN

"What was he doing so close in the first place?" an angry male voice said. The distant sound came through almost inaudible, and the wide open spaces of the connecting maze of caverns didn't help.

The cave was damp and cold, but Quin could feel Noam's warmth, being tied back to back with him. Covered in darkness and hands bound, Quin could hear bits of people talking, catching a word here and there, and sometimes getting a full sentence. She was straining to hear, but thought she might get enough information to figure out where they were, or at least what these stranger's intentions were.

Noam had obviously seen something down in that cavern that she had not right before they were assaulted, judging by his gasping reaction. She very much wanted to know what he'd seen but couldn't ask him, for their mouths were gagged with a foul tasting cloth. The most she could do to communicate with her friend was grunt and moan, which would award her a kick in the side from her captor, so silence seemed the best option.

Leaning her head to the side, as if it would somehow enhance her hearing, Quin heard the words, "duty," and "gathering information," and "murder." She jerked at the word "murder" and could feel the ropes that tied her hands behind her back chafing her skin raw.

Although she couldn't make out everything that was said, she could tell by the tone and inflection of the voices that there was a large group of people and that they were arguing heavily.

"Alright, you two snoops, *get up!*" The gruff voice jerked at the rough ropes that bound their hands and jolted Quin and Noam unsteadily to their feet. "We're going to see the king. You'll be lucky if you leave with your heads."

The king? King Thunderdyn is here? But I thought Father had summons to the King's Castle to meet with him. Why would the king be here on the complete opposite side of Merenia?

If Quin had ever felt disoriented, now was one of those times. With a bag over her head, gag in her mouth, and not having her bearings, she felt completely lost. She just couldn't puzzle together what was happening.

Quin and Noam, stumbling clumsily all the while, were pulled closer to the voices, which echoed and bounced off the cave walls.

The heated conversation grew clearer. "Aren't you forgetting that *we* are the ones keeping *your* secret so that history does not repeat itself!" a nasally voice said.

Then another booming voice spoke, solid and commanding, "Enough of this hostility. We are members of The Peace Protectors and it is our purpose to *keep* peace, not create tension!"

The argument was obviously over, for the voices were now silent, as the two prisoners were half-walking and half-dragged along. Quin could sense that they were now further down in the vast cavern, as it was cooler, and she could hear the soft lapping sounds of the lake water.

"Your Majesty," her captor said boastfully, "I beg your pardon. I did not want to disturb the meeting, but… "

"Out with it man. What is this all about, Sir Tornbuckle?" A loud but familiar and kind voice asked.

"Well, Captain, we were going about our rounds, and found these two… ruffians sneaking about." the man said, his voice full of pride.

"Spies!" one of the voices from the earlier argument hollered.

"Should we take care of them, Captain?" Quin could feel her guard, now known as Sir Tornbuckle, move one of his arms, and pictured him making a slicing motion across his throat.

"Well, let's have a look first and see who these little informants might be. Do ye agree, Your Majesty?" The familiar captain queried.

The solid and booming voice spoke, "Yes. Bring them forward. Reveal their faces." Quin and Noam were roughly jerked forward and pushed a few more steps before coming to a stop. The entire place was quiet, except for the little sloshing ripple sounds coming from the water. Quin could almost feel the others' anticipation while she waited for the dark material to be ripped off of her head.

And then it happened. Quin and Noam were thrust into reality, a blinding light shown in their eyes. In all actuality it was a dim light from an array of soft glowing lanterns, but it was very bright and painful to the stowaways and their dark-adapted eyes.

Blinking against her hazy vision, Quin turned to look back at her captor. He was a tall and slumpy man with a golden tooth that gleamed from within a dirty and scruffy face. Tornbuckle flashed her a sinister smile. She turned back and could make out two groups of people on either side of a large stone slab table coming out of the lake near the side wall. One group sat on what looked to be a bench carved right into the stone wall, dangling their feet into the rippling water. The other half waded in the shallow pool of water, making small ripples in the lake.

What an odd meeting place... and odd people. And who on earth are The Peace Protectors?

She focused in on one member, sitting on a small rock island in the water that was closer to her side of the lake. He held some sort of rod or staff and wore what seemed to be a white crown. She could not make out his features for it was a bit dark and her eyes had not yet adjusted to the lantern light. The muscular man had a long silver beard and hair and wore strange clothes that glittered blue with hints of turquoise and green.

She heard one of the hazy members loudly draw in his breath in shock.

"What is it, Captain?" someone asked.

There was a pause. "It's me... granddaughter... " And then there was nothing. Not a word was spoken and silence hung thick in the air.

As Quin could not see anyone's features or details, she could not tell the reaction of the group but she could sense being watched, the lot of them more than likely contemplating the new arrivals.

Quin, having an overwhelming feeling of relief at knowing she had found her grandfather, was also still a bit frightened as to what might happen next. She started to call out his name, but it came out more like, "Mmmmphmm," forgetting that her mouth was still gagged.

"Well, don't just stand there, bring them here I say." Captain Longship commanded. When the two guards brought the children down and around the lake, Gaderian rushed to meet them.

As he uncovered Quin's mouth, he whispered, "It'd be best if ye don't speak a word, Quinnie, let me do the talkin'.'" He motioned a shushing sound to Noam, laying his finger gently across his lips, and the boy nodded in understanding as a guard untied the gag from his mouth. Quin's eyes settled on the distressed captain's face. It was not his usual expression and didn't suit him well. She didn't like it, the lines of worry creasing his brow. As a matter of fact, she didn't like it at all.

By now the blurred veil began to lift from Quin's eyes as she began to regain focus and she surveyed her surroundings. Her mouth dropped open in awe, for what she saw was unreal. She thought for a moment that she might be dreaming.

The blurry man she'd seen sitting atop the water-surrounded rock was now a clear vision, which she eyed from top to bottom in shock. The white crown he wore was made from sea coral that had been sanded smooth and polished to shine, carved in an intricate detail of twisting and crashing waves that curled around his head perfectly. He had a handsome face that seemed molded from rock with sharp features, arched brows, and dark entrancing eyes the color of acorns and leaves. Flowing out from the bottom of the crown was his long white-silver hair that touched his bare and tanned chest. The staff he held in his right hand was made from a long chunk of driftwood, shining with the gloss of lacquer, with a similar white coral carving on the top to match his majestic crown.

This man, who she assumed was "the king," was not garbed in the sparkling-colored clothes she had thought earlier with her hooded eyes, but wore a tail of cool colored glimmering scales of blue, turquoise, and green that shifted their colors in the pale light.

"Granddaughter?" one of the members questioned haughtily. "Longship, what is the meaning of this? You know the rules —this could jeopardize everything!"

Another interjected, "Anyone that so much as catches a glimpse of a merperson, *must be killed!*"

All of the Council members start speaking at once, shouting, and talking over one another, tempers rising.

Quin was gaping at the half-fish man when his voice exploded. "Enough!" He slammed his staff into the water causing it to ripple and wave wildly, the ground vibrating, and small pebbles and rocks rained down from overhead.

Covering her head against the shower of dirt, Quin scanned the room quickly, eyes darting back and forth. *They are merpeople! Oh, my bloody goodness!*

The ones swimming in the water that she had thought human, were actually like their king, with tails of glistening gem-like scales, each different and unique from the next and every hue in the color spectrum.

Heads snapped towards the king. The anger on his face melted into kindness as he looked at Quin. "Girl, come here to me."

The merman king gestured to her with his abnormally large hand, as she looked at her grandfather for reassurance. He nodded his approval and smiled warmly. Quin slowly walked to the edge of the lake, her hand nervously feeling for the lump in her pocket just to make sure it was still there.

"Don't be afraid, child. I only want to have a look at you." The merman king motioned for her to come closer. Looking down at her toes touching the edge of the water, she raised her head and looked at the strange fish king.

"It's only water, little one." The fish-man's voice was deep but kind.

Quin glanced at Captain Gaderian once again as she anxiously rubbed the soft fur of the rabbit foot that she tied to her skirts, and he nodded her on encouragingly. She looked at the merpeople in the water, as she caught herself biting her lip, their faces studying her as if *she* were the strange one. *Oh my,* she thought, *they are so beautiful!*

Only a short distance now from the rock, she took a few steps further into the water, which was surprisingly warm. Shaking, she looked into the merman king's eyes.

"What is your name, child?"

"Quinlan, daughter of Lord Emrys Castlecray," she said proudly if not a bit tremulously, "of Castlecray Keep."

He studied her thoughtfully for what seemed to be an eternity and turned to regard the captain. The captain nodded his head and smiled as if answering the king's unspoken question.

The king turned to Noam. "And you, boy?"

"Noam Finbar, guard and protector of Lady Quinlan Castlecray… Your Majesty." Noam stuck out his chest confidently, trying to hide his fear.

The crowned merman chuckled in spite of himself.

"Children," he said looking back and forth between the two, "Can you keep a secret? One you must keep until your dying day?" Quin and Noam looked at each other and nodded apprehensively.

The king's soft side changed to rock again. "Everyone, meet at the shore, it is almost sundown. Quickly now!" At his urgent words, the humans moved up towards the narrow exit of the cavern and the mermaids and mermen who sat upon the rocks dove into the water only to disappear.

As Captain Longship, Quin, and Noam begin to leave, the king called out, "Quinlan of Castlecray!" She turned.

"Take heed," the king said cautiously. "This is only the beginning of your journey." He gestured to the two children, "You will now play a very important and dangerous role, one that causes others to rely on *you* for their lives."

BANON

Banon was very cold, his fingers frozen like blocks of ice under his leather gloves. The ground was covered in white blankets of snow that glistened like diamonds and the world was still and beautiful, though Banon had a gut-wrenching feeling of dread. He didn't understand why, but the dark feeling enveloped him, pulling him further into sadness and sorrow. He was riding a white horse down the banks of the river, looking for something, but he didn't remember what. The snow crunched loudly in the silence under the white gelding's hooves, as the fluffy falling flakes obscured his vision, but he searched the surrounding trees anyway. He felt a longing to find something, an urgently severe tug, and kept heading east.

The silence was now being filled with a soft chiming song, melodic yet also poisonous voices coming through. A choir of airy tones blended in perfect harmony, lulling Banon and drawing him on. He felt calm, but the inner dread remained tucked away in a small corner of his mind. *I must not forget. I must keep searching.* But what was he searching for?

The enchanting melody grew louder as he ran his horse down the riverside, watching icy crystals fall into the water, making small sparkling ripples circle outwards until they disappeared, only to be replaced by another. And clearer yet the sound came to his ears, tempting him and teasing him into a state of bittersweet bliss.

And then he remembered. A young woman. He was searching for the one he loved. A scream filled his ears, meshing with the soft musical chanting; a scream of hopelessness. Banon frantically drove his horse harder towards the shrill screaming, as the melodic voices tried to pull him in, tried to make him forget. *I must not forget. I must keep searching.* And just then, as his horse hurtled a rocky mound, he burst through a group of trees and saw her.

Submerged in water up to her neck, she reached to him from the middle of the river, blurred by snow and ice. How beautiful she looked, and terrified, surrounded in a world of white. *But who is she?*

Banon knew he loved her, and that he must save her. Throwing himself from the horse, he landed hard on the ground, breaking through the top crust of the snow.

But she wasn't alone. Figures surrounded her, crooning and purring a seducing lullaby, the sound of a thousand voices coming together, though there were only a few. The young woman, whom he noticed wore a crown of white waves, looked desperately into his crystal blue eyes, searching for safety, for rescue.

Banon started for her, but was unable to move, his foot stuck in icy slush. He struggled and pulled as the figures closed in on her. He felt helpless as his scrambling attempts caused him to fall into the cold wet snow. *Nooooooo!* He tried to scream, but the bewitching song seemed to fill his mouth and choke off his words. The only thing that came out was a low growling sound.

The girl reached for him again, slowly sinking, her mouth now being covered by water. Banon rose to find his foot still caught, and again came a growl. But it was not his growl.

Banon woke in a cold sweat, disoriented as to where he was. He couldn't shake the dream from his mind or the strong feelings that he had towards the mystery woman. Was he still dreaming? He glanced to his side to see the other men sound asleep, snoring heavily. No, this was not part of his dream. They had been on their journey for days now and camped in many places. *Snakewood.* That's right. They were camped a bit north of Snakewood village, high in the mountainous forest hills. Banon remembered now; he had had that dream before. He felt relief at knowing that he was now in reality and not in that terrible dream. He breathed in the cold misty night air deeply and let his tense body relax.

And then it came again. The low rumbling growl he had heard in his dream. Banon's eyes shot to the edge of the clearing, scanning the trees for the source of the noise, his body tensing again. He didn't see the guards that were to be posted in shifts to watch the camp overnight and the site was dark, except for the glow of the dying fire.

Banon's ears perked up as he heard a rustling in the bushes scoring the forest edge, the moon casting a silver lining over the forms of men sleeping under their cloaks, lined neatly on the ground. No one stirred. Was he hearing things? Something didn't feel right. Captain Leof snorted loudly as he shifted under his wrap, mumbling something in his sleep.

The hair on the back of Banon's neck stood on end, and goose bumps prickled his skin. Hearing another sound like the crunching of leaves underfoot, he slowly moved his hand to the hilt of his sword, concealed by his cloak. *Maybe it's just one of the guards...*

As quick as a flash, a giant form came bursting from the trees, snarling and bolting towards the sleeping men.

"To arms!" Before Banon had finished yelling, the large heaving form locked yellow glowing eyes on his target. The prince, now up with sword in hand, watched the grey beast charge at him, slimy skin gleaming in the moonlight. The ground vibrated as the heavy feet pounded in angry fury. The closer it came, the better Banon could see its features, ugly

and bumpy, fangs dripping with blood from its recent kill.

Trembling, the young prince waited for the bulky monster, looking like a sack full of boulders, to rush at him. Just as Banon could feel the beast's hot stinky breath on his face, it lunged at him with clawed hands outstretched. Quick as a cricket, the prince dodged under the pale grey arm, pivoting and striking the beast through its side in one soft fluid motion. The monster had armor-like skin, but slimy, just like the bard had described in his story of the Crag Trolls, but the blade cut sure and true. The reptilian creature stopped, gripping its wounded side as though it had only been stung by a bee, and turned, fuming, to find the one who'd done it. Banon, now quite a bit less confident, backed into a tree. The troll-like thing started at him again, but this time with caution.

Just then, Lord Emrys appeared out of nowhere, sword at the ready, shining in the moonlight, a sinister smile upon his rugged face. The foul-smelling monster, with razor-sharp spikes running down its back, turned to Emrys, distracted by the newcomer. Banon, cornered against his tree, heard Lord Emrys whistle to the thing, as if he were calling a hound, and saw him curl his finger for the beast to come closer. Irritated and angry, the oversized revolting head looked back and forth between Emrys and Banon, finally deciding on the older and more annoying of the two.

The beast, roaring thunderously, charged and swung his arm at Lord Emrys's head, missing and making an airy swooping sound as the man ducked just in time. Banon saw Sir Captain Leof sneak up behind the fighting fiend, locking eyes with the crouched Lord Emrys. Simultaneously, as though they had come to an understanding, the men took their positions. Captain Leof brought his broadsword in a downward arcing motion through the beast from the nook between neck and shoulder to the opposite side of its ribs. At the same time, Emrys, with his sword hand crossed over his knees, diagonally sliced across the beast from thigh to hip as he stood, the monster blinked in shock and then slid apart into four pieces.

The three of them, panting and shaking from exertion, smiled at each other in victory, but whipped their heads around to the sound of metallic shearing, times a dozen, accompanied by that familiar throaty growl.

Another revolting and stench-ridden creature came crashing through the clearing at hearing its brother's cries, and went straight towards a line of Goldenshields, their swords quickly leaving their scabbards. Now the entire camp was in pandemonium; men in fighting stance, hair on end and sleep in their eyes, fighting unknown monsters in the dark. Banon could see Jack Piper swinging his dirk wildly, making the trinkets weaved into his long matted hair jingle and sparkle in the moonlight.

The second creature was surrounded by half a dozen golden shields, and seemed to be taken care of rather quickly. Two more appeared, one on either side of the camp, snarling and spitting through sharp, rotten teeth, ears pointing up towards the sky.

While Lord Emrys and Captain Leof were diverted towards the beasts to join the Goldenshields' fight, Banon heard a quiet sniveling whimper nearby. He looked to see Lord Aurous Goldcoin huddled under a thorn bush next to a large crooked oak, his jewel-crusted and golden gilt walking stick raised above his head to keep away the drooling savage troll that stood hovering over the little man. The monster did not seem impressed, and didn't hesitate to start for Lord Aurous.

Banon searched for anyone who could help, but he was the only one close enough to do anything in time. He was frightened. No, he was scared out of his mind, but heard his father's voice ring through his head. "Courage is not the lack of fear. Courage is facing the fear that you have… like a madman."

Banon felt an odd sensation rise up within him, a courage he'd never felt before. Running his left hand straight back through his hair, leaving it to spike up in all directions, the prince smiled…like a mad man. With the prickly thorn bush in the way, Banon did the only thing he could, and gave a running start towards the tree. Barreling as fast as lightning, the prince's feet left the ground and continued up the side of the leaning tree, bounding up the bark. Two, three, four steps Banon went up, and just as he reached the peak, he pushed off the side of the tree hard and went further into the air, sword arced high above his head, and in a swooping motion sliced down through a thick low-hanging limb. As he hit onto the ground, legs bent, he watched the tree limb clout the monster square on the head with a loud *thunk!* The troll stood dazed, its heavy grotesque body swaying to and fro before finally toppling over backwards as straight as a board and landing with a hard blow, shaking the ground. Banon rushed around the shaken treasurer, jumped up, and came down thrusting his sword into the center of the troll's chest. The large body jerked and then lay lifeless, putting out an acrid smell.

Banon surveyed the other groups and all of the fighting seemed to be coming to a halt. Jack Piper hooted something inaudible and then pulled a small tankard from his tunic, leaning his head back, and drank deeply —*no doubt, whiskey*.

No more evil creatures crawled out of the forest, and there appeared to be minimal injuries to the other men. The prince stumbled to his knees, body strained and exhausted. Chest heaving up and down, he glanced up to see Emrys running to him with Captain Leof Brawnmont, a group of guards, and the bard trailing behind.

"I'd lost track of you in the fight, my boy. You alright?" Emrys asked in concern.

Banon shook off the blurring fatigue. "Yes, I'm fine."

Leof, grabbing Banon's shoulder with a muscular hand, tugged him off the ground and patted his back proudly, saying, "That was some trick you pulled there, Your majesty! Hahaha! I thought you might just sprout yourself some wings and keep on a'flyin up that tree and right up into the clouds!"

The men all chimed in, talking of Banon's astounding feat. Even Aurous Goldcoin, who had bravely ventured from his hiding spot, excitedly congratulated the young prince with an over-exaggerated handshake. Banon was still pumped with adrenaline and excitement over their triumph, but felt that further measures still needed to be taken.

Banon held up a hand to still the lively group and they quieted.

"We are not quite in the clear yet," he said as the men watched him, panting. "Men, keep on your guard and watch each others' backs. I will not have another surprise attack." Banon scanned the group. "Who was on guard shift this night?"

"Johnson and Demiere, Your Majesty. We haven't seen them anywhere," stated one of the older Goldenshields matter-of-factly.

"I want two scouts to fan out and circle the area." Banon pointed towards the small massacre on the campground. "Make sure there are no more of those... *things* around." Two of the men bowed their heads and darted off into the trees.

Captain Leof took a step towards Jack Piper and looked him straight in the face. "I'm sorry for giving you such a hard time back in the village, bard." The captain smiled and shouted, "Three toes!"

Leof pointed at the foot of a nearby fallen beast and then grabbed the scrawny singer by his shoulders and shook him. "It seems you really *do* know what you're talking about. That's sure a Crag Troll if I ever saw one! You've got my trust bard, you're a good man!"

"Aye, aye!" yelled one of the men, and "Three toes!" exclaimed another.

"I's alright Captain, you're not so bad yourself." Jack said, grinning. The men talked amongst themselves, reliving the fight, invigorated by the small battle.

Banon didn't know what to do next. It was like he was walking in the footsteps of a storybook character. He had never been through anything like this, the tiring journey, the vivid dreams, and now a fight with fabled trolls; it all seemed so unreal! Would today's events be written in legends for years to come? He fell deep in thought, proud of his courage, but feeling weary and homesick. He missed his father. The king would've known exactly what to do. He even missed the comfort of his brother, Tolan's, company, irritating as he might be.

Just then, two breathless scouts, ran back into the clearing and up to the prince, both of them covered in troll blood from the skirmish. "Your Majesty... " white as a ghost, the first leaned a hand on his knee, breathing hard, "I think we... found

Johnson and Demiere." Men began gathering around to hear the news.

The second scout, looking only to be a boy, said tentatively, "Well, we're not quite sure."

"How are you not sure?" questioned the prince.

The first scout grimaced, "The only thing that was recognizable was their swords and the official goldenshield broach. The rest… "

"Mutilated," the younger of the two finished.

Banon was hit with a wave of grief. He felt that he should have done more, pushed harder. Maybe they could've arrived a day earlier and protected these people.

"There's something else." The first scout raised a strip of green cloth. "We found it about ten paces into the woods." The man handed it to Banon.

The prince studied the scrap thoroughly. "It looks to be the remains of a coat of arms. Of which house, I'm not sure." He held the cloth up and asked, "Does anyone recognize this coat of arms?" The group was silent, some shaking their heads. Banon handed it to Lord Emrys for a second opinion and Jack Piper stepped in for a closer look.

"There are many houses in Merenia with green as their color, but there seems to be a bit of a black figure here at the tear," Lord Emrys declared.

Jack Piper reached for the cloth, "May I?" Lord Emrys gave it over as men closed in around them, curious about what might be their only clue to who was in charge of the brutal attacks.

"Emrys is right," the Bard mused, "There are many houses with green as their color…but green with a black ensign? That might narrow it down a bit, but there are still sure to be quite a few with similar colors."

Banon took back the cloth and, folding it neatly into a tiny square, placed it in a hidden pocket within his surcoat. "Upon arrival at the Castle, I will go straight to Elder Wylie at the Golden Library. If anyone would know whose house this represents," Banon patted his pocket, "It would be the Grand Elder."

Although the group knew that they were one step closer to discovering who was behind the rebellion's rising, they were still in dark moods over all of the deaths that had occurred.

"Lord Emrys. Bard Piper." The prince looked at the two men in question. "I will have you both accompany me when we reach the King's Castle." Lord Emrys bowed to the prince and Jack Piper made his own clumsy attempt.

"It is settled then." Somberly, the prince walked over and picked up a log from the pile of chopped wood and threw it on the fire, sending glowing sparks to flutter in the cold night air. In an instant, the fire blazed brightly. "I imagine none of us will be taking to sleep well tonight."

QUIN

"I, Quinlan of House Castlecray of Merenia, solemnly swear that I will faithfully and honestly…" Quin mimicked the strange king's words.

"Support the Protectors of the Peace and protect its loyal members from all enemies…" the merman king's voice echoed over the water like a drum.

"Support the Protectors of the Peace and protect its loyal members from all enemies…" Quin spoke softly but confidently.

The sun was setting on the horizon, creating golden yellow and orange waves shimmering far out to sea. The sea king sat on a rock in the shallow bay of the lush magical island, covered partly in water to his glittering scales.

Quin stood by Noam, warm water to her middle, while merfolk and humans gathered around them, silently watching, all half submerged in water.

"And will keep the balance of land and sea..." The king said with Quin repeating after.

"By holding close to my heart the merpeople's secret until my dying day." Quin finished the words of her oath, breathing in deeply the cold sea air, her brown hair fluttering in the wind.

A young fair-skinned, light-eyed mermaid swam to the two children and handed them each a large conch shell. The young mermaid spoke in a melodic watery voice, "And now you will drink the brine of Mer Ocean to symbolize your union with the sea."

Quin and Noam exchanged looks and with heads tilted back, drank the liquid down in one gulp. Quin licked the salty water from her lips and again gave her attention to the silver-haired king, his tanned muscles gleaming from the sun-reflecting water.

"I, King Nerius, of the Wavekeepers of Tidebreak Tower, of Mer Ocean and all surrounding oceans and seas, by under oath of the Protectors of the Peace, hereby deem you members of The Peace Protectors." King Nerius motioned for Quin and Noam to approach. They slowly waded through the water and he put a medallion looped with thin hemp rope around each of their necks.

Quin reached her hand to her neck and felt of the strange necklace, rubbing its smooth metallic texture between her fingers. The charm was a round flat seashell, winding in on itself like a spiral staircase, dipped in a thick metal, the color of ravens.

She quickly glanced up at her grandfather and realized that he too was wearing the same medallion and it shone like shiny black silk in the setting sun. She'd seen him wearing it all of her life, but never realized what it was. Looking around at the other members of the Peace Protectors, she now saw that they all wore the symbol threaded around their necks or tied to theirs belts, swaying with movement.

And then Quin's jaw dropped as she looked at the king's necklace. It was different from the others, but not unlike anything she'd ever seen. As a matter of fact, she *had* seen it somewhere else. *The stone!* It was the exact twin to the inky black rock she had found in the tunnels under Castlecray, the rock that was now sewn into the pocket of her skirt. She gripped it fiercely, remembering how she'd felt when she first held the glowing rock—calm, but full of emotion. She'd almost forgotten and left it in Aaric's bedchamber when she readied herself to sneak away in the dark, but decided better of it and went back, tiptoeing in to fetch it up.

The clumpy dark rock dangled from a brown braided cord that hung loosely on King Nerius's strong neck. But it did not glow, Quin noticed. *Why would the same stone be locked up in a chest underneath Castlecray?* Something wasn't adding up. Quin thought best that she not say anything yet, until she had her grandfather alone. She didn't know these strange merpeople, and though she had taken an oath to protect them and their secret, she still didn't know how far she could trust them.

"Members of the Protectors of the Peace, listen here!" The merman king raised his staff of waves, the smooth wood and coral top glittering, reflecting the colors of the sea. "This is a very trying time and we must make haste to see that our secret stays concealed and with what happened in North Harbor that makes it very difficult. Reach out to your brothers and sisters through the Whisper Web, and spread word of what has happened; we need to clean up any suspicions those fisherman may have started. My fellow merpeople, tomorrow we will convene at Tidebreak Tower for a meeting of all of the kiths of Mer Ocean. Please spread the word, we need everyone in attendance."

The king gestured to the group, "Now go and begin preparations." The mermen and mermaids vanished into the water of the bay, leaving behind sunset-colored bubbles that rose to the surface. The sun was now well below the sparkling horizon as the humans began to walk the beach towards rocky cliffs and disappear behind ridges and crevices in the darkening scene.

The mer king looked to Noam and Quin, still standing in the water next to the captain. "I would like to formally welcome you to Invisible Island." With a bow to the children he continued. "The official headquarters of the Protectors of the Peace. Please make yourselves at home. Nimbus Nooney will be seeing to your needs. It pleasures me to have such promising new members grace our presence."

Pausing, the king looked at Quin and said, "There is something special about you, Quinlan of Castlecray. I cannot put my finger on it, but I deem we shall find out sooner than later. I'm sure we will be seeing each other again in short order."

Nerius nodded to Quin and Noam. "Goodnight and may the power of the waves be with you to lighten your dreams." He then nodded to Captain Gaderian, and with that, the majestic half-man half-fish dove into the now dark water, silver ripples trailing behind with the light of the first stars.

The three made their way up the soft beach, feet sinking slightly in the sand. None of them spoke; they walked in silence, reveling in the strange and recent events. Coming to a crevice in the wall that looked very much like the one Noam and Quin went into when first arriving on the island, they slipped inside to find themselves by a fast flowing small river with a group of little wooden row boats lined neatly next to it in the hollow.

"We must be silent as we ride." The captain whispered as he chose a red dingy and untied it from a post and pulled it into the water. Giving Quin his hand, she hopped over the side, steadying herself as the boat rocked back and forth finding its balance. Noam followed, and then her grandfather. They all sat huddled together as the captain pushed off the wall and they began traveling swiftly through the cold, dark, and narrow stone passage.

The current whipped them around like a toy boat in a whirlwind; up and down, in and out, down and around the winding curves they flew. Quin liked the damp and cool musty smell; it reminded her of the tunnels under Castlecray. Surprisingly, as they traveled further on, the tunnels grew warmer.

They began to tilt back a bit, and coming upon a small upturn, Quin's heart leapt into her throat as she saw the river racing down a steep drop off in front of them into a deep, dark tunnel. Before she had time to think, they were rushing down the dark waterfall underpass, droplets of mist spraying them in the face. She gripped hard to the sides of the boat, eyes closed and head ducked.

Whhhooooosh! Quin's stomach heaved with fright and excitement at the zinging cascade. She turned and cracked her eyes to see the falling water behind them and the current of water, now slowed, bringing them through a grand opening to a still lake in the center of a large cavern. The sound of soft lapping water echoed through the vast chamber, but no other noises could be heard other than the fading sound of the waterfall.

"Oooooohhhh, it's beautiful!" Quin exclaimed at the wondrous sight, her voice bouncing off the tall walls and the high jagged rocky ceiling.

"And here we are," Captain Longship said happily extending his arms, "Headquarters of the Protectors of the Peace."

The first thing Quin noticed was that they were surrounded by tiny twinkling lights like the ones they first saw covering the island. It gave a magical feeling of stardust and diamonds hanging on the thick, damp air, and the lights moved, sparkling, in quick little motions, zig-zagging up and down and back and forth. Quin and Noam's heads turned upwards, moving this way and that, taking in the beautiful starry lit stone cave.

Everything was made of the existing rock, mazes of twisting and turning stairs carved into the walls, winding up so high that they faded out of sight. There was a web of paths straying across the ground floor, crossing each other, going over small rocky hills and streams in little bridges and pathways.

Their little boat eased while it went down one of the streams and Quin looked up to see an enormous chandelier of hundreds of twinkling candles overhead, hung from a ledge on a massive rusty pulley system that gave off a warm and cheery glow in the otherwise dim cavern. Surrounding the chandelier, the ceiling was full of downward pointing icy spikes that pulsated in an iridescent array of colors, reflecting the water's movement, the dots of light swirling around their points.

"But there's nobody here," Noam said, his voice echoing through the cave.

"On the contrary Noam, many people are here. Don't let yer eyes fool ye. There is much more to this place than meets the eye," the captain answered.

The small stream pulled them further on, under a large rock shelf and into another dark tunnel.

"Grandfather," Quin bit her lower lip in contemplation, "Why couldn't we see this island? And what were all the tiny stars surrounding it and back in the cavern?" Quin, despite the cover of darkness, pointed back from the way they had come.

"Aaaaaahhh, lightning bugs." Her grandfather's husky voice explained. "But they are a very special kind o' lightning bug only indigenous to the Invisible Island. They are enriched wi' a certain kind o' magic, one that draws them to surround the island, therefore making it invisible."

The blackness of the tunnel cloaked Quin's eyes from sight, but she could still feel their slow movement in the water.

"But wouldn't people see the bugs glowing? And wouldn't they wonder what it was? How is it that no one knows this place exists?" Noam asked one question after another.

The captain chuckled heartily, his voice bouncing loudly through the tunnel. "That's the trick, young laddie. Not just *anyone* can see 'em, only true believers may see the island."

Quin could see the dim flicker of torch light at the end of the tunnel as they approached their destination. The mouth of the narrow passage opened to what looked to be a docking station. The ceilings were low, but the cave was wide, and on either side were small little wooden piers with boats perched at the ends, rocking merrily in the water. Behind each dock, there was a set of stairs, carved right into the wall, climbing through the ceiling, lit by the glow of an iron lantern and a tiny wooden sign hanging below and a painted number on each one.

"And here we are." The captain stopped the small rowboat at an empty dock, with a black nine brushed lazily on the sign behind it.

They exited the dingy and clambered up the rickety pier to the bottom of the stairwell. Captain Longship started right away up the narrow stone steps, followed by the two children. The climb was long and they passed three landings before stopping at the fourth, coming out into a hallway of sorts.

Huffing and puffing from exertion, Quin glanced to her side, where there were various paintings lining the passage, hung in arched niches in the walls. Lit by small hanging lanterns, some of the art depicted aquatic scenes with mermaids or mermen, and some, studious and well-dressed lords and ladies with serious looks upon their faces.

The captain, obviously in great physical condition for his hefty size, was breathing normally after the climb, pointing at a number of doorways that were spread out down the long rock corridor. "Each member of The Peace Protectors gets his own room. Nothin' too fancy, but they're cozy and serve their purpose. We still have a ways to go yet to me room."

Like the docks were numbered below, the rooms were also painted with a series of numbers. The one Quin looked at now was 9-2. She supposed that would be the dock number, and then the room number. There must be hundreds of rooms here! But how strange that they had yet to see a soul. The place appeared to be abandoned, except for the fact that there had to be *someone* there to light the lanterns.

Quin, gazing at the paintings as they walked, saw one that caught her eye and stopped. It was a merman sitting on a rock, and as she had recently discovered, that was their preference when residing above water. The half-man half-fish held a rod in one hand, his other hand by his side in a fist. Powerful waves crashed in around him, brushed in strokes of blues and whites. The merman had rich wavy brown hair and sparkling blue eyes that hinted at a smile, but the face looked stern otherwise. There was something familiar about this painting. She felt as though she had seen it before, but knew that she never had. She couldn't stop looking at the merman's eyes, seeming as though he knew something that she didn't, like an amusing secret he wouldn't tell. *Hmmm. What a curious painting.*

Quin pulled herself away from the painting and started down the passage again to find that her grandfather and Noam were gone. Quin's head darted left and right down the empty corridor, but she could see nothing except a few lanterns giving off a yellow circle of light, and in between the small lighted areas, nothing but pitch darkness. Her heart began to beat faster, as she walked quickly so that she might catch up to the other two. She was now at room 9-7, and had no idea how far they had gone.

"Grandfather?"... No reply. "Noam?" Her voice trailed off down the tunnel, being sucked into darkness. No one answered.

Quin felt panic begin to rise up through her chest and into her head, expanding to her arms and legs, creating a tingling sensation. Faster she walked, her legs starting to ache from exertion. Heart racing and mind spinning, she began to trot. Doors flew by. 9-9. 9-10. 9-11, and so on until two arms reached out from a dark spot and grabbed her by the shoulders. Quin squeaked like a frightened mouse and frantically pulled away from the firm grip.

"Let go!" She screamed. "You dirty, no good, son of a motherless... "

"Sssssshhhhh!" The voice that went along with the arms said. "You'll create a scene!"

Quin wriggled and fought with all of her might and kicked the stranger in the shin. "That is exactly my intention!"

With a yelp the strong man gripped her mouth and closed it tight. "Quite the little thunderbolt you are," the man said in a strained voice and then spoke again. "I'm not going to hurt you. It's okay, Quinlan, I'm a friend."

Quin stopped struggling and mumbled something from behind the hand that covered her mouth.

"Yes, a friend. I'm a Peace Protector also." The voice was warm and kind now, easing Quin's fear. "Now, I am going to lift my hand from your face. And you're not going to scream, right?" Quin nodded.

The hand lifted away from her face and she took a deep breath of air. The mystery man took a step in front of one of the doors, letting the lantern light wash over him, revealing a surprisingly short person. Quin was almost eye to eye with him.

"Nimbus Nooney, Protector of the Peace, Master of the Whisper Web, and Keeper of the Invisible Island at your service, m'lady." The short man bowed to her, his bald head reflecting the lantern light, tufts of dark hair sticking out on either side by his ears.

"I have been anxiously awaiting your arrival, Lady Quinlan of Castlecray." Quin looked at him curiously. How did he know that I would come here, when *I* didn't even know?

"It is a pleasure to finally meet you, Quinlan." Nimbus Nooney was very short, but by no means thin. Quin gaped at the compressed man, with a stocky build garbed in grey robes that hung to his feet. He too, wore a black glossy seashell hung about his neck, proving that he was, in fact, a member of the Peace Protectors.

Trying to remember her manners, Quin curtsied clumsily, saying, "It's a pleasure to make your acquaintance… Master Nooney." She wasn't sure how to address the little, yet powerful man, and she still felt hesitant after just being scared out of her wits.

"Oh, just call me Nooney, we are not so formal around here." He rubbed his head thoughtfully, studying Quin. “On your way to the captain’s room, I assume?”

“Yes...”

“Let me show you the way, my dear.” Nooney put a gentle arm around her shoulders and they began to walk slowly down the flickering pathway.

Trying to think of what to say, Quin offered, “It’s quite a... nice place you have here.”

“Why thank you, my dear. I do what I can to keep it running as it should, though it gets harder through the years as we lose more and more members of the Peace Protectors, giving me less help.”

The stunted man gazed off as though in memory. "Did you know that many, many years ago, in the time of the Red-Bearded King, just about every room here was filled? Things have changed greatly since then.” Nooney looked sad, but his face lightened as he remembered something. “Oh! I meant to ask you, Quinlan, did you find what you were looking for?”

Quin tentatively asked, “What do you mean, ‘what I was looking for?’”

“In the old chest.” Nooney said matter-of-factly. Quin was dumbfounded. *How does he know?* Should she trust him and was he the one who unlocked the chest that held the magical stone? She was silent as she looked straight into the little man’s eyes.

“Quin,” Nooney said with a curled lip, “you were the one meant to find the rock.” And then she remembered.

"It was *you!*" she said in realization. "I saw you talking to my father at Aleena's feast! Were you the one following me around? Did you put the rock there for me to find? What is it? What does it do? Why…"

The short balding man cut her off, "One question at a time, my dear." Nooney paused, thinking, and then continued, "Yes, it was I who was talking with your father, and it was I who was making sure that you found the rock, and no one else."

"You scared the daylights out of me!" she cried.

"That was not my purpose, Quinlan. I was, in a way, protecting you. The rock you found, if in the right hands, is very powerful, and if in the wrong, very dangerous." They began walking again with the Island Keeper's urging. He looked at Quin. "Have you told anyone about the rock?"

"No!" Quin said startled by the question. "Well, yes. I mean… I only told my brother Aaric… but…"

"Good. Keep it that way. Tell no one else. *No one,*" Nimbus Nooney emphasized the words "no one" considerably. "There are eyes and ears everywhere, not all good. And although I hate the thought of it, there are possibly spies even here on the Invisible Island."

Quin thought for a moment. "But aren't you a spy?" she asked dubiously. "As well as being an Island Keeper and a Peace Protector, you said you were the Master of the Whisper Web. That sounds very spy-like and suspicious to me."

Nooney harrumphed. "Sharp little one, aren't you?" He rubbed his gleaming head in thought. "Am I a spy? Yes and no. The Whisper Web is used for only defensive purposes. It's a small sub-group of the Peace Protectors. It's just a secret network, really, where we can connect with other members of the Peace Protectors across Merenia and other lands to transfer important information. It is only used for good and for the safety of us all."

Quin's curiosity was brimming, "What about the glowing stone? What is it? Why does it only glow for some?"

Nimbus began to answer but a large figure suddenly blocked off the path, as well as the light of the lantern.

"Quinnie-fish!" Captain Gaderian suddenly came bursting from the dark and swooped Quin up in his arms, leaving Noam trailing behind.

"I was so worried when we couldn't find ye! This place is like a giant maze!" Setting her down, Captain Gaderian gave a huge sigh of relief and looked up to see Nimbus Nooney.

"And there's the Island Keeper! Nimbus blazin' Nooney! Great to see ye again so soon." The captain's voice spiraled in booming echoes down the cold rock hallways.

"Likewise, Longship! Always a pleasure, old friend," the very short man said to the very tall one. The odd couple hugged and thumped each other loudly on the back.

Nimbus stepped back and continued, "The lot of you must be hungry, cold, and exhausted from the day's excursions. Go ahead and get settled into your rooms; there's already a fire blazing, and dry clothes set out." Nimbus Nooney began to walk away, backwards into the dark. "Dinner will be served shortly in the dining hall. I expect I'll see you hungry bunch of tattered travelers there after you clean up."

Quin looked down at herself as the small man disappeared in the dark, and realized just how tattered she was, if not more than usual. Her skirts were ripped and torn from crawling through jagged tunnels, her hair sopping wet from waterfalls, mist, and sweat, and her skin smeared with dust and mud.

Today had proved to be a day unlike any other she'd ever known, and she hesitated at the thought of what tonight might bring. She and Noam exchanged smiles as they went through the heavy wooden door painted with the numbers 9-19, leading to their room, firelight crackling in the dark.

AARIC

Hagglers Way was the long road that connected Castlecray Keep to the waterfront fishing village of South Harbor, lined by a tall stone ocean-side wall that protected it from the high tides and unpredictable waves. Hagglers Way was a bustling mishmash of small lean-to shacks and vendor carts open to the public for buying or trading goods. Aaric trotted his horse through the muddy and crammed street, pulled in by the aroma of savory meat pies and sweet cinnamon pastries and the yells of the merchants calling out their wares. The market hummed with sound and movement as Aaric stopped to let a horse-drawn cart full of eels and freshwater fish cross by. The ringing of the blacksmith's anvil struck rhythmically with a *clang clang* as dirt-smudged children ran in circles giggling and playing games, getting underfoot and being reprimanded by the traders trying to do business.

Aaric had fond memories of coming to market with his mother when he was young. Before shopping, they would always sit on the grass across from the market, sipping cider, and people-watch.

As well as farmers with their pigs and chickens, and craftsmen with their array of wooden and metal trinkets, there were entertainers. Jugglers juggled, flutists fluted, and fire-breathers would breathe fire in long drawn out crimson flames. It was a lively and magical place, but knowing that his littlest sister was missing, Aaric couldn't enjoy the atmosphere as usual.

Once finding a clear path he kicked his horse to a faster pace, galloping down through Hagglers Way and out to the piers at the dock. There he saw her, *The Fair Maiden.* His father's majestic boat rocked gently in the shallow water, sails flapping loudly in the wind, crewmen and servants running up and down the gangway loading provisions and going about their duties.

Upon rising that morning, Aaric had sent word ahead to have the ship readied to set sail immediately. He couldn't wait any longer. Quinnie was missing and the numerous searches that had been conducted by the house guards and workers of the castle had turned up unsuccessful. He had a feeling that he knew where she had gone; with Grandfather to North Harbor.

Quin idolized Captain Longship and had always begged him to take her on his journeys and he had no doubt that she had climbed aboard and off they went. Aaric knew she would be safe, if she was in fact with Captain Longship, but he didn't know for sure, and Quin seemed to find trouble wherever she went.

There had also been reports that Noam, Quin's friend the kitchen boy, hadn't shown up for his kitchen duties yesterday morning. *Darn you, Quinnie! Why'd you have to go and run off like that? Especially when Father's not here to do anything about it.* Word had been sent to Lord Emrys, but with the terrible icy storms that had been hitting east Merenia and sweeping across west, the message wouldn't reach him until a fortnight after he'd already arrived at the King's Castle, and that just might be too late. It was up to Aaric to take care of matters and he'd already made up his mind as to what he was going to do.

He'd wished he hadn't been so hard on Quin the night she came to show him that mysterious stone. He laughed as he thought about looking in the pocket of his cloak the day before and finding the rock missing. She'd probably taken it before she stowed away on grandfather's boat. *The little sneak.*

There was nothing to be done now but to make way for North Harbor, the captain's usual route, and bring her back home safely. He hated to leave Aleena behind with the stuttering Prince Tolan, but King Thunderdyn had wanted him to stay behind to protect the soon-to-be princess, seeing as times had grown dangerous, and for them to get to know each other better before the royal wedding. A lot of good he would do. Maybe the prince could scare off the enemy with his oversized teeth. Aaric shook his head, feeling a bit guilty for thinking such thoughts. Tolan wasn't such a bad guy; Aaric was just in a fitful and irritated mood, nervous about Quin's disappearance.

"The boat's just about ready, m'lord," the captain of *The Fair Maiden* called out.

"Thank you, Captain Bottlesby." Aaric replied. And the man was shaped like a bottle, with a small head and upper body, and then rounding out like a ripened pear on the bottom. He waddled this way and that, shouting orders to the deck hands, his black floppy hat waving in and out of his eyes in the cold morning breeze. It had been unusually cold that morning and people bundled up in their cloaks and gathered around various fire pits.

The spring rains seemed to have never ceased during the graduation into summer, but actually increased greatly, making it a wet and oddly cold season so far. Master Dunley had been saying that the sea was angry, and that something must be awry for Mer Ocean to be acting the way it was.

Oh no! Aaric had forgotten about Master Dunley. He had meant to leave a note, telling him of his decision to set sail to North Harbor and find Quinnie. Well it was too late for that now.

"Aaric!" a weak and raspy voice called out. Dismounting his horse, Aaric turned to see Master Dunley riding towards the dock on a white horse.

Speak of the storm and it will rain, Aaric thought. He looked quite uncomfortable; the old man hanging on for dear life, long white hair flowing out behind him. At that age, anything more than sleeping must be uncomfortable.

"Lord Aaric," the old boney hound said with relief at finding the boy. "Where in good graces are you going?"

"I'm going to North Harbor to find Quinlan." The Master halted right before him and Aaric helped him down off of his horse very carefully so as not to break any of the elderly man's bones.

The old man stopped and rested his hands on his knees, breathing hard from the effort of riding so frantically, puffs of cold air appearing every time he exhaled. "If I may be so bold, m'lord, it is a dangerous journey and you have never sailed by yourself."

Captain Bottlesby hastily came waddling over to Aaric and took his pack, handing it off to a worker headed towards the boat, and scuttled off in the opposite direction, yelling at some other men who were handling a crate improperly.

"I've sailed to North Harbor with Father many times, and he has a very good captain and crew. Besides, Father taught me very well, and I know my way around the coast."

"And what of your lady mother? Have you told her of your plans?" Master Dunley objected again, looking concerned.

"My lady *stepmother*," Aaric corrected, "need only to worry herself with the household duties. I will be back before you know it, with Quinnie, safe and sound." Aaric handed the reins of his horse to a stable boy who had been patiently waiting.

The old master was interrupted from voicing his concerns when they spotted Aleena on horseback, wildly dashing her way towards them through the crowd of Hagglers way, Prince Tolan trailing behind. People darted out of the way from the reckless duo, as Aleena didn't seem to care who or what obstacle was in front of her.

"Aaric! Thank goodness you're still here. I was so afraid you'd already left." Aleena spoke with sweet sincerity as she brought her mount to a halt, but there was a tone of frustration behind her voice.

"Aleena, what in blazes are you doing here?" Aaric scratched his head. All he wanted to do was board the ship and get going.

"I'm coming with you," Aleena stated confidently.

"No, you're not," Master Dunley and Aaric said in unison.

"I am not letting you go off on your own to find our sister," Aleena said and then making an overly dramatic gesture towards Prince Tolan she continued, "Besides, the very brave prince Tolan will protect us on our journey." Looking at Prince Thunderdyn she added, "That was your father, the king's, wish, wasn't it, to protect me?" Aleena fluttered her eyelashes slightly.

Prince Tolan, all puffed up with confidence from Aleena's praising words, answered, "W...why, yes. I g...g...go where you g...go, m'lady." Tolan bowed awkwardly to his betrothed.

The old master looked wary. "Pardon me, Your Majesty, but I don't think that that was exactly what the king had in mind. It's just... very dangerous."

Aleena, spoke again, more determinedly, "Being cooped up in an old keep is no way for a prince live, especially one with as much skill, and... and... brawn as Prince Tolan." She patted Tolan's scrawny arm muscle and then pulled away quickly.

"Aleena, you are not coming. It isn't safe." Aaric said with as much authority as he could muster.

"But Quin needs me. I'm the only mother figure she has ever known." Aleena looked pathetically at Aaric, and then at the prince.

Tolan, feeling that he should defend his lady, spoke to Master Dunley and Aaric, holding his hand on his sword. "Sh... sh... surely we won't be gone long. And I will p... p... protect Lady Aleena with my life. Besides, one day she might be queen, and it would b... b... benefit her to see her lands and her people."

Aaric couldn't believe this. All he wanted was to get sailing and find his sister. He really didn't want Aleena, and especially Prince Tolan, tagging along... although it wouldn't be so bad having the extra help to find his sister. And if anyone *could* find Quin, it would be Aleena.

"Alright. Alright. Let's go. Quickly now, before the tide." Aaric said hastily, waving them towards the gangway.

Master Dunley, still uneasy, said, "Aaric, m'lord. I don't think this is a good idea."

"Master Dunley?" Aaric questioned.

"Yes, m'lord?"

"What would Father do in this situation?"

Dunley looked uneasy about answering the question. "Well, he..." the master sighed in resignation, "he would leave no stone left unturned until he found the Lady Quinlan."

Aaric smiled. "Exactly."

And then they were off, sailing away with the rising sun, looking back at the lively dock of South Harbor and the bustling Hagglers Way. Aaric could see the top towers of Castlecray in the distance reaching towards the clouds in the icy sky, and he felt a sense of sadness at leaving his home.

ALEENA

Aleena began passing around salt pork and hot mint tea to the crew members and then brought some for Aaric and Tolan to the quarter deck where they were standing with the heavy-bottomed captain.

"The sea hasn't been herself of late," Captain Bottlesby observed. "She's a trifle angry, and doesn't care who knows about it. It's as though she's going to punish us humans for our unholy behavior." The captain tugged on his wide-brimmed hat. Aleena regarded his words as just a silly sailor's superstition, but began feeling a little uneasy as she thought more about the recent and unwarranted cold spells in the middle of summer.

To the east, the sun was rising, spraying out colors of purples, pinks and oranges into a clear sky. To the west, inky black thunderheads were boiling and growing larger by the minute, shooting bright flashes of lightning into the ocean. The captain waddled off, yelling something about the sheets being too tight, and Aaric tagged along, leaving her and Prince Tolan standing alone.

Aleena glanced up at Tolan, him being very much taller than she, and her light grey eyes, fringed with dark lashes, contemplated what to say. She was being forced to marry the poor sap; she might as well try to get to know him better. She asked politely, "Do you travel a lot, your highness?"

Smiling a toothy grin, Tolan answered, "Y… yes. My father sometimes lets me go with him on his hunting trips in the King's Forest, but he mostly takes B… B… Banon with him on trips of official business." Aleena, trying to look engaged in the conversation, regarded the prince with a delicate smile.

Tolan gazed out at the expanse of water in front of them, his brown eyes longing. "I *wish* Father would take me on more tr… trips. But he says I need to spend more time on my lessons at the castle with the M… M… Master of Articulation." The prince's face gave a hint of frustration and then instantly went back to a smile.

"Master of Articulation? What pray tell is that?" Aleena asked curiously.

Tolan flinched. "It's for my… " Slumping, he looked down at his feet, gripping the mug of warm tea nervously. "My st… st… stutter."

Aleena had a sudden feeling of pity for the poor boy and found herself telling a "little white lie," as she would call it. "Stutter? Oh, I hadn't noticed." She wrapped a ringlet of her long brown hair around her finger, glancing out at the water.

Tolan looked a bit surprised, "Yes, well, it has gotten a l…little better, since I started my speech lessons." He stood up a bit straighter now.

"I imagine that must have been very hard on you, as a young child," Aleena said sincerely, almost wishing she hadn't encouraged the conversation.

Tolan nodded as he took a sip of the steaming mint tea and then said, "The children at court used to call me Teetering Tolan and T…Troll-Tooth." He wiped his mouth with the back of his hand. "Of course, not to my face, me being a prince and all. But I heard them, laughing and mocking me."

Aleena tugged sheepishly at her skirts, feeling badly for the unkind thoughts she had had of him. "But honestly, it just got harder as I got older." Tolan licked his dry lips. "I used to go out to the streets with Grand Elder Wylie and the Acolytes to hand out bread to the less fortunate. And that's when I realized how bad it was, when the poor began to take pity on me. I could hear them saying, 'Oh that poor stammering Prince Thunderdyn. It's a good thing he was second born, and not the first heir to the crown.'"

Aleena stepped close to the prince saying thoughtfully, "Oh, I'm so sorry, Tolan. It must have been terrible." She looked into his sad dark eyes and felt a humility she had never felt before.

"And now, it's not much better. Father began to bring me in on matters of the Golden Crown; royal business, you see. But no one would take me seriously." The prince shuffled his feet. "It doesn't much help that I'm not fair to look upon like my charming brother, Banon. I guess it is a good thing that he was born first, charming, well-spoken, and handsome as he is."

Aleena began to feel angry at all of the hurt Tolan must have felt over the years. "Oh, bother! Don't you worry a bit about it! You're not so bad to look upon, believe me, I've seen worse." Aleena laughed nervously and tried to recover. "I mean... you've got nice hair, and very intriguing eyes." She caught herself gazing into his deep rich brown eyes and looked away quickly, wrapping a long brown lock of hair around her finger.

The prince looked at her earnestly. "Why thank you, m'lady. That's the nicest thing anyone has ever said to me." The prince reached inside his shirt and pulled out a small brown parcel and handed it to her. "I almost forgot. I have something for you." Aleena silently raised an eyebrow in question as if to say "for me?" and Tolan nodded, encouraging her to open it.

She slowly unfolded the brown linen and gasped at its contents. It was a small golden dagger that fit in the palm of her hand, encrusted with red rubies and glimmering moonstones. "Oh, my oceans, it's beautiful!" she said as she held it up, turning it back and forth, the sunlight catching the gems and making them sparkle.

"It's not quite as beautiful as you," he said, his cheeks flushing bright red. Shaking off his shyness, he added, "And I thought it would be something to help you feel safe. It's small enough to keep tucked away in your boot."

Aleena's delicate face flashed a brilliant smile, "I love it! Maybe you can teach me how to use it sometime?" she said as she whipped it back and forth through the air.

Tolan, dodging her movements, quickly brought his arm up and gently lowered her hand and the dangerous weapon. "Yes, sometime." He smiled widely. Aleena now thought that his teeth were starting to look more like a cute bunny's rather than a donkey's.

She straightened up abruptly. "You know what?" The prince looked at her blankly. "You haven't stuttered at all in the last few minutes!"

Tolan cocked his head, thinking, and then his face lightened with sudden insight. "Oh, yes. I stutter mostly when I'm uncomfortable or nervous." He tenderly put his hand over Aleena's, which was resting on the deck. "I guess you make me feel comfortable."

Aleena felt a tingling sensation from his touch and warmth traveled up her arm and throughout her body. She shivered at the nice feeling, and felt her stomach flutter as though it were filled with butterflies. *He really isn't so bad to look at, and he's kind.* She'd never felt like this before and didn't know what to make of it. Tolan leaned in close to her, puffs of warm mist rising each time he took a breath, smelling like fresh mint. Aleena closed her eyes, letting the warm pull of emotions envelope her and then suddenly jerked away at the lookout's urgent call.

"Sail ho!"

The captain came scrambling up the ladder, followed by Aaric, to the quarterdeck where they stood. "Where away?" he called back, hand cupped around his mouth.

"Two points straight ahead!" the voice answered.

The group all stood peering out over the bow at the great expanse of sparkling water ahead, to see the outline of a large boat.

"What ship?" The captain was rummaging through a leather pack strung to his hip.

The lookout paused and then yelled out, "A Galley, Captain!"

Finding what he was looking for, Captain Bottlesby pulled out a brass looking glass, extended it, and raised it to his right eye, the left one closed tight. "The North Harbor war ships don't patrol this far south, and they don't look to be merchantmen…" Leaning over the railing as he further studied the oncoming ship, he muttered, "It can't be…"

Aaric stepped up beside the captain, his chiseled jaw tense with concern as his golden hair waved in the breeze. "What is it, Captain?"

The captain shook his head in disbelief, "It looks to be that they fly the flag of the Black Rebellion... but that's impossible. The black knights haven't been around for centuries. My deep blue sea, they haven't been around since the first of the Thunderdyn Kings vanquished them."

"You haven't heard the rumors?" Prince Tolan stepped forward.

The captain looked around nervously repeating, "Rumors?"

Aaric chimed in. "That was why Father was summoned to Merene, to the King's Castle. There are rumors that someone has brought the rebellion back to life and has been pillaging and plundering towns and villages in the west."

Aleena strained her eyes to see the large galley heading their way growing larger against the now storm-darkened horizon. She could see a black flag flapping but could not make out the details. She remembered from her studies with Master Dunley, the signet of the black rebellion was a black background with a silver sword, laid diagonally, dripping with drops of red blood. She shuddered.

Aaric, taking the looking glass from Bottlesby, peered through and said, "If the rumors *are* true, and that *is* a black rebellion galley, we may be in trouble. We plainly fly the Castlecray crest, and it is well known that Castlecray is one of King Thunderdyn's largest supporters."

Aleena looked up to see her house crest, a great white castle on a blue background, flapping majestically above them in the wind, making the blue fabric look like waves surrounding the embroidered keep.

"Well, I won't sit here and sail straight into those bastards," the captain said gruffly, and then yelled out to his crew, "Make due west, ye dumb fisherboys! We're going to swing this maiden wide around 'em!"

The once delicate waves surrounding the boat had increased to surging and roaring whitecaps from the growing western storm, and Bottlesby had to lean hard on the helm. "Turn, damn you!"

Aaric and Tolan both bolted away to help the crew adjust the sails, and the men swarmed the boat frantically.

The clouds had grown darker with bolts of ragged electric lightning fraying across the sky and Aleena watched the large galley approaching closer as they slowly swung west, and gripped her dagger tight in her fist.

Tolan and Aaric came scuffling back to help Bottlesby with the helm. "That galley there is a bottom-heavy tub and our *Fair Maiden* can outrun 'em at this distance," said the captain, leaning further into the helm.

Prince Tolan, now with the looking glass, shouted, "They've got rowers! Three sets on each side. It looks like they're going to try to c… c… cut us off."

"Damn!" The captain exclaimed. "If ye've ever been good to me, lassie, now's the time," the captain said, patting the boat.

The galley was now in clear sight, the black rebellion's banner waved, depicting exactly what Aleena had remembered from her studies, a black background with a bloody silver sword.

"Tighten those sails!" Bottlesby shouted to the crew. He turned to look at Aaric. "We've turned enough that the wind is now in our favor. We might just have a slim chance of outrunning those rogues, but best be safe and get the prince and Lady Aleena down below." He talked to Aaric as though Aleena weren't standing right there.

"I'm not going anywhere. This is my father's ship, and I will not be locked below deck to be kept wondering." Aleena looked the captain straight in the eye.

"Have it your way m'lady, but when those..." The captain's hat was zipped off of his head suddenly. Time stood still as he reached up to his balding head and followed everyone else's eyes behind him to see the black floppy hat stuck to the mast by a quivering arrow.

And then the rain came. Not water falling from the sky type of rain, but a rain of arrows pelting the wooden deck, sounding like a stampede of hooved animals.

Aleena heard a whizzing sound coming straight for her, and before she knew it, was on the ground with Prince Tolan's weight pressing her down. She could hear the frantic yells of the sailors on board and a cry or two of wounded men. Gasping for breath, she pushed Tolan's body off of her and he rolled over with a *thump,* landing on his side. Sitting up, she could see that the prince had been struck in the back with an arrow, and his shirt was slowly changing color from a crisp white to a muddy red. *He saved my life.*

"Tolan! Tolan!" She shouted, shaking him. "Tolan!" His face pale, he looked up at her through slanted eyes and she could see the pain on his face. "Oh, my prince, you're going to be alright. We'll get you to a healer, just hang in there." Holding him in her arms she could feel him shivering, and she grabbed his fallen cloak and covered him, pressing her hand against the wound.

Aaric had grabbed the lid off of a barrel and was using it for a shield at the head of the boat, dodging zipping arrows and helping the captain with the tiller. Men darted back and forth from behind crates and other objects, ducking low to the ground to avoid the deadly flying weapons. The fall of arrows had subsided to a trickle, but she knew the Rebellion's galley was still near, by the victorious shouts of the men across the water.

Tolan moaned as she held him tight in her arms.

And then there was silence. Her mind was turning in circles, trying to grasp the recently chaotic conditions that had now turned to an eerie quiet. *No more arrows?* It was very strange and quiet, like being in the eye of a storm.

Aleena cautiously laid Tolan against the side of the rocking ship, his breathing labored but his body still warm, and slowly began to rise, seeing men coming out of their cover, like little rodents peeking out of their holes. She peered over the side rail to check their assailants' mysterious lack of presence and her heart stopped in her chest, for what she saw could only be described as supernatural.

"Wave!" She screamed as other sailors began to look upon what she saw. The mountainous curved mass of white foamy water was as tall as a bell tower, traveling towards them and the other galley at increasing speed, the watchers frozen in shock.

"Wave approaching!" was one among many yells she heard as men scurried about, battening the hatches, and securing the safety ropes.

Aleena's arm was suddenly jerked away from the rail and she looked to see Aaric dragging her away from the side. "We've got to get you below deck quickly!" he said in a frenzied voice.

Aleena dug her heels in. "No!" Aaric gave her a puzzled look.

"We can't leave Tolan, he's hurt." Aleena broke away from Aaric's grip and dashed back to the wounded prince. "Here, help me carry him," Aleena said frantically, stooping over and putting the prince's arm over her shoulder.

"There's no time!" Aaric shouted.

A low groaning sound came from low in the sea, vibrating the timbers on the boat, and Aleena's feet became unsteady. A man ran by, his foot getting caught in some loose ropes and he fell flat on his face, and was trampled by the other crew members. Not only could she hear the frightened yells of the men on her boat, but the distressed shouts from their enemy as well.

"Aleena! We must go *now!*" Aaric pulled her away from the prince and made way towards the hatch. An enormous dark shadow covered the boat and Aleena glanced up as Aaric stopped. The wave, now hovering high overhead, blocking out the sunlight, the clouds, the storm, and the sky, looked to be an unreal dome of watercolor brushstrokes surrounding them. The deck screeched and shifted under her feet as the boat began to tilt sideways, reluctantly climbing the steep underbelly of the monstrous wave. Aleena instinctively brought up her arms to shield her head from the oncoming concussion, and *The Fair Maiden* protested in wooden creaking groans, as the wall of water closed in all around them.

KALAYA

There was a feeling of anticipation emanating from the castle and its inhabitants in the false dawn light. The crowds surrounding the outskirts of the entrance buzzed like humming-fish with a low drone of conversation. From a hill just outside, Kalaya took in the sight of the Tidebreak Towers and their majestic ivory spires reaching towards the sky as if in search of sunshine. The outside of the grand castle was picturesque, with soaring towers, rounded domes, magnificent arches, and a maze of intermingling bridges and parapets, glowing eerily in the bluish-grey dusk. Workers moved this way and that, preparing for the coming events of the day. Her father was to give a speech that morning, and she could feel tensions running high.

Kalaya could see the beams of white light starting to form and shoot diagonally into the water, a touch from the world above, waving kisses of sunlight. Though she was unable to breach the surface, this was her favorite time of day because she felt connected to the world above. She could sense it awakening in all of its bright glory, the world that she so dreamed to see... the human world... full of light.

"I knew I'd find you here," Kai said, appearing from out of nowhere in the dark. He swam a circle around his sister, his sea-blue fin very much like her own curving around as he twisted about.

"So, what do you suppose all of the fuss is about?" he asked.

Kalaya felt very close to Kai, as he was her twin, but there was always an underlying tension, for Kalaya was heir to the Coral Crown because she was born first, only moments before her brother. Under rule of the Mer kingdom, the line of succession was passed to the first born merperson, not mattering whether it was male or female. Although Kai never spoke of it, Kalaya knew he felt that he should have been the heir to the crown, and was quite jealous of her.

Kalaya followed her twin brother with her rich brown eyes, "It's probably about Amias's death." Amias was a member of the Shapeshifter's Kith and had been caught and killed by a group of humans off the coast of North Harbor. The details were hearsay, and everyone had a different notion about the event, some thought it to be an accident and some murder.

The Shapeshifters were the only merpeople allowed near humans, and only with a disguised form. Although the Shapeshifters were not under her father's rule, they worked hand in hand with the Peace Protectors and the Whisper Web by gathering information from the world around them, land and sea, and ensuring communication and safety.

Kalaya had met Amias many times while accompanying her father to meetings of the Council, and remembered his fiery red eyes, matching his crimson-colored scales with flecks of gold. He was a very powerful merman and said to be one of the greatest Shapeshifters ever known, but was otherwise cold and detached. He had scared her sometimes just by the way he looked at her, those glowing eyes peering out from behind his dark salt and pepper hair. It was known that most of the Shapeshifters were of a strange breed by nature, coldhearted and pathologically secretive about their whereabouts and their alias forms.

"Those land walkers are trouble. It's always violence and killing with them, walking around all swelled up with pride and self-admiration." Kai snorted his opinion as he gracefully moved through the smoke-colored water.

Kalaya lived in a world of dark, darkness, and near dark, from the moment the sun rose in the world above, giving them hints of dim illumination, to the moment the sun set at night, casting Mer

Ocean into pitch blackness, except for the meager luminescence that the Lightkeepers provided.

Kalaya watched her brother. His striking brown eyes, a lot like their father's, were mischievous, and his dark hair swayed and moved about as though it were alive itself.

"Nobody knows what *actually* happened, Kai." Kalaya knew of her brother's strong distrust of humans, but she wasn't quite sure how she felt about it. "Merpeople have been known to kill at times also." She stated plainly. "Are you saying that all of *us* are violent and full of ourselves?"

Her brother's face turned a shade of red. "Oh, Kalaya. That's different."

Kalaya's long, dark chestnut hair swirled slowly around her shoulders as she shifted. She resembled her brother greatly, and their father even more; all of them had the same sloping nose and sharp dark brows. When she was young she remembered her father's hair being the same as her's and Kai's, a dark brown as rich as the sea soil, but as he was now centuries old, it had turned a beautiful shocking white-silver.

"How? How is it different?" She spoke to Kai indignantly.

Just then, the Light Keepers with their brilliant bright yellow hair and yellow tails, the color of lemons and sunshine, came in like the dawn, in groups of three from all sides of the fortress, holding glowing glass blown bulbs, like enormous crystal bubbles, full of twinkling lights — little Lantern fish.

The luminescence of them was warming to the dull grey, slow motion world Kalaya lived in most days and she smiled at the angelic sight. The bulbs of Lantern fish were only brought out during grand festivities or gatherings of importance; otherwise, single jellyfish would be harnessed sporadically around the Kingdom, like fluctuating lanterns, to give general task lighting for everyday duties.

One of Kalaya's favorite pastimes was to come to this very hill, in the dark pre-dawn, and watch from afar the release of the jellyfish. They would slowly rise, hundreds of little warm yellow balls of light in the slate-colored sea, towards the sparkling surface of the water to live freely, unsuspecting that they just might be recaptured again that night for their very useful skill.

As the Light Keepers secured the luminescent orbs, casting a golden light over the grand facade of the great white castle, Kalaya could see a dozen Mer guards lined up in front of the castle at the top of the rise, mounted importantly at the back of the terrace near the wall.

Mother Pearl, her grandmother, the oldest mermaid in the ocean, arrived at the terrace at the top of the great incline leading to the castle entrance escorted by four Mer guards. Then came Ormon, Kalaya's uncle, and the king, her father, followed by Silvana, the enchantress of Shadow Rock. It was quite an odd group that gathered on the dais, her grandmother, father, and uncle, being Wavekeepers and in the same kith, all were in close resemblance, their blue-green scales sparkling like the shimmering water in which they resided. But Silvana, the Enchantress, with her long jet black hair and eyes almost as dark, looked a sharp contrast amongst all the other brilliant colors. Kalaya knew the sea witch to be quite old, though younger than the king, and she was stunningly beautiful, with her fresh youthful looking skin as white as seashells. Merpeople aged slowly, and because they lived to be centuries old, their appearance betrayed their true age.

The crowd hushed as Pearl raised her delicate hand, her silver hair wound around her head in a large knot and her blue-green scales glittering in the light of the lantern fish. She bowed her head slightly to the King, as if she were giving the go ahead to speak.

King Nerius cleared his throat. "Thank you all for coming." His voice was deep like distant thunder. "I would like to personally welcome those of the Kingdom of Mer, the merpeople of Shadow Rock, and all that have traveled long distances from other seas and oceans."

Kalaya's father bowed his head in sadness. "It is unfortunate that we must meet under such grievous conditions; the loss of one of our own, Amias of the Shapeshifters of Shadow Rock."

A few cries came from the gathered merpeople. "Murder!" and "Butchery!"

The king, ignoring the comments, continued, "Although the merpeople of Shadow Rock are under different rule, we have worked side by side with

Shadow Rock and their Shapeshifters to keep peace in all of the oceans in our realm and others. They are our closest neighbors, and in their time of sorrow, we grieve with them, and for Amias's widow, Silvana, Enchantress of Shadow Rock."

Kalaya's father raised a hand to Silvana, who gave a quick nod of acknowledgement.

"Amias was one of the most powerful shapeshifters known and he will be greatly missed. Let us now give a moment of silence for our beloved fellow merman." A silence rang across the waters, all minds thinking the same thoughts and questions. *Was it an accident or cold-blooded murder?*

King Nerius lifted his head. "May he pass to the deep blue beyond with peace in his soul and love in his heart. Fare thee well, Amias."

The entire group repeated after their king, "Fare thee well, Amias."

King Nerius, his silver hair flowing weightlessly in the water, spoke solemnly, "I know that the last thing we want to do is talk of business just now, but because of this unfortunate event, there are pressing matters to be seen to. Now that Amias has... left us, there is an empty seat in the Peace Protectors Council that will need to be filled by a member of the Shapeshifter's kith." Nerius looked to the group of Shapeshifters amongst the crowd. "Have you decided amongst yourselves?"

Silvana waved in a merman from the front of the crowd and bent over as he whispered in her ear. The Enchantress, raising her head high, spoke in a voice like thin broken glass, sharp and crisp. “Lar of the Shapeshifter’s of Shadow Rock, please come forward.”

All eyes went to the young merman, who had crimson scales on his tail, brilliantly shimmering as he swam towards the terrace. His bright red eyes, big and eager, searched Silvana’s face. Again the beautiful enchantress spoke. “I will now hand you over to Nerius, to perform your induction to the Council of the Peace Protectors”.

“*King* Nerius.” Ormon, Kalaya’s uncle, spouted impatiently, correcting Silvana with a firm voice. Ormon had a likeness to the king, with his silver hair and scales the color of the sea, but was not as tall and muscular, and his features were smoother, as Nerius’s were sharp. But Ormon had a very rigid personality and felt that rules were to be abided by, never to be broken.

Silvana’s face turned, her dark eyes almost as black as night, flashed to the king’s brother, and then she smiled widely. “Yes. *King* Nerius. Thank you, Ormon.” The enchantress all but spit out the words, her long black hair wavering ethereally.

Kalaya could almost see the thick angst between her father and Silvana, the sea witch, as her father performed Lar’s induction into the Peace Protectors. There had always been an unspoken tension between the merpeople of Shadow Rock and the ones of the Mer kingdom. For many years now Shadow Rock had been exempt from the rule of the kingdom and King Nerius, but had been led by

Silvana. It was plain to see that now, looking out over the crowd, an invisible line down the center, Shadows, with their tattooed skin on one side, and merpeople of the Kingdom on the other.

Nerius brushed off the small confrontation and continued again. "We have discussed everything amongst the council members and will be implementing new rules for safety reasons. Shapeshifters, you will now be traveling in pairs. No one is to go near the surface of the water by him or herself, for any reason. For all of the other kiths, mainly in the kingdom, please see your head member of the Peace Protectors."

Kalaya could tell that her father hadn't slept much; the lines of his face were deep and his eyes dull. "The Tidebreak Towers and all other roofs in the Kingdom of Mer Ocean have most always been peaceful, and we intend on keeping it that way. If we work together, our children and our children's children will have the beautiful and harmonious world we have loved for so long."

The Tidebreak Towers had always been Kalaya's home, as it was for many generations of the Wavekeepers, and ever since the strange disappearance of her older brother, the responsibility of being heir to the Coral Crown fell to her. It was thought that the oldest son of King Nerius had been murdered years ago, but there was no proof.

A shout came from an older female in the crowd. "For those who don't remember, this is how the slaughter started years ago. We need to defend ourselves against those bloodthirsy land walkers!" *A shadow, no doubt,* Kalaya thought.

Silvana moved forward to address the caller, her black tail swaying back and forth like the feathers on a raven. "Yes, my sister. You are absolutely right. We cannot stand for this. The land walkers will see this as an invitation for bloodshed; for war. We are in immense danger, and I say we strike first!"

King Nerius, holding up a halting hand, addressed the numbers of merpeople. "I understand the fear you might have, but be comforted that we have everything under control. The Whisper Web is communicating with all of the others across our realm to stop the rumors and provide damage control. And it is unconfirmed as to what actually took place. For all we know, Amias's death was an unintentional act; an accident, with no intent to harm."

A murmuring swept through the crowd. Whether they were agreeing with her father or not, Kalaya did not know.

Upstaging the king, Silvana boldly pushed to the front of the terrace, a look of anger and determination on her face. "I say that we unite the stone tablet, call upon the Power of Mer, and wipe out the humans! We have not much use for them and the ones with half a brain or a bit of skill we will keep for slaves!" A loud roar came from the crowds of merpeople, the shaking of fists accompanied by shouts of obscenity and cursing, amongst ones of encouragement.

Kalaya had heard the story of the stone tablet many times in her youth and remembered it well. A great wizard of the sea who lived over a century ago, Pontus, the oldest merman at the time, kept this tablet hidden away, knowing the great power that it held.

On it was inscribed a poem, or a riddle of sorts, that told where the four elemental pieces would be scattered throughout the realm once the Prophecy began its course. The Prophecy stated that a great star would create these four pieces, and when combined with the tablet and the spell etched into the stone, could invoke the greatest power ever known: control of all waters of the world. Pontus, knowing that the Prophecy would in fact take place, had grown very old, and knew that his time had come.

He trusted no one but himself with the tablet and the choice to keep its magnificent power tucked away, so with his great magic he broke the stone tablet in half, and bestowed one side to Silvana's mother, who was Enchantress of Shadow Rock at the time, and one to King Nerius. Because the old wizard knew of the legendary dislike between Shadow Rock and the Mer Kingdom that had gone on for generations, he believed that neither side would be likely to hand over their half of the tablet to be reunited, therefore negating any chance of it being combined with the fallen stars, once the Prophecy had come to pass.

In response to Silvana's comment, Ormon broke through angrily, "This is absolute nonsense! It's insanity! We are a peaceful people, not ones to start wars!"

"Stop the threat!" yelled a merman from the crowd. "Unite the stone tablet!" Ormon glared at the ridiculous merman.

Emotions began to build throughout the water, like a slowly moving inky black cloud. There were no smiles, only grunts and frowns and hurtful words that passed through the crowd. Some of the younger mermen began to argue, on the brink of physical confrontation; the two separate sides coming together like an angry magnetic pull, sparks flying. Kalaya was afraid that a riot was beginning to break out, like an unpredictable storm that crashes heavily without warning. She watched her brother, Kai, shoot away in a hurry towards the mass, and called out to him. Ignoring her shouts and without a backward glance, he disappeared into the crazed scene.

Silvana began to shout out to the crowd, her sharp crystal voice ringing out over the water, loud as though magnified by some unseen magic, her dark hair waving wildly in all directions. "If *King* Nerius had done something about this sooner, Amias would have never been killed." Putting a little too much emphasis on the word "King," Silvana gestured to Nerius.

"*He* has a say in the Peace Protectors, as I do not. *He* was the one pushing the Shapeshifters to gather more information, therefore putting them closer to danger." The Enchantress gracefully turned her head to the king and, addressing him, said, "It was *you* who murdered Amias."

The unfavorable relationship that had carried through the years between her father and Silvana had always been civil, but Kalaya could see that single shred of harmony that *had* been there shatter right before her eyes, as the calm on her father's face broke. King Nerius's chest began to expand and contract with deep breaths, his tan skin turning shades darker, as the crowd, *shadows mostly,* began to chant "Murder! Murder!"

It was understandable that Silvana was upset about her loss of love and it was well known that Amias was everything to her, but in the few times Kalaya had met the Enchantress, she had never seen her like this, unrestrained, cruel, and outright vicious. Her charcoal tail whipped quickly like a sea snake and her face was drawn tight with fury. Kalaya thought that she looked almost... evil.

Tensions grew greater and small fights broke out in the large mass of merpeople beneath the grand castle. Kalaya could hear screaming and shouting as bystanders darted away to get clear of the brawling. The line of Mer guards, holding their eclectic collection of rusty swords and spears gathered from various shipwrecks, swept towards the front of the terrace, pushing back some of the shadows that began to rush the podium. Kalaya scanned the scene, which had become complete chaos in a matter of heartbeats, fearing for her family upon the dais.

Kalaya leaned her spinning head forward and brought her hands up to cover her ears against the ear-piercing noise, as she felt a strong hand grab her arm and jerk her close. Startled, she glanced up to see Cade, the captain of the Mer guard and her personal protector, holding her, and she relaxed.

Kalaya had almost forgotten that he was standing there behind her the whole time. She felt silly for her fright, because she was *always* accompanied by a guard, and it was almost always Cade. She looked up into his emerald green eyes, set into a chiseled olive-colored face, and realized just how safe she felt.

He was handsome, for sure, but Kalaya had grown up with him since she was just a little swimmer and almost felt him to be a brother. As she gazed into her guardians' face, she remembered him as an awkward merboy, not the strong and mature merman he had become.

"You're safe now, princess. It's alright," he said in a reassuring voice, barely heard over the fighting screams.

If it was at all possible the crowd grew angrier, two sides of a mob crashing together into a blind rage. The chanting grew louder and louder.

"Murder! Murder!"

The Mer guards at the terrace were now swinging their weapons defensively to keep back the throng of nettled shadows, and she could see her father holding up his staff trying to vie for calmness.

And then amidst the chaos came her father's voice, amplified as if by some unseen magic, booming across the waters, vibrating her to her core.

"SILENCE!"

Her father's staff immediately began to glow, the intricate carved waves at the top emanating an electric blue color, like a pulsating heartbeat of mad energy.

Suddenly, the king slammed his staff into the ground with a deafening blow that echoed loudly, bolts of energy, sufficient to destroy an entire city exploded in a spectacle of color, beyond the grasp of mortal eyes to comprehend.

Then as if by two giant hands, a hole was ripped in the sea, wide like the opening of a mouth, starting small around the king, coming from the point of the staff's contact and then growing and generating upwards like a wild underwater tornado, whitecap surges flowing outward into bigger and wider waves as it evolved. Kalaya could hear a low groaning sound as the expanding giant whirlpool picked up speed as fast as lightning; schools of fish were being swept away, and sea trees and plants leaned intensively sideways against the water's strong pull.

Cade, holding Kalaya tight in one arm, grabbed for a narrow rock jutting from the hill to brace them against the fast approaching blast. Kalaya peered out from nearly closed eyes, to see mermaids and mermen covering their faces, hanging on to each other or anything they could grasp in the raging current, their clothes of braided grasses strewn with seashells and capes of woven seaweed being torn off in the process.

And then there was stillness, like the calm after the storm. Kalaya peeked out to see a mind-blowing scene of clear and vivid tranquility. Like a tall funnel of water, the ocean surrounding the Tidebreak Towers had receded upwards, reaching towards the sky, with a blinding brilliant sunbeam, the size of the enormous gap, blasting down on their air-covered circle. She lay on the seafloor, like all of the others, as there was no water to hold her up.

She felt heavy and sluggish with bodily weight, the dry scene a shock to her body. Glancing upwards, the walls of water around them looked to be holding a brewing storm, flowing with a rise and fall of brilliant colorful energy and white clouds of sea foam. It was as if an invisible force of the beautiful blue sky above was drinking in the storm of water and light, leaving a gateway to the world above.

Time stood still.

Kalaya saw her father's arms stretching outwards, commanding the water, palms flexed as though he was holding the weight of the retracted sea from crashing down around them. His face was tense with concentration while he slowly lowered his arms and, as if in reply, the huge cylindrical ocean wall slowly began to lower itself, and water began to cover the muddy ground, oozing in all around them, filling in the hole that the king's displeasure had created.

She had always recognized her father to be the strongest merman known, but had never witnessed such a display. Even the powers of Silvana, the most powerful Enchantress of the sea, could not compare to her father's exceptional strength. It had been said that the staff of waves, which he held, was like a conduit, magnifying his own sea-born magic even further, though he never much talked about it.

The slushing sound of liquid filled her ears as it also filled the immense gap. Kalaya could feel her body lift weightlessly with the rise of the water and she stabilized as it quickly rolled past her head and advanced upwards. A great dark shadow loomed overhead as the sunlight was shut out through the usual slate-colored sea, clouding the scene once again. Gradually meeting itself at the top, the calm water was whole again and satisfied.

All of the merpeople, with their crazy whipped hair and tattered and torn clothes, were shaking off their confusion, looking around at each other as if in wonder at what to think about the experience.

"Now, if I may have your attention." Looking none at all ashamed of his actions, Nerius spoke more quietly, but with great care and composure.

"This is not a time to lay blame; this is a time to take precautions. And the solution that has been agreed upon by the Peace Protectors, who represent all of us and all of the realms, is to keep the stone tablet separated and not to meddle where we merpeople do not belong: the human world. And in exchange, the humans will continue with their side of the agreement, keeping our identities secret and ensuring the peace between land and sea."

Kalaya watched Silvana, a look of restrained fury on her usually beautiful face, and wondered what the sea witch must be thinking.

The king's voice continued matter-of-factly with a strong layer of authority, "Now. I may not have jurisdiction over all of you," the king markedly looked at Silvana and some of the shadows, vines of ink crawling up their arms, necks, and faces, and continued, "and I do not presume to make any decisions for anyone but the inhabitants of the Mer Kingdom. But I can assure you that the Peace Protectors represent *all* sea blood and land walker blood and their word is *final*."

The king, hovering tall, scanned the disheveled crowd. "Is there anything anyone else would like to say?" A thick silence swept the ocean as he paused.

"No? Good. Now, I would like my Mer guard to escort Enchantress Silvana and her shadows back to Shadow Rock. As for the rest of you, not from the Kingdom, please make yourselves at home."

Kalaya, upset and frazzled by the morning's events, swam off in the opposite direction to find solace amid the wide open ocean, Cade close behind; tiny lines of sunbeams brushed their glittering tails as they made away in the dusky water.

AARIC

A red hot pang shot through Aaric's temple where it had been struck with a blinding force. His hands instinctively groped his head as if to ease the searing pain, a wave of nausea sweeping over him. His body was being thrown around uncontrollably like a rag doll in the wild current and he felt himself being pushed further down, away from the surface of the water. He reached out both of his arms frantically to find something to grasp onto. His eyes were closed tight against the powerful thrusting waves, blood reds and bright whites flashed behind his lids simultaneously with the throbbing in his head.

Aaric's lungs began to burn and tighten with desperation for air. Again and again he tried to swim upwards, but with every attempt it seemed he was pulled further and further under the pitching and rolling waves, unable to stabilize himself.

As Aaric became panic-stricken, he could concentrate on only one thing: survival. He knew he had only enough energy for one last effort and brought his arms and legs close into his body and then with all his might, thrust them up, out, down, and around in one fluid motion, like a water frog pushing up skyward against the current. He then reached one arm up high and felt air on his fingertips, breaching the surface of the sea, only to be shoved forcefully back down by the reverberating tide.

The need to breathe became imperative as Aaric had the feeling of a horse standing on his chest and pressure in his throat. His body began to jerk and twitch in struggle when all of the sudden, bleakness fogged his mind, and his weak body floated like a feather on the breeze, no longer fighting the shifting motion. The feeling was peaceful and euphoric, a relief of the heavy burden of life. *So this is what it feels like to die?*

Memories of his short life started to flood Aaric's thoughts — beautiful memories of his family, and especially of his mother, like the pages of a picture book, coming in flashing chapters.

The sound of thunder quaked through the cold stone castle corridors and flares of bright white and polished purple lightning flickered in squares upon the walls coming through the paned glass windows. He was frightened at the sound and walked the hall seeking comfort; the dim light of a single hanging lantern danced his enlarged shadow upon the wall.

Mindlessly padding along, his leather houseslippers made soft tapping sounds that echoed through the halls, his feet leading the way. Coming to a heavy wooden door, washed in blue, he stopped, hesitant to enter. Father had been gone on business matters for a fortnight now, and he didn't want to wake his mother, for she had been very ill after the birth of his littlest baby sister, only a few days ago. Master Dunley, being an extremely talented healer, had been with her day and night since the birth, using his herbs and potions to no avail, and only took short breaks for sleep.

Aaric had heard the chambermaids talking as they worked the night before, saying that she had birth fever and didn't have much time left. He didn't know exactly what that meant, but it gave him a dreadful feeling.

Thunder cracked powerfully making him jump in the unreal half-light and, unthinking, he quickly opened the door. Candles sputtered in the dark making undulating pools of yellow light, little beacons of safety from the storm.

She was curled up in his father's chair that had been pulled to the wide open balcony doors, wrapped in a blanket, her hair whirling around her gaunt but beautiful face in the late night breeze. She gazed out at the black world, quick razors of fire-bolts frayed colorfully over the ocean water, illuminating her sweat-beaded pale skin in quick and distorted jerky movements. Her head turned slowly to him, light gray eyes locking on his, and smiled the warmest smile he'd ever seen. She raised her hand, and with slender fingers, called him to her.

He looked to see that the swaddled baby had been laid in a small wooden rocking cradle, her little pink lips opened and closed and her tiny chubby hand grasped the air in her sleep. From the glow of the candles, he thought she looked like a little angel from the stories that Nunny told.

His mother patted her blanketed legs slowly and as he climbed into her lap, her long golden hair tickled his face. She wrapped her frail arms around him; he could feel her shaking. Wishing and praying with all of his power that his mother might be healed, he knew helplessly that there was nothing he could do.

He wished his father would come back soon. Master Dunley had told him that riders were sent out with the speed of the wind to find his father and bring him home. He hoped his father would make it in time, for he would know what to do.

He felt safe now in her arms, sheltered from the angry storm. And that is where they stayed for the rest of the night, burrowed in a pocket of each other's warmth, watching the spectacular display of lightning reflecting out over the twinkling black and silver water.

After a while, he didn't know if he'd fallen asleep or just watched the storm pass in a timeless bliss, but he heard his mother speak, soft like a breath of wind through his hair. "Breathe my son... just breathe."

Mother, I miss you so much. Everything has been so difficult since you left. Aaric felt his body floating and weightless. *I'm so cold, mother.* He saw curtains of bright yellow light pass by from behind his closed and heavy lids. An immense contraction of burning pressure rose into his chest again.

Breathe my son... breathe.

And breathe he could not, the weight of his lungs crushing within his chest. Aaric could feel a presence, but could no longer see her. *Mother, wait!* A rushing silence hung over him. *Mother, don't leave!*

"Breathe..." Aaric heard her voice again, but... wait, that was not his mother.

Like trying to listen to someone talk through a pane of glass, he could only make out low droning and soft mumbling sounds, but no words. His head seared in red hot pain, throbbing and pulsing in time with his weak heartbeat. Cold water was brushing up and down his legs feeling like the seashore. *Where am I? Aleena?*

There were two voices, fading in and out, one light and soft, one low and baritone. Were they arguing? Aaric thought. The one that sounded like a female seemed to be urging Aaric on, coaxing him.

"Breathe," she said, "just breathe." The myriad of sounds started to narrow, coming together as one, making sense to him now.

"This is preposterous!" The male voice huffed.

The pressure that Aaric felt was overwhelming and painful, his body tensing. And then his chest began to heave, blood rushed to his ears, like waves pounding on the beach.

"That's right. Breathe." Aaric turned over on his side and vomited hard, water projecting from his opened mouth.

"It's alright, let it all out," the kind voice said.

Aaric coughed fitfully, his head spinning.

The male voice spoke again with irritation. "This is a terrible idea. Don't say I didn't warn you. If your father finds out... "

The lighter female voice cut in, "He *won't* find out if you don't tell him."

Between fits of hacking up water and convulsing Aaric could hear the sweeter voice continue, "The girl has already seen us. If there is any risk, it has already been taken."

He could feel a light touch on his back, fingers rubbing and patting. Aaric tried to sit up, but lightheadedness took him back down to the ground, to what felt like wet sand.

"Take it easy. That's right." The female laid his head upon her lap, his eyes still closed with violent episodes of coughing.

"Trouble. That's all this is, is trouble in the making!"

The female spoke gently. "I felt something. Something drew me to them, like a pull."

Aaric could hear the sounds of the ocean hitting the beach somewhere close by and could see blinding sunshine through slanted eyes.

"I know it sounds silly, but it just seemed the right thing to do." The female paused as if thinking, "Any longer and they would've..."

Aaric's chest spasmed and he coughed again, progressively spitting out more water. The tightness of his lungs eased and he took a deep breath, his head still wavering in dizzy circles.

"Aleena..." Aaric began to form words, as though he had forgotten how to somewhere along the way. "Where's Aleena? What happened to the b..b...boat?" His teeth began to chatter with the bitter cold of the biting wind against his sodden clothes.

Aaric peered out of small slits, his eyes not yet adjusting to the light, and saw a blurry face with long dark curling hair, hanging over him.

The voice was compassionate. "Your boat capsized. You and your sister almost drowned." And then it came all rushing back at once. Aleena. Arrows. Prince Tolan. Water. Lots of water.

"Aleena!" Aaric cried out, his voice cracking. He again tried to sit up, but was still too weak, the visions before him cloudy and revolving. He let his head roll to the side limply.

"She is just fine," said the voice. "She went to fetch some water for you from the stream. Just rest now."

Aaric relaxed a bit. His breathing was deep and even now, and his heart felt stronger. He could hear the lapping tide, the crackling of a fire, and smell the roasting of fish. His mouth began to water.

He gazed up at his savior; the blurred lines creating the shape of her face began to sharpen, her detailed features popped crisply in his vision and became more vivid and colorful. Dark hair curled long down her back and dark brows highlighted her acorn-colored eyes, like a dust storm cresting the sea, and her face was kind, with plump salmon-colored lips forming into a wide grin. She was quite fair to look upon, Aaric thought, as his sight returned swiftly.

The young lady turned her head to her companion. "He's coming to, I think." She looked back at Aaric. "That's some bump you've got there." She reached out to touch Aaric's injury lightly. He sucked in his breath painfully and flinched away.

"We are friends,"she said reassuringly, "Don't be frightened."

He became confused for a moment. *Why on earth would I be frightened of this lovely and kind lady that saved my life?* And then he took a second look at her. She wore strange clothing, looking to be some sort of brown braided sea grass woven with tiny cream-colored shells. She lounged beside him, near the shore, the calm tide retreating and advancing and then slowly receding again to reveal a blue-green glimmering tail, like that of a fish, on the woman's lower half of her body.

Aaric popped straight up to sitting, his eyes open wide. He rubbed them furiously with the backs of his fists, as though rubbing the sleep out. He opened them again. Yes, still there, a shimmering tail of scales the color of the ocean.

"It's alright. We're friends." At that, he looked to the man and was seeing double. The male, who was sharpening a rusty spear on a rock caught his surprised look, shrugged and went back to work, his naked upper body oily and muscular. Aaric looked down to see that he also had a tail, his being the color of wet moss.

"Who... what... what are you?!" Aaric exclaimed with disbelief.

"We're merpeople." Aaric's mouth hung wide open at the strange creature's words. He began to scoot backwards in the sand, resisting the urge to get up and run, his legs still feeling numb and feeble.

"Oh, Aaric! I'm so glad you are alright!" Aleena returning to the site, came running to him. "I was so afraid you'd never wake up."

Aaric lowered his voice, almost whispering to his sister. "Aleena, where are we? Who are these... creatures?"

Aleena took Aaric's hand in hers. "It's alright Aaric, they're friends."

"But they're... they're mermaids!" His face was all screwed up in confusion and disbelief.

The fish man cleared his throat. "Correction. I am a merman. Captain Cade of the Mer guard of the Kingdom of Mer." The man bowed his head.

Aarric shouted in question, "Merpeople?"

He started to laugh like a crazy person and after a moment he stopped abruptly.

"Alright, enough of this." Aaric shook his head, tapping his forehead lightly as if to erase the visions he was seeing. "This is not real. I'm dreaming. It's just another hallucination. Before I know it, I will see my dead mother again soon. I just drank too much sea water, that's all." He lay back down on the ground, covering his face with his hands. "I'll just go back to sleep and when I wake everything will be back to the way it was."

"No, Aaric" Aleena said touching his shoulder, "You're not dreaming."

The mermaid lady said, "I assure you, we are as real as the air you breathe. My name is Kalaya, daughter of King Nerius of the Wavekeepers, heiress to the Coral Crown."

Aaric just lay there, silent, as if ignoring the situation might make it go away. He finally spoke, interrupting the silence, his voice muffled by his hands. "This is unbelievable."

His sister, moving his arms, put a damp rag on his forehead. "Aaric, Just take a deep breath and relax. They saved us. We'd have drowned if not for them. Don't be afraid."

Aaric felt strange as he sat up again. "You know, I could swear this was a dream... because I feel like I've seen this before... like I've been here before. This is so... curious. Have you ever had the feeling like you've lived a moment for the second time? I swear... this has happened before."

"I agree with the boy," Cade said plainly. "He swallowed too much sea water."

Aleena grasped her brother's arm, "No, Aaric I sort of felt the same way. Like we're reliving a moment a second time..." She walked to the crackling fire and pulled a stick from the coals, skewered with fish.

"Anyway, just rest now." She brought a piece to Aaric. "What you need is some food. Here." He took the fish anxiously and started to eat.

Aaric stopped. "Wait, where is Captain Bottlesby? Where's the rest of the crew?"

Aleena, as well as the two strange merpeople, or whatever they were, all had their heads down, avoiding his questioning gaze.

"And Prince Tolan?" There was a long pause of silence.

"Where *are* they? Aaric demanded.

The strange lady spoke. "They didn't make it. You and your sister are the only two survivors." Aaric looked over at Aleena and saw a single tear run down her cheek and drop into the sand.

Aaric put his head in his hands and sighed. He spoke solemnly, "It's my fault. They're all dead because of me."

Kalaya says, "You couldn't have done anything about it." She exchanged glances with the merman captain. "It's not your fault... it's... it's..." Her words trailed off.

Cade, his attention now on the ocean, suddenly yelled, "A boat!"

The small group looked out to see the dark outline of a ship sailing towards them, contrasted by the shining gold horizon, and fluffy cotton-white clouds hanging in the air above.

"Humans. And where there are humans, there's danger. We must be on our way, Kalaya." The guard was inching himself further into the water.

"No," Kalaya said sternly, "We can't just leave them. This is a small desolate island and there's no one else to help them."

"We've done all we can for them," Cade said, and then adding for emphasis, "against *my* better judgment."

Cade seemed to be getting very nervous, his moss green eyes stuck on the approaching boat. "Now it is time we part ways. Let them wave down the boat themselves."

Kalaya stayed where she was, ignoring her guard's suggestion, eyeing the ship that was slowly closing in on them, with its white sails waving in the wind.

"Kalaya! Now!" Cade pulled himself towards her and grasped her arm roughly.

She wrenched her arm free with a tug. "Wait! Look at the boat! They are Peace Protectors; they fly the banner."

Aaric could now see the bleached canvas sails flapping, and a banner that displayed a large spiraled black seashell. The people on board seemed no more than slight stick figures cut out against the sun that was now beaming after its escape from the storm.

Cade lowered his head, yielding, and let out a breath. "One day, Kalaya, you're going to be the death of me." Kalaya looked at him and laughed.

Aleena stood at the edge of the ascending water and waved the dirty rag she had used to cool Aaric's head, in the direction of the boat. There was no mistaking; it was headed right towards the little island that could not have been any wider than the dining hall back at Castlecray.

"Looks like Sir Theodore Tornbuckle," the merman mused. "What in the deep blue beyond are they doing this far south?"

The man Aaric supposed was Theodore, stood at the bow of the ship and waved an arm at them. The vessel, in all of its massiveness, crept up to just a stone's throw from the reef.

"It's safe. Come, let's swim them out to the ship." The mermaid gestured to her guard.

Aleena helped Aaric to his feet and kept a firm grip on his arm as they walked into the shallow water, Aaric swaying unsteadily. He felt a bit better after eating the fish, though his head was still pounding and his legs were like jelly. Aleena released her hold on Aaric and, looking back, waded out further to Kalaya and put her arms around the mermaid's neck. They skimmed out into the crystal clear sea, little ripples around them catching the honeyed sunlight.

"Well, landwalker, what're you waiting for?"

Aaric looked down into the water at the merman hesitantly, his muscles as solid as rock, gleamed; the body of a natural-born swimmer.

May as well. This day could not get any more curious. Once Aaric was in position, he felt them shoot out effortlessly into the water, weightless like floating oak leaves.

"Good day, Sir Theodore!" Kalaya called up to the boat. "It's a good thing you were near, we've some need of your help."

Sir Tornbuckle bowed awkwardly to Kalaya, his swollen paunch belly restricting his flexibility from beneath his faded red surcoat, emblazoned with the silhouette of a merman's body, apparently being his house crest.

"Princess," he addressed the mermaid formally as a golden tooth flashed in the sun, "How may I be of service?"

Aaric thought the man looked to be a knight; a rather sorry one at that, his rusty chainmail armor peeking out from behind the surcoat, which was stained with sea salt, tattered and weather-beaten, the stubble on his face almost indistinguishable from the smudges of dirt.

Aaric began shivering again as they floated in the cold water and Cade explained the great circumstance of their need to the shabby knight. The captain told Sir Tornbuckle, whose greasy brown hair floated like matted webs in the breeze around his swollen face, of the boat crash and of Aaric and

Aleena's survival, pointing out that *he* was in fact in favor of leaving the humans to be.

Kalaya chimed in, "Will this vessel be making its way towards South Harbor?"

Aaric frowned. Aleena must have told their rescuers where they lived while Aaric was unconscious. What else had she told them, he wondered.

"And will you please see these children to safety?" Aaric was starting to get frustrated at being called a child. He was almost a grown man, at sixteen name days old, the mermaid looking to be not much older than he.

The has-been knight spoke under his breath, his voice as hard as stone. "I'm not going to be able to do that." He picked at his golden tooth nonchalantly.

Kalaya eyed Tornbuckle coldly, as though she had turned into burning ice. "And *why* might I ask, can you not?"

"I cannot." He said plainly, avoiding their skeptical stares.

"By order of the King Nerius and the Coral Crown, I command it," Kalaya said firmly. Theodore just stood there staring into her eyes.

Aaric touched the painful bump on his head and sensed that something was wrong. And, as if Kalaya were reading his mind, she queried, "What is going on here, Sir Tornbuckle?"

The knight's tattered strips of what used to be his undershirt flapped in the wind. "Sometimes things do not work out as we planned."

Kalaya looked suspiciously at Theodore, as Aaric, still hanging on to the Mer guard, felt him bring his spear up and at the ready.

"It is for the greater good," Theodore growled.

Just then, a dozen merpeople appeared from nowhere, their tattooed faces just cresting the water surrounding the boat. Aaric jumped with a start and looked at Aleena. She held her composure, still atop the mermaid's back, rocking softly in the water, but he could see her hand shaking.

"Shadows? What is the meaning of this?" Cade ordered.

Theodore gave a nod to his crew and the merpeople that Cade had just called shadows, and commanded, "Capture the princess and the captain as well."

Aaric's body tensed, as the odd tattooed people in the water were on them in a blink. Making a startled noise, he struggled to hold on to Cade, as two large mermen were trying to rip them apart, the dark ink etchings on their face recalling black vines creeping up a garden wall.

He kicked the smaller one in the stomach as a last-ditch effort, but his fingers slipped from the muscled guard's arm.

Aaric could hear Aleena screaming and he saw that she was giving them the fight of their life. She had hold of a mermaid's long hair, the color of spiced pumpkin, and yanked hard. The mermaid howled, and the black scrawlings on her face stretched out as

Aleena pulled harder and Kalaya punched the pumpkin-haired shadow in the nose.

At just about the same time, both Aaric and Aleena were ripped away from their only safety, the strange merfolk they had just met, and were held tightly in the grip of two Shadows.

Shouting and arguing resounded over the water; hands, legs, hair, arms, and fins were all in a tangle during the commotion and Aaric couldn't tell what belonged to whom.

The tattoo-faced merman who held Aleena shouted up to Theodore Tornbuckle, asking, "What do you mean to do with the children, Sir?"

A hand on his tubby midsection, the leader looked down over the side at them, with a flash of irritation on his face and said, "They were not expected." The scruffy knight's lips, chapped from sea and wind, moved as if in thought. "Bring them along as well. Silvana can decide their fate."

Aaric could hear frantic splashing in the water and looked to see Kalaya covered in a fish net, held by two large mermen, flipping her fin wildly.

She glared up at Tornbuckle, "Silvana?" She spoke with disgust. "You're working with Silvana? You traitor!"

A loud gasp came from a male voice in the water and Aaric saw Cade elbow one of his captors in the face and run another through the throat with his spear, the end coming out the back with surges of red blood mixing with the splashing water. As Cade ripped his spear from the bloody flesh, two more shadows charged at the Mer guard. Aaric then saw a blur, as fast as green lightning, and Cade had the two assailants in an arm lock. In one swift movement he let go of one and speared him through the eye, the merman gargling and sinking below the foam-crested waves. He then took the other with both hands and abruptly broke his neck with a bone-popping crack. And then Cade was away with a flash and headed towards his princess.

"No!" She screamed. "No, Cade!"

He stopped.

"Go!" Kalaya, on the brink of tears, spoke with a wavering voice. "Go tell my father! Go warn the king!"

Cade looked back and forth between the stalking shadows on either side of him and decided that he had not much of a choice and called to her as he swam off, "Don't you worry, Kalaya! I will come back to save you!" And with that Aaric saw a moss green fin dive into the water and disappear into the great wide blue expanse.

"Shall we go after him, sir?" One of the shadows queried of the knight.

Theodore answered in a grim voice, "No. Let him go. That's exactly what Silvana wants."

"A trap?" Kalaya realized. "You're setting a trap for my father!"

Theodore, ignoring the mermaid, turned and with a sweep of his hand said, "Haul her up. Haul them all up."

Some of the shadow merpeople had gathered together and were carrying the dead bodies of their brothers off in the water, blood trailing behind making it look like red wine had spilled in the sea.

Aleena, being held tightly from behind, looked at Aaric and spoke, "It's alright, Aaric. We're going to be alright. Someone will come looking for us soon." Aaric nodded, as he was being pulled closer to the ship, unable to speak for fear of what might come out, and hoped she was right.

Men grunted as they hauled Kalaya over the railing and onto deck, throwing her to the floor with a wet smack. Aaric and Aleena, just a moment behind, landed hard on their backsides with a thud, strings of Aleena's long brown hair covering her face. Their hands were quickly bound behind their backs and they were tied, standing back to back, to either side of the main mast.

"When my father hears of this you will be dead meat, Sir," Aleena said calmly to the bedraggled knight as if they were having a conversation over tea. A big hairy-chested sailor laughed and coughed intermittently and then spit a large glossy blob at her feet. "Aaahh!" She bellowed with disgust.

Still on the floor, the mermaid smiled at Aleena and gave a reassuring nod to Aaric. She then glared at Sir Tornbuckle through the fishnet covering her face, her acorn eyes burning with hatred.

"You will pay, Sir Knight. Just wait... just wait and see. You will have the wrath of the Wavekeepers crash down upon you, and you will wish that you'd never made this treacherous decision." Aaric shivered at her words.

He closed his eyes for a time as they sailed off towards the horizon, trying to comprehend the day's events. It was just so unreal, and yet he felt a connection to these half-fish people. He wondered where they were taking him and his sister, who Silvana was, and why did they have to get dragged into the middle of this storybook escapade? He couldn't imagine what his father would do when he found out that Prince Tolan, his boat captain, and entire crew were dead, all because Aaric had to play the hero and take the ship in search of Quin.

Oh, goodness, Quin. He hoped and prayed that she was alright. More than likely she was with their grandfather, Captain Longship, headed back home to safety, unlike Aleena and him with their own unforeseeable future. How did he get them into this mess?

Furthermore, what would King Thunderdyn do when he found out that his son, second in line to the Golden Crown of Merenia, was first impaled by an arrow on a "borrowed ship," and then tossed into the sea by a monstrous wave, ending his short life.

And poor Aleena, she also had lost her betrothed prince because of him. He knew that she had really started to have a liking for Tolan, but now it was too late. Aaric shook his head side to side with frustration, and could feel the tender egg that popped out from the side of his skull throbbing.

Looking over at Kalaya, her blue-green scales sparkling with water and sunlight, her rich eyes wild and angry, Aaric felt a sense of calm. Although they were tied and bound, and the outcome looked hopeless, he somehow felt it comforting that he was on the side of the Wavekeepers, whoever they were.

BANON

Grand Elder Wylie?" Banon called out to the shadowed form hunched over a small candlelit writing desk. It was early morning, but the library was as dark as night, with thick velvet draperies drawn closed over the tall windows.

The dark figure slowly raised its head revealing a thin worn face beneath a long fibrous snow-white beard, with deep crow's feet and a pointy crooked nose. He smiled a toothless grin at Banon when he saw him.

"Your Majesty!" The voice all but croaked and the frail man stood shakily, outstretching his arms from under a long puddle of white robe, a stiff white hat sitting bulbously on his tiny skull.

"Elder Wylie, this is Jack Piper," Banon said, introducing his companion. "Traveling bard and history keeper." Jack bowed dramatically to the small Holy Man. "And you might remember Lord Emrys Castlecray?"

The Grand Elder's bristled white eyebrows furrowed together in thought, "Why, yes, of course I remember Lord Castlecray. He had a hand in helping his Highness during the Snell trials." He nodded his head slightly to Emrys.

"A pleasure to see you again, although it is under most unfortunate circumstances." The Elder shuffled out from behind his desk, "Am I right to presume you are here for the Gold Council Meeting?" he asked Emrys.

Banon interjected, "Yes, the meeting will start shortly after midday. But we have a most urgent matter that you may be of some help with, Grand Elder."

"Yes, I see." The Elder studied the small travel-worn group, showing signs of a sleepless night and lack of food and bath. "How may I be of service, Your Majesty?"

Banon ran a hand through his short cropped and dirt-matted hair. "We need information on a specific coat of arms and which house it may belong to. We are looking for a green background with a black ensign which we cannot quite make out." The prince reached inside his surcoat and pulled out the scrap of fabric, holding it out for Elder Wylie to see.

Elder Wylie's mouth moved open and closed involuntarily as he fixed his eyes on the textile, his stiff pointed beard following along. "Yes, that is a problem easily resolved."

He shuffled towards two carved bookshelves that flanked either side of the immense cobbled fireplace, radiating warmth and yellow light. Deciding on the one to the left, he ran a pointed finger softly up and down the bound book covers, finally landing on a red leather one, tattered from years of use, and pulled it from the shelf.

Banon glanced around at the majestic library, lined with rows of floor-to-ceiling bookshelves filled to the brim with colorful bindings. The Golden Library never ceased to amaze Banon, although he had spent many a winter day there huddled up with a good novel, and at the desks for his daily lessons with Master Brooks, pondering the histories of Merenian battles and politics.

Grand arched windows swept with luxurious curtains lined the eastern wall and crystal chandeliers hung in clusters at every joint of the painted barreled ceiling, depicting numerous starry constellations and wispy white clouds. The smell of old parchment, ink, wood, and leather always brought back a flood of nostalgic memories to Banon.

Brought out of his dreamy recollections by the group's movement, Banon followed them to the golden tufted chairs that sat merrily, washed in the light of the sunset-colored flames that cut through the dark shadowed room.

The men huddled around the Elder as he sat and began to thumb through the pages. "This is the more recent registry of Merenian Houses, and if my memory serves, there are quite a few with green impressions." He stopped and tapped a finger at the page. "This one is House Adlam with the green and gold adder...no, that's not right." Flipping further through the pages they went on for quite some time finding close similarities to the scrap and different combinations of black and green, but they were paired with other colors of reds, blues, and yellows. They finally stopped on House Birdhill.

"That could be it, by jove!" Jack Piper exclaimed as the charms and bells in his gnarled hair chimed. The house crest was a solid green shield with a jet black raven, beak opened and wings ready for flight.

Banon thought of Lady Maeveen Birdhill. She was quite an odd woman, always nervously jerking about. Aside from her daughter, she was the last of the Birdhill bloodline.

"Let us keep looking," Emrys suggested, "and we'll keep a list of all of the possibilities."

On they went to discover House Nooney, which took a black crescent moon rising on a green field, and House Snell, whose sigil was the black sea snake on the solid forest green shield.

Hmmm. Trenton Nooney has always been extremely loyal to the Gold Crown, but how deep does that loyalty lie? And House Snell, now that is quite a possibility with such a dark history. As Banon mused over their potential enemies, he and Lord Emrys exchanged glances and Elder Wylie snapped the book closed.

Banon had only been a young boy, clutching to his mother's skirts, at the time of the Snell Trials, but he remembered the stories well. He rubbed the grit out of his sleepy eyes as he thought about the story of the last Council Meeting that had been held years ago.

It was per a judgment upon House Snell, where Lord Lavoy Snell of SeaWatch had committed treason against the Gold Crown, and Beaumont Thunderdyn being a good and just king, called the meeting for a fair hearing of his peers. After many weary days of judicial proceedings, Snell had finally been found guilty by the Council, and sentenced to beheading. The rest of his family had been pardoned with the exception that they had to evacuate Castle SeaWatch and move into Tumbledown Tower, allowing their previous home to be given to a more formidable family: the Castlecrays.

"That looks to be it for the recent registrar..." The little Holy man paused, scratching at his wiry white beard, "Although, if you want to be a bit more thorough, there is a more complete compilation of houses and their coats of arms down below, some of which have died out or, for whatever reason, have not been used for a number of years." His white robed arm pointed towards a large bookshelf at the very back of the library, half hidden by an exotic painted screen from Braisia, intricate birds and vines brushed onto the thin material.

Banon searched Lord Emry's tired face, stubbed with hair and smeared with dirt, and then looked towards bard Piper, who also looked the worse for wear, his matted long hair sticking out in every direction, clothes torn and splattered with blood. The other men of the traveling party had already receded into their quarters, for very much needed nourishment and sleep, but his two loyal companions, bone-tired and ready to drop, still followed him without complaint.

"Alright then," The prince said. They could all rest when they were done with their research, Banon thought. "Grand Elder, lead the way."

The older man looked down at his lap hesitantly. "Your Majesty," His hands shook as they held the leather bound book, "Unfortunately, I must stay aloft, for my knees do not serve me well as they used to, and the climb is steep and narrow."

The Elder looked sadly regretful for, as well as the Royal Bethel, the Golden Library had been his keep for many years. "But please help yourselves. The chambers are still kept up by Chamberlain Darcy and the torches are lit daily."

Jack Piper and Lord Castlecray agreed and followed Banon through the Grand Library, looking around for a supposed staircase to lead them "down below" as the Elder had stated.

Stopping at the ornate bookshelf behind the painted screen, Banon made a fist and pounded on the side twice with a wooden *thunk... thunk* and then gave it a nudge with his shoulder. With a groaning sound, the console shuddered and slid sideways, revealing an arched doorway that disappeared into darkness, with flickering torch light. His two companions eyed the passageway warily, but despite their inhibitions, followed the prince down the cold stone steps, venturing further and further underground, their dancing shadows thrown against the confined rock walls by the torch light.

Banon knew of the extent of the Golden Library, and by comparison, it was the largest in all of Merenia. Books were very costly, and a castle of even the highest of nobility usually only held a dozen or so. Scholars would delve eagerly into the unique plethora of knowledge. But no one outside of the Royal Family, aside from a chosen few, came down to the secret underground wing of the Library.

Jack Piper, along with being a singer, musician, and storyteller, was also a historian, and made himself at home amidst the musty close quarters of the shelf-lined catacombs. The bard, already immersed in the search, was humming a song that sounded a lot like *Stink Bottom Meri*, while Banon and Emrys spread apart into different sections, fingering the many books that looked to be centuries old.

Since Elder Wylie's decline in health, it seemed that the library had suffered as well. Sections weren't as organized as they used to be and books were stuck haphazardly out of place. Banon picked a shelf at random and began to read off the titles as he heard Jack Piper, a row over, doing the same out loud.

"*Merenian Courtois, Song of Lo Blanc, Digenis Nikaydian, Chanson de Gusto.*" It sounded like the bard was in the song and poetry section.

Piper continued naming off works of literature excitedly. "*Acolyte Hymns, Golden songs, Toubadours of the Realm.* Now these are my kind of books! Haha! If my insides weren't growling like a starved lion, I could stay here all day." The bard seemed as happy as a pig in new mud.

Banon could feel his own stomach turning with hunger as he read some of the titles on the shelf in front of him, *Anselm of Snakeden, Petre Plowman, Legends of Gold, Tales of Braisia.* He was in the reading for pleasure area. Coat of arms would be with the historical documents and records, Banon thought, as he moved on towards Lord Emrys.

Lord Emrys was crouched on the ground, his lean muscles taught with intent. He called out a few works as he swiped a sweat-matted string of brown hair from his face. "*Theological and Philosophical Treatises, Knights of the Eagle, Book of Hours?*" It sounded like he was in the general area that they needed. "Ah!" Lord Emrys stood abruptly with a large volume in his hand. "Could this be it, *A History of Heraldic Devices and Merenian Crests?*"

Jack Piper rushed over to them hastily as the men grouped together in the dim light. The book seemed to weigh as much as a boulder, and looked almost as old as one, but was a work of art in itself.

The cover was bound with boards of fine beechwood and encased in a supple and powder-colored, tawed skin. The title was in elegantly inked calligraphy and the end band was elaborately detailed with metalwork, twining and curving up the side, inlaid with ivory miniatures of some of the predominant house symbols of that time. The bard gasped in awe, as Lord Emrys gently ran his fingers over the detailed embellishments.

"This would be the one we're looking for!" Jack Piper exclaimed excitedly as the men took the book to a wooden table that was nestled in a corner, sitting under a set of shelves stuffed full with rolled-up papyrus scrolls and long bundled maps.

Banon scratched at his head, wondering if he hadn't gotten a case of itch mites, given that their traveling conditions weren't very hygienic. He stopped when he noticed the other two studying him and quickly shifted the topic to the current search. "So far we have three possible matches to the crest we are looking for. How many more do you suppose could be in here?" he said, tapping the book.

"This is a very large book," Jack said as he opened the cover with a flurry of dust and continued, coughing between words, "but keep in mind…it will be repeating most of the coats of arms we went over upstairs."

Emrys waved away the dust cloud and began to ever so carefully turn the brittle yellowed pages as Banon stood and pulled a flaming torch from the wall. With his free hand, he opened the small glass door of a lantern, held the torch to the wick, and with a popping sound the fire caught.

Except for the beautifully illustrated coats of arms, the book was really quite boring: lists of family trees, dates of births and deaths, amongst other uninteresting notations. The three men searched for what seemed to be hours, bathed in a small pool of warm yellow lantern light, when they finally came to a very unusual coat of arms. The crest was a shield rippling with blue and white, and a pearly white crown atop made of undulating whitecap waves that twisted and curled this way and that. The picture seemed vaguely familiar, like the lingering of a dream between sleep and wakefulness. And then it hit him. Banon's heart jumped into his throat, and firmly laying his palm flat on the book, he stopped Emrys from turning the page. *That's right, a dream!*

Banon flashed back to his recurring dream, as enchanting melodies filled his ears. Through the forest, down the riverbank, over a mound of rocks and through a group of trees, there she waited for him, tragically submerged in water, beautiful and tortured with a crown of white waves on her head. She reached out to him, her features blurred and her eyes searching his face for some semblance of hope, a suggestion of safety.

A hot surge rushed through the prince's body, making his cheeks flush and his fingers tingle. *What could this mean?* He searched the page, his eyes trying to take in as much information as quickly as possible, although there was not much information to take in. There were no dates, no list of names, just three words. *Custos de Fluctus.*

"Is everything alright?" Lord Emrys asked Banon, who was now pale and sweating, as the blood slowly drained from his face.

"Your Majesty," Jack added. "You look as though you've seen a ghost."

It sure felt to Banon as if had seen a ghost; a beautiful one who haunted his dreams. "Er... no, I'm fine. Just thought I recognized something." The two other men studied him dubiously.

Banon took a deep breath to calm himself. There was no need to tell them about his bizarre dreams and this ironic coincidence, they'd just think he was mad, or probably blame it on lack of sleep. Best to just focus on the task at hand. "Really, I'm fine, let's keep on looking."

The three of them continued searching through the endless pages, stopping at possible matches, only to be passed over due to small discrepancies.

"Here we are," Jack Piper said, his former enthusiasm had waned with time, leaving his voice tired and scratchy. "House Brumble." The coat of arms was a green shield with the silhouette of a front-facing black horned bull.

"I've heard of that House," Banon stated. "Weren't they the ones that were killed off in a bloody battle of Songstone River?"

"Yes, you know your studies, m'boy!" Piper thought twice about how he had addressed the prince and corrected himself, "Uh... Your Majesty."

The bard went on instructing, "That was many years ago when House Tallhart of Castlebridge and House Brumble of Torro fought over the crossing at the Songstone river."

"Yes," Emrys interjected, "and House Brumble was defeated, thus leaving Castle Torro uninhabited and in ruins for near on a hundred years now."

"They say it's haunted by the ghosts of House Brumble," Jack Piper added, "seeking retribution for their untimely demise." The bard made a theatrical impression of a ghost, as a child might do while camped in the woods telling scary stories, his hands flowing upwards weightlessly at his sides.

"That battle is what inspired the well-known *Song of Souls*." The bard began to hum the eerie melody to himself, and the humming morphed into a drawn-out yawn.

Flipping through the last few pages of the book, with no luck, Banon rose from his seat. "We have what we came for; four possible matches." The prince, tucking the scrap of the mystery house crest in his surcoat, staggered on his feet. "Let us go rest and wash up before the meeting; it is going to be a long one."

And with that, the men parted ways, Banon too tired to eat, threw himself on the fluffy feather bed in his private chambers and drifted into a deep slumber, his dreams haunted by a beautiful nameless girl with deep eyes and a crown of waves upon her head, along with the words *Custos de Fluctus*.

NOAM

Ah! Here they are; our newest...*and youngest* members of the Peace Protectors!" Nimbus Nooney spread his arms wide in welcome as Noam and Quin entered the large dining hall doors, trailing behind Captain Longship. The first thing that Noam noticed about the great room was the ceiling, or lack thereof. The room had no roof! It was open to the starry night sky. Curious little lightning bugs twinkled and flitted above their heads, creating ever-changing pinpoints of light that filled the room and made it look alive.

"And as hungry as two little sharks in a fish pond, I imagine!" A short plump lady, sitting near the door, chirped, her large grin flashing bright white teeth against her dark smooth ebony skin. She had eyes shaped like a cat's, deep and dark, and big puffy brown hair that she pinned up with a fancy little hat that was crusted with sparkling gems.

Captain Longship gave a short hearty laugh, patting his round belly. “I don’t know about *them*, Amabel, but *I* could eat a shark all to m’self!”

Noam lagged near the entrance, Quin just beside him, nervously playing with something in the pocket of her skirts. Captain Gaderian took a seat near the end of the table, and was greeted by the other members, all of whom wore the gleaming black seashell around their necks, wrists, or tied to their belts. Nimbus Nooney waved them in jovially. “Come, come! Have a seat. We have a feast prepared for the occasion!”

Down the center of the long cave room was a wooden table that ran the entire length, made of the same natural material as the knotty wooden doors. An eclectic assemblage of chairs were perched neatly underneath, all of different sizes, shapes, and colors. Quin chose an intricately carved chair, with gold gilt and a velvety upholstered seat, to the left side of the captain. Noam took a simple blue painted wooden chair to her other side and glanced sideways to notice that the walls seemed to be moving.

The sides of the cave were covered in twisted and intermingling rocks that looked like tree roots and stone icicles, trickles of water running over them and disappearing into crevices along the corners where the walls met the ground. The sheer sheets of blue water glimmered and shined with sparkles of gold, reflecting the movement of the lightning bugs, like little stars surrounding them.

"Things have been terribly hasty; we haven't had a chance for a formal introduction yet," Nooney said as he gestured to Noam and Quin from his head spot at the table, his lips curling into a smile, and dots of fluttering light shining on his balding crown.

Captain Gaderian stood and cleared his throat. "Uh, um. Yes. This enchanting young lassie," he pointed at Quin, "is Lady Quinlan Castlecray, daughter to Lord Emrys o' Castlecray Keep." His eyes lightened as he added, "Me granddaughter."

Quin stood and curtsied awkwardly.

"And this strapping young lad is Noam Finbar, Master o' Kitchens at Castlecray Keep." Noam blushed at the introduction, which made him sound so very much more important than the usual calling of "you there boy," or "kitchen rat."

Various nods and a repetition of greetings echoed through the vast cave, some members even coming to hug Noam and Quin. Everyone seemed so nice and enthusiastic about the two newcomers that Noam felt at ease right away.

People began to take their places, as serving women and men brought out lavish trays, toppling over with an assortment of mouthwatering foods. Noam licked his lips at the sight, unable to remember the last time he had eaten. A savory aroma filled the cave and added to its surprising warmth.

It had been unusually cool lately, for summer; actually downright cold, but the invisible island had seemed to keep a comfortable temperature. There were no fires lit in the dining hall, but hanging lanterns lined the walls, throwing pools of warm yellow light onto the sparkling walls of running water and spiraling fingers of stone.

"Now," Nimbus Nooney looked at the children, "This here is the human half of the Peace Protectors, with exception for a few missing members." He glanced around the table, explaining, "Lady Dilantha Lovelyn and Lord Norman Willoughby have both responded, but have other urgent matters that need tending to. But what of Sir Tornbuckle?" His little brown eyes darted around the room. "Has anyone heard word from Sir TheodoreTornbuckle?"

"No," said a tall thin man. "It seems that he just up and disappeared."

"Hmm," the Island Keeper mused, brown tufts of hair sticking straight out from behind his ears, making him look like a pudgy rabbit.

"Alright, alright. Back to business." The short tubby man looked back to the children and gestured to his side at the tall thin man who had spoken earlier. "This here is Bardolph Belecoat and his lovely wife Betha." The thin man's lanky arm rested on top of his wife's large one. She must have been wider than her skinny husband by two-fold and almost as tall. Although they had quite opposite statures, their faces shared a lot of similar features, light blonde eyebrows, pinched little mouths, and high cheekbones, Betha's being full and Bardolph's boney. The happy couple smiled and nodded quietly.

"They are very well known wine merchants," Nimbus continued, "from Belecoat Keep in Knos. They and their ancestors have been a part of the Peace Protectors for centuries."

Nooney waved a hand further down the table at a mid-sized, quirky woman with dark thick black hair, and a long thin nose drastically humped in the center. Noam thought she looked like a bird, and her nose a beak. "This is Lady Maeveen Birdhill."

Birdhill, that's appropriate. Noam chuckled under his breath and exchanged a quick look with Quin. The Island Keeper continued, "Lady Birdhill, wife to Randolph Birdhill of Songstone."

Lady Maeveen cocked her head at Quin and Noam, and all but squawked a nasal, "How do you do?"

"And here to the other side," Nooney gestured at the seat to his right, "is Sir Winchell Tallhart. He is a retired knight from Castlebridge, and a tourney champion of Merene, if I may boast?"

"Yes, thank you," the chiseled man spoke in a monotone voice, his posture rigid. "It is a pleasure to make your acquaintance." The knight spoke with absolutely no inflection or emotion, combined with a very non-expressive and plain-looking face, fanned with thick blonde hair. *Champion,huh? A champion of snooze-ville, I suppose.*

Noam made a mental note of each member in the colorful group, putting on his best imitation of what he thought to be noble character, sitting up straight, nose slightly pointed into the air.

"You, of course, know Captain Gaderian Longship, a very true and loyal member. What you may not know of your grandfather," Nooney said looking at Quin, "is that the Longship name is very highly regarded, for it was Gaderian's great ancestors who began the Peace Protectors in the time of the Great Hunt, and drew up the formal treaty and documents." Noam saw Quin gaze up at her grandfather in awe, finding out another one of his many secrets.

"And last but not least, our fair Lady Amabel Diamond, from House Diamond in Goldbridge." Nooney bragged. "The wealthiest widow in North Merenia." Lady Amabel had been the one to call Noam and Quin "hungry little sharks" upon their arrival. She beamed at them, waggling her fingers in a delicate wave, every one with a precious sparkling gem or jewel bigger than the last. "Hello, my darlings!" she sang. *One of those rings could feed Castlecray for an entire winter!* Noam decided that he liked the woman.

"And we have been acquainted," the short Island Keeper put a hand to his chest, "but in case any have forgotten, I am Nimbus Nooney, Head of the Merenian district of the Whisper Web, and Keeper of the Invisible Island." Bowing to the children he stated, "Let me be first to welcome you home."

"We are your family now, and don't you forget it." Lady Amabel Diamond's laugh was like the ringing of chimes, beautiful and melodic, and made Noam and Quin smile.

Captain Longship pushed back his chair and raised his glass high. "To Lady Quin and Master Noam!"

The whole grouped mirrored the captain. "To Lady Quin and Master Noam!" Everyone cheered and then broke out into excited conversations.

Sounds of dinner commenced with the clinking of silverware, plates, cups and bowls. Serving people buzzed around, pouring water, ale, and wine where needed, while Noam took a huge bite of a chicken leg, and the grease ran down his chin. He looked over to see Captain Gaderian's plate piled high with honeyed ham, steaming buttered turnips, and biscuits smothered in gravy. The captain was happily chewing on bits of ham and washing it down with a mug full of ale as he talked with Lady Amabel and Nimbus Nooney in between bites.

Noam caught the end of Nimbus Nooney's hushed sentence, "... is up to something. There's no other explanation for her strange behavior." The little broad man brought a piece of meat to his mouth on the end of a sharp knife.

Lady Diamond spoke low, as people do when repeating scandalous information, "It is quite odd that the Tinkers have settled down near Shadow Rock. Some say that Silvana has been overly friendly with the travelers."

The captain dipped a hunk of biscuit in the creamy gravy and gulped it down. "That's verra unlike the Tinkers." He wiped his mouth with a linen napkin. "They are an independent people and have always avoided close contact wi' any organized group, unless it's to trade or barter as they are travelin' through."

Quin looked up from her plate of mashed turnips and roasted chicken, her bright blue eyes lined with thick brown lashes. She looked at Captain Gaderian. "Grandfather, what's a Tinker?"

The captain stopped abruptly as though just noticing that Noam and Quin had been listening. "The Tinker's are a specific kith o' merpeople. They wander from mangrove to mangrove in the depths of the ocean, never staying anywhere too long."

"What's a kith?"

"What's a mangrove?"

Noam and Quin both spouted questions simultaneously.

Gaderian chuckled, "I know, I know. There's so much ye still have yet to learn, and that will come in due time, my wee ones."

Nooney interjected into the conversation. "The most important thing for you two to remember is to keep your stations."

Noam and Quin looked at each other; confused. The Island keeper continued, "When you go back to your home at Castlecray, you must resume your previous lives as normally as possible. Quinlan, you will continue to be a Lady of House Castlecray. And Noam, you will continue to be Master of Kitchens."

"We have to go back home?" Quin looked disappointed as she pushed back a stray strand of hair from her face.

"Aye, me Quinnie-fish. Eventually," her grandfather said as a spunky little serving woman topped off his cup of ale.

"But don't you live here?" Noam asked.

The captain scratched his scruffy salt and pepper beard. "No. Well, aye. This is me home away from home, when I'm no on merchant business, stationed in South Harbor."

Lady Amabel Diamond swirled her wine in her cup as she spoke. "Every Protector of the Peace gets his or her own room at Invisible Island. But, like your grandfather was saying, you must keep your station in your normal life. Most of the members stay here for a time, but when business is finished, they go back to their own homes. Otherwise, people might start to get suspicious."

"So it's like leading a double life?" Noam asked in between bites. He was ravenous after their travels.

"Quite right, young Master." Nooney looked at Noam and Quin. "And you too will have your own rooms the next time you visit."

Noam and Quin caught each other's glances. "Wow!" they said in unison.

Dinner seemed to be wrapping up as Noam looked around to see yawning and sleepy faces amongst the group. Workers were clearing empty plates and bowls, busily hurrying the remains of the feast into an adjoining room, which Noam assumed to be the kitchen. The group began to part ways slowly, one by one leaving the magical room with its undulating walls of seeping water and twinkling lightning bugs, for the dark honeycomb of stone caves and pathways leading back to their designated chambers. Nimbus Nooney escorted them down the sparse dark halls, walking ahead with Captain Longship, talking in hushed tones, leaving Quin and Noam to walk behind.

Quin edged close to him and whispered, "I've been meaning to show you something." She opened a pocket in her skirts and reached in, a dim blue glow radiating from the folds of fabric, reflecting onto their faces. The conversation of the two men in front of them ceased and Nooney looked over his shoulder, but just before, Quin jerked her hand from her pocket and they were cast into darkness again, only the few and far between lanterns left small warm pockets of light sporadically down the passage. Quin and Noam walked along quietly as if immersed in the peculiar paintings on the walls.

The captain and the Island Keeper resumed their in-depth conversation, speaking low so that Noam could only hear an occasional word or two. Quin breathed a deep sigh, as though in relief. Whatever it was, the two men hadn't seen.

"What in the world was that?" he asked Quin in a forced whisper.

"Remember me asking you if Aaric had spoken with you on the day of the feast?"

Noam thought back. So much had happened since then. "Um... I think so."

"He was going to test you."

"Test me?"

"Yes, with the magical stone." Quin pointed to her pocket. "I found it in a locked chest under in the tunnels back home at Castlecray. You can't say anything about it to anyone. Nooney warned me to tell *no* one. Not even Grandfather."

"Why would he do that? What does it do?" Noam pondered the pulsing icy blue glow. "How did he know you had it?"

Quin grabbed his arm tightly and brought him even closer as they walked, their shadows being thrown large onto the bumpy cold walls. "It's a long story. But it glows only for certain people and I wanted to see if... "

"Nooney! Captain Longship!" A shout echoed down the hall, footsteps clomping along behind them.

The group stopped and, turning around, saw a young boy wearing brown robes. "Come quick to the rooftop! Something's happening." The young boy turned and ran in the opposite direction, the sounds of his running feet trailing off down the corridor.

"Let's go have a look, shall we?" Nooney turned around, and with quick little feet shuffling under his long robes, the short man was scampering down the hall like a grey rabbit, the captain, Noam, and Quin running to keep up.

Cave doors and numbered signs whizzed by, glowing lanterns brightened and then faded as the group ran this way and that through the twisting tunnels, finally coming to a stop.

"The only way is up!" The squat man made a sharp right turn into a crevice in the wall, which opened into a small hollow, the floor a square wooden platform. Captain Gaderian planted his feet hard onto the plank, making it rock back and forth, like it was hanging in mid-air. Noam hesitated, Quin beside him, looking at the unsteady little room.

"It's safe," the huge bearded captain said, as he began to hastily unwrap a coiled rope from a metal hook on the wall. "Hop on!"

Noam looked at Quin. She was biting her lip as she gazed at the wavering wooden contraption, strung with heavy ropes.

Nooney theatrically waved them in. "Quickly now!"

Quin returned Noam's look and they both hopped on, feet teetering, and tightly grabbed the nearest rope. Gaderian began to pull the rope he held and Noam glanced up at the sound of high-pitched creaking coming from the invisible darkness high above. He could feel them begin to move slowly upward and then faster with increasing speed. Up and up they went, a small lantern above them rocking and swaying, the contrivance creaking and grunting, and Captain Longship sweating with effort.

Noam felt as if they were miners mining for gold (from the stories he'd heard, at least, considering he'd never actually been on a mining expedition). *What a brilliant invention. Wish I had one of these at the Castlecray kitchens. It would sure beat the constant running up and down endless flights of stairs.*

Suddenly, a cold blast of air hit them, his blonde hair whipped him in the face, and he assumed they were close to their destination. Moonlight began to trickle in and Noam looked up to see the thick rope that the captain held, running up and over a metal wheel, squeaking as it went about its job. *Ah, so that's how it works!* The small hollow in the rock then opened wide to the grand night sky, glistening with thousands of stars. The platform came level with hard ground and the captain secured the rope tightly to another hook in the rock.

Dozens of people stood on the rooftop balcony: some Protectors of the Peace, and some servants and workers, all huddled in groups. Noam's breath caught in his chest as he gazed around them at the sparkling ocean and surrounding rocky mountain peaks. He thought it likely that you could see the whole world from up here.

Poised near him was the robed young boy who had called them up from the passage, standing stock still, his head raised to the night sky. Noam studied the people around him; everyone was looking upward in awe. He arched his neck back, and among the heavenly stars, like diamonds tossed across the velvet black sky, was one, more intense and bigger than the others. It was unlike any other star Noam had ever seen! It shone brighter and grew larger with every breath he took. The celestial sparkle grew even bigger, swelling with light, outshining its neighbors ten-fold.

Noam asked of no one in particular, "What in the deep blue is that?"

Suddenly the star exploded with supernatural force, the rumble being felt on the earth beneath them, light beams shooting apart into three pieces. "Bloody Hell!" Quin yelped as she grabbed Noam, hugging his ribs so tightly that he thought they might crack. She nestled her head into his neck, hesitantly peering up at the sky from under her long dark brown hair. Noam glanced down at Quin, holding him close. *If it weren't for unexpected exploding stars,* Noam thought, *I could get used to this.*

He was brought back to the blinding scene and squinted his eyes at the triad of star pieces, each began to wave and shimmer into different colors. The first turned into a radiant yellow, like sunlight, winking and trembling, followed by the second, a hot burning red, like fire. And the last piece burst into a blazing emerald green, glittering like a precious jewel. The magnificent three-pointed constellation reflected out over the water, unfolding like a blooming flower with luminous and electric light.

"Well, I'll be a dancing dolphin," Captain Longship mused.

The pieces then began to fall towards the earth and sea with fiery tails, a spectrum of bright colors trailing behind them.

Noam looked to see a cold sweat beading across Nooney's head, reflecting the sky's brilliance. The Island keeper reached a hand up towards the sky and spoke in a foreboding tone, "The Prophecy begins its course... "

ALEENA

"There's just got to be some way we can…" Aaric grunted, as he pulled with all of his strength against the iron bars, "break ourselves free." He let go and released his breath, slumping his head and shoulders, and sloshing his feet back to the cold rock bench and sitting down heavily.

"You've been at it for some time now, Aaric. There's nothing we can do but just hope someone will come to rescue us." Aleena was beginning to feel less confident about her statement as she gazed through the metal rods of their cell upon the endless expanse of ocean, caressed by red and gold sunset clouds, making the sky appear to be on fire.

The three captives had been brought to Shadow Rock, which was literally a mountainous rock stretching from the depths of the ocean floor all the way up into the clouds, honeycombed with dark caves, underwater and above. The rock was surrounded by a small beach of craggy terrain, making an uneasy climb and hard footing for any human, except for where Aleena, Aaric, and Kalaya were held.

Their cave, resting right off a small shallow inlet edged by water, was at sea level and welcomed the cold surf to rush in through the steel bars under their feet, a couple of finger-widths deep.

Aleena shivered and her teeth chattered with cold and damp, the bottom of her skirts mopping up the water like a sponge and weighing her down. She sat on the stone pallet, the only thing in the empty cell, and curled her legs into her chest in hopes of creating more warmth.

"Let's hope someone comes soon." Kalaya spoke dismally as she cupped her hands into the water on the floor and poured it over her iridescent scales which sparkled in reflection of the colorful sunset.

"When the tide rises in the morning, this cave will be filled with water." Kalaya was leaned up against the wall, looking quite ill, her glittering tail laid flat on the floor. As she had explained earlier, merpeople could not be kept out of the water for very long, or they began to dry out, causing them to get very sick.

Aaric, feeling another wave of anger, popped up and ran splashing to the bars, then jumped up and hung on, shaking them like a wild monkey.

"Hey out there!" he yelled to the merpeople who had been guarding them. "This is absolutely immoral! We've done nothing! At least let my sister go; she's a lady of House Castlecray! I demand it!" Aaric's blonde hair was sticking up in all directions, spiked by sea spray, his eyes mad with fury.

"Hush up in there, you filthy landwalkers!" one of the guards called out. Aleena could see them lounging in the water on either side of the cavern entrance, one sharpening his knife on the side of the dwelling, making a ringing sound that echoed out over the ocean.

"That scrawny little walker just never shuts up, does he?" The other one asked, a black twisted pattern on his skin, running up the back of his neck.

"You smell like rotten fish, the two of you!" Aaric howled, his gray eyes gleaming with mischief. The comment seemed to strike a nerve with the first guard, his neck tensed as he looked over his shoulder back at the captives, his black eyes smoldering.

"Aaric, stop it!" Aleena cried out. Lowering her voice she added, "You'll just make things worse."

Just then, another merperson swam up to the guards, a female. She had large kinky curly hair, adorned with braids and bells and all sorts of trinkets that chimed when she moved, twisted with strips of different colors, looking like some sort of exotic striped animal. She spoke to the two mermen with a hushed voice, occasionally looking back at the three prisoners, her purple eyes twinkling. She handed one of the guards a large gold coin that flashed in the sun, and they swam off into the darkening water without looking back.

The mermaid gingerly moved to the opening, held onto a bar, and studied the three of them.

"A Tinker," Kalaya said dryly.

"Why, yes, princess, some would call me that." The strange mermaid looked quite the spectacle, with her wild hair, and layers of golden and silver bracelets, rings, and necklaces with sparkling rubies and moonstones.

She wore human clothes too; a purple corset, laced tightly with green ribbon, and a cream shirt underneath, as opposed to the other merpeople Aleena had seen. If they wore any clothes at all, it was usually scraps of natural woven grasses, plant life, and sea shells.

"What do you want with us?" Kalaya said scornfully. "Talk is that the Tinkers are now siding with Silvana and her Shadows."

The woman made a *tsking* sound. "Our kind sides with no one. We only work towards our own means."

The Wavekeeper princess snorted. "Selfish, you mean."

Ignoring Kalaya's remark the woman pulled a package out from behind her back and handed it through to Aaric, who had backed up a few steps upon the stranger's arrival. Wrapped with brown twine, the shiny yellow package dripped water like off a duck's back.

"Don't take it, Aaric," Kalaya warned, her long dark hair hanging in waves around a face looking paler than Aleena remembered.

"I can only imagine how hungry you all are? The shadows don't usually like to feed their captives. They feel it's a waste of food on the soon to be dead." The stranger's eyebrow wiggled with the offering, as she held out the wrapped parcel.

Aleena's stomach, as if in answer, grumbled voraciously. Aaric eyed the package and then lunged forward and swiped it from the Tinker's hand. He brought it over to Aleena and sat down beside her, looking over the package of strange material.

The mermaid spoke, as if reading Aaric's mind. "Beeswax. It's a fantastic little invention of the humans; keeps the water and damp out."

Aleena looked down and felt of the bundle, seeing that it was in fact fabric that had been coated with wax. Aaric untied the string and unfolded the package, displaying hunks of salted fish and seaweed. Normally, Aleena would have not been too keen on the dish, but at this point there was no better option. Her brother and she took their share and then passed it on to Kalaya, who grudgingly took a bite of fish.

"Humans are the most interesting of creatures; so resourceful and quite brilliant." The Tinker pushed a bright orange strand of curls from her face, joining it with the blue, green, and purple ones.

"Who are you, anyway?" Aaric questioned the mermaid.

"Oh, how rude of me not to introduce myself." She bowed her head. "My name is Moselle, of the Zebrata kith."

"How did you know we were here?" Aleena asked as she chewed the stringy seaweed.

"The Zebrata have quite a few merpeople who are closely knit into the Whisper Web. News travels fast."

"I thought you took no sides," Kalaya repeated as she ate sparingly.

Moselle looked thoughtful. "Oh, we don't. The Whisper Web is universal and has no sides. We just pass on information as we receive it, sometimes in exchange for... treasures," she spoke as she adjusted a golden comb in her hair, inlaid with rubies.

"Well, then, why are you here if not to help us escape?" Aaric questioned.

"If that I could, young human. Silvana's Magic is much too powerful. It surrounds this place like a barrier. Good thing our friends out there," she said, pointing to the two figures floating on the horizon, "are interested in gold." The Tinker turned her head back, her hair jingling. "I came to bear news."

Kalaya lifted her head lethargically at the Tinker's words, her brown eyes dim with weakness.

"King Nerius has been instructed to bring his half of the stone tablet here, by high tide tomorrow morning, in exchange for the heiress." She gestured to Kalaya.

"It's a trap," Kalaya retorted. "Silvana won't let me go alive. Nor my father."

"And that is what I've come to tell you, so that you may be warned. Also I wish to tell you that..."

A loud whistle came from the two dark mounds floating out in the water, looking like cutouts against the grey twilight. Darkness had now fallen and Aleena blinked, her eyes adjusting to the night sky.

"I must go now." She looked at the small group, catching each one's eyes. "Be strong." And with that the strange mermaid was off into the water, bubbles cresting the surface from where she dove.

The guards were back in a flash and the first one put his head up to the steel bars, tattoos framing his creepy dark eyes. "You had better keep your mouth shut if you know what's good for you." The guards turned to their spots on either side of the cave, staring out to the first stars of night as if nothing had happened.

Aleena could see a disturbance in the dusky water to the right side of the small cove that their cell rested in. As the wrinkles in the water moved closer, she could tell that it was a procession of merpeople, one mermaid higher than the rest, being carried by the others.

Aleena watched intently as they came close. The one that was being lifted had dark inky black hair and eyes to match, but skin so soft and fair as beaches of white sands that it stood out amongst the darkness. Her tail sparkled in the moonlight, black as jet, and she held herself royally.

There were half a dozen mermen, who looked very much like the guards, with patterns and drawings etched into their skin, all differing from each other. The dark-haired mermaid was carried effortlessly through the water towards their cell, tracings of silver moonlight reflecting out behind them all, furrowing in the water. Aleena saw Aaric quickly shove the package of food behind the stone bench and then bring his hands to rest lightly on his lap.

"Halt!" the dark-haired mermaid commanded as she was brought in front of the barred cave. Aleena's teeth chattered furiously now, but she wasn't sure if it was from the cold rising water that was now a hand's width covering the floor, or from the uneasy feeling she had at seeing the female leader. Aleena hugged her legs tightly to her body.

The mermaid, sitting up high on the shoulders of two mermen, looked down at Kalaya with deep eyes, like black velvet pools of the night sea. Waving off the rest of her escorts, she studied her for a very long time.

"You don't look quite so majestic *now*, princess. Are you ill?" The mermaid japed, knowing very well the answer.

Kalaya glanced up wearily and quietly laughed at the mockery. "You will not get away with this, Silvana. My father knows better. He will not be baited as you wish."

"Oh, on the contrary." A smile flashed across her graceful face. "As you very well know, you are the next heiress to the Coral Crown, not likely to be left rotting as a prisoner without a fight. Nerius has agreed to come before sunup on the morrow and bring me what I desire in exchange for you."

"He will kill you. You cannot match his strength."

The mermaid, who Kalaya had named Silvana, laughed. "Without his staff of waves, he is nothing more than a regular Wavekeeper."

Kalaya looked away with dim anger, her tail flapping against the ground, making a splash.

Seeming amused, the charcoal-eyed fish woman turned her gaze to Aaric and Aleena. "And these must be the landwalkers I was told you were harboring. I doubt your father will be happy when he finds out."

"You leave them be!" Kalaya shouted, her voice cracking weakly. "They've nothing to do with this. Just let them go!"

"And where shall I let them go to?" The cruel mermaid made a sweeping motion around her. "Shadow Rock is an island surrounded by ocean with no land in sight. Besides, they are human. *They* are the reason Amias is dead. They do not deserve to live."

Aleena made a sound as Aaric grabbed her hand tightly.

"You can't kill them, it is not their fault! You're taking this too far!" Kalaya was now sitting up straight, with color flooding her face.

"Oh, I won't be killing them myself. I will let the power of the Ocean do its work. By high tide tomorrow, your lovely little landwalkers will be drowned." Aaric opened his mouth as if to speak, but Aleena stopped him with a firm grip.

"You're nothing but a heartless, evil sea witch!" Kalaya yelled.

Silvana smiled at the princess and sneered, "Why, I'm glad you think so highly of me."

A shout came from the water, a stone's throw out in the inlet. "Enchantress, look!" Silvana turned her head and instinctively the whole group looked to the caller.

Just above, in the murky sky, a bright star began to grow. In intervals, it expanded and pulsed with light, twinkling as a fire does when first kindled. Aleena heard Kalaya draw in a deep breath, and looked to see her mouth open and eyes wide, face highlighted by moonbeams shooting through the prison bars.

"Could it be?" The Enchantress's voice was intrigued and sick with lust. "Gibson!" the wicked mermaid called out and a small merman with long red hair came to her side, looking out at the sky. "Recite to me the first part of the Prophecy."

"Um." Gibson was a spindly little merman with anxious eyes darting from the sky to his master. He cleared his throat and spoke with a nasal voice. "Yes." He paused for a minute, anxiously rubbing his smooth chin in thought. Aleena looked up as the small red-headed merman spoke. "*When need is great and balance in peril, a celestial being will be brought forth from sleep. The true born savior far from birth, will rise from the shadows, waves they will keep."*

And just at that moment, the shining orb burst apart in the sky, the water rippled and the rocky earth grumbled in reply to the powerful thrust. Aleena and Aaric held tight to one another and Kalaya sat staring as if seeing the end of the world. The great star had broken apart into three smaller ones that hung close together, blazing with luster.

"Go on!" The Enchantress demanded impatiently to her lesser companion.

The nervous little merman spoke, *"Air, as bright as flight."* Aleena could see the first piece flare with bright yellow light.

"Fire which burns the night," continued Gibson as the group watched the second star erupt with a red hot radiance.

"Earth of brawn and might." The third piece shot out its vibrant glow, like a sparkling emerald.

"Water with the speed of light." And then there was no movement, the waters thick with silence.

Silvana looked at her assistant in question. "There should be four parts." Angrily she grabbed Gibson's shoulder. "Where's the fourth star?" Aaric glanced at Aleena, distraught, tiny star lights glittering in his eyes.

The little merman spoke uneasily. "I don't know. There should be Air, Fire, Earth, and Water." *Silvana's right*, Aleena thought, *it didn't add up*. The Prophecy *had* spoken of four parts of nature, and only three shown in the sky.

Silvana, looking flustered, shook her hand at the frail red-head, "Alright then. Continue."

"Elements will part their ways. Falling from the sky for days," Gibson's voice squeaked excitedly, rising to a higher pitch. *"Touching the earth and kissing the sea, setting the true one powerful and free."*

The little merman looked away from the three stars and to Silvana. *"High and low the winds shall go, four corners of the sea and earth, far and wide the fires will blow, revealing the blood's true birth."*

"Now speak the last part." Silvana demanded.

Gibson went on to finish the Prophecy, *"Clouded breath, stricken to take. Freezing dark and burning wake. Amethyst Cedars Grown of Old. The Eldest..."* He stopped in mid-sentence and then explained, "And that's where it ends. That's where the tablet was broken apart."

Silvana looked at Kalaya as though to reassure herself and then spoke softly. "That's alright. We will have the other half of the stone tablet tomorrow and will be able to put the prophecy whole again."

What on earth is going on? Aleena's mind began to spin in circles around all of the day's outstanding events. It was as though she had been thrown into a whole other world, where ambushes, mermaids, and prophetic exploding stars were an everyday occurrence.

And what had happened to her Prince Tolan? She had barely had a chance to mourn for him. If only she could just see his face once more, none of this would matter. But he was long gone. A single tear fell from her face and landed on her hand. Looking up through watery eyes, Aleena saw the three brilliantly colored stars begin to fall, fiery tails trailing behind them.

"It has come to pass," Silvana waved an arm towards the three glimmering fire-tailed stars dramatically, "The ancients have heard my call and named their true savior! Follow me and be saved!" The sea witch laughed maniacally like a wild woman. "By tomorrow we will have the stone tablet in one piece, and once the four elements have been gathered and brought to me the spell can be activated!"

"Father won't let you have his side of the tablet. Without it, the fallen stars cannot be found." Kalaya growled.

"We will see about that, my pretty little Wavekeeper. We already have the first three clues; it is only the fourth that Nerius holds. And we *will* get the tablet from your father."

Turning to her guards, Silvana waved to them. "Gather all of the inhabitants of Shadow Rock together." She stopped in thought. "And Moselle, I wish a word with the Tinker's leader, I have a proposition for her. And don't forget the landwalkers who are loyal to me. They will be needed as well. By tomorrow at sundown we will begin the search! No one sleeps until those fallen stars are found!"

The sea witch and her followers gathered together and made their way back around the bend of the island, leaving the captives alone except for the silent guards. Aleena, cold, frightened, and exhausted, laid her head on Aaric's shoulder, and with the repetetive sound of the soothing waves, felt herself fall into a fitfull sleep.

EMRYS

"Will you be needing some extra towels, m'lord?" The young chamber maid asked as she poured hot rose water in the wash stand basin, the flowery aroma filling the guest quarters. Lord Emrys hadn't been to court in many years and had forgotten how luxuriously the guests at the King's Castle were treated. Beside the basin lay a cake of soap, smelling of aromatic herbs, *imported from Nikaydia no doubt*, a newly-sharpened silver shaving knife, a silver comb, a green hazel twig for teeth cleaning, and a woolen cloth.

Emrys glanced down at the footstool with a stack of neatly folded towels on top. "No, thank you. Everything is satisfactory." The girl nodded with eyes down and left the room, shutting the door behind her.

Although Emrys was the lord of his own keep and was regarded highly as nobility, he was not accustomed to such royal comforts as these. Looking at his worn and ragged reflection in the mirror that hung on the wall over the wash stand, he dipped the soap into the water and then rubbed it between his hands creating a foamy lather. His twin in the mirror reflected his band's treacherous and wearisome journey north, accompanied by Prince Banon and his Goldenshields. The summer storms were not light and welcomed as usual, but had turned cold and wintery, causing their travels to slow considerably. Not to mention the shocking ambush on the camp by Crag Trolls, appearing as if out of an evil fairy tale.

Emrys smoothed the lather onto his stubbled face and tried to concentrate on carefully scraping the knife across his dirt-smudged skin, but his thoughts were back at Castlecray with his family. He pictured Aaric at swordplay with Captain Swordsby in the practice yard, his face flushing with effort, and Aleena, sitting ladylike on the knoll, watching while she practiced her stitches. And goodness knows what Quinlan was up to; probably off with Noam at the stables harassing the stable boys.

Emrys chuckled to himself as he cupped his hands in the warm, bubbly, sweet-smelling water and splashed it over his face. Grabbing a soft towel and rubbing hard, he looked up to see a chiseled jaw and a shiny pink face looking back. He let out a deep breath and felt much better after rinsing the grime off. Though they corresponded by letter often, it had been a decade since he'd seen Beaumont Thunderdyn, a good friend of his, and he wanted to look presentable for the upcoming meeting.

Emrys picked up the silver comb and began brushing the gnarled knots from his brown waves, thinking about the last time he'd been at a Gold Council meeting for the Snell trials. Lavoy Snell had been a cruel and wicked man who had been sentenced to beheading for treason against the Gold Crown. His remaining family had been pardoned, but as punishment they had been made to leave their keep and move to a ruined tower, giving up their Castle to Lord Emrys and his family. And it was no secret that Lavoy's only son, Malvin, had a deep grudge against the Castlecrays, for he blamed them for House Snell's disgrace.

King Thunderdyn, being one of the only friends who truly knew Lord Emrys and his struggling past, had put his trust into the Lord by giving him a step higher in society and granting him the castle Sea Watch, which had then been re-named Castlecray Keep for its new ownership. Aaric had just been a little one then, Aleena, toddling around sucking her thumb, and Quinlan just ready to be born.

A commotion from the grounds below brought Lord Emrys back from his memories and to the cold fogged window streaked with raindrops and icy slush. He wiped a section of the wet film off with a swipe of his hand and peered out to see a Caravan of three carriages, horse-mounted guards, and pack mules stopped at the castle gate, being let through by the Royal Gatekeeper.

Emrys noticed the brightly colored banners of each House with its coat of arms, and stopped dead in his tracks, comb hanging from his hair. The first two flown were not of much importance to him: the earthy brown willow branch on a forest green background of House Willoughby, followed by House Lovelyn, who took the black masked love bird with his mate as their sigil, bright blue with a dark mask on a heather gray banner. But it was the last carriage to come through that had Emrys's pulse quicken.

It was a dark black buggy with matching black bay mares driving it, and flapping above in the wind was an emerald green shield yielding a black horned bull: House Brumble. Emrys remembered that crest well, for it was one of the matches to the clue they had found near the wreckage of Snakewood village, and not only that, House Brumble had supposedly been killed off in battle over a century ago, never to fly their sigil again.

Emrys took a second look, astonished at the long dead family's coat of arms, the black bull moving lifelike in the strong breeze. *Yes,* Emrys thought to himself, *that is unmistakably House Brumble.*

But who could it be? Emrys strained against the cold glass trying to see into the carriage, but dark curtains had been pulled tightly closed, and there was no sign of anyone inside or emerging.

Though there was no movement from the mysterious black carriage, a small hunched figure emerged from the first buggy and Emrys recognized him as Norman Willoughby.

The last time Emrys had seen Lord Norman Willoughby was at the last Gold Council meeting, many years ago, and he had been well into his seventieth name day old at that point. *I can't believe he is still up and walking.*

And then there was House Lovelyn. Lord Willis, an older gentleman and recently a widower of his first wife, had just been married to the young Lady of House Lovelyn; young enough to be his granddaughter. She would be a woman now, after so many years.

Emrys watched the carryings-on of the group below as he buttoned up the top of his blue tunic with the white castle sigil on the front. Stable hands took lathered horses to be groomed and watered, castle servants carried away bulky belongings, and lords and ladies flitted about conversing in small groups beneath the muddled gray sky, their breath coming out in puffs of mist.

Lord Emrys was anxious for the meeting and, rather than waiting to be summoned, figured he would investigate the mystery representative of House Brumble. As he made way towards the door, he felt his boot kick something with a light fluttering sound and looked down to see a folded piece of parchment beneath the footstool. Bending over to pick it up, he realized that it had not been there before and must have fallen out of the towel he had used. Unfolding the paper carefully, his eyes read the quickly scratched words.

"Do not meddle in matters that are not of your concern... or your secret will be told."

Emrys stood up straight and rigid, his face turning a deep red. *There are only a few in all of Merenia who know my secret, none of whom would go about threatening me in this manner... or would they?*

Angrily, he crumpled the paper and threw it into the hearth; the flames licked the note turning it from blue to red and then smoldering ash. Storming from the room, Emrys slammed the door and before he knew it, in his quiet rage, found himself in the garden outside of the Great Hall, royal servants bustling this way and that, going about their duties.

Something just isn't adding up. I've got to find out who is here from House Brumble... Emrys's thoughts were interrupted by a cheerful greeting as he paced back and forth in front of the solid wooden doors, decorated with the Royal Crest, a golden crown with a silver lightning bolt inlaid on the front.

"Lord Castlecray! What a pleasure! It has been too long." Emrys looked up from his internal stewing to see the warm smiling face of Lady Lovelyn who was being escorted by the captain of her house guard. His temper cooled as she warmly hugged him, the white fur that lined her velvet sky-blue dress tickled his ear. *Definitely not a girl anymore*, he thought.

Emrys took her hand and bowed his head. "Dilantha. You haven't changed a bit. Why, you were just a young lady last time we met, new to court and freshly married to Lord Willis. How fares your lord?"

Dilantha Lovelyn, who couldn't be any older than thirty-five name days, turned her eyes down, her lips and cheeks flushed a rosy pink from the cold against her fair white skin. "He…passed away…just a fortnight ago."

"I'm so sorry for your loss," Emrys said sincerely.

"Yes, thank you." Dilantha rubbed her white gloved hands together for warmth. "He was a good man. But he was ready to go, being of his advanced age and with his ill health."

"He was very good man, and will be deeply missed." Emrys consoled.

Lady Dilantha nodded her head. "I'm assuming you are here for the Gold Council meeting." She smiled shyly. "Would you be my escort?"

Lord Emrys looked at her face, pretty as porcelain, and bowed. "It would be my honor."

As if on command, the grand doors, sparkling in gold gilt, opened to the great hall, and members of the Gold Council, appearing like magic, trickled inside towards the warmth. Lady Lovelyn and Lord Emrys followed arm-in-arm.

Normally upon entrance, the court herald would be announcing the arrivals of nobility, but because of the urgent and secretive nature of the meeting, only Gold Council representatives were told of the meeting, so as not spread alarm through the Royal court.

The hall was just as monumental as Emrys had remembered, if not more so. Striking crystal chandeliers hung down the center of the vast barreled ceiling, their facets sparkling with golden candle light. Every inch of the vaulted roof was gesso-painted in intricate designs, picturesque with battles, lovers, mystical creatures, all amongst the dreamy brushed clouds and stars. Regal gold gilded chairs lined the oblong lacquered table, their seats puffed with luxurious upholstery. The table had already been set with small pastries and cakes, breads, fruits and cheeses, to ease the rigors of a long assembly.

There were small groups of people gathered by the two hearths on opposite sides of the room, thawing themselves from the bizarre frosty weather. Emrys recognized most of the faces, but some were missing.

"Welcome lords and ladies! Take your seats." Lord Emrys knew the man who spoke to be Master Brooks, the king's right hand man, overseer of all domestic and court affairs of House Thunderdyn. As well as being of such a high title, Brooks was an herbalist and healer, and gave the Princes of Thunderdyn and children of court their lessons. Though he was a bit older than Lord Emrys, the man had the stamina of a young boy.

People began to take their seats at the lengthy oak table, and serving maids brought around pitchers of warm cider and ale, filling the gleaming golden goblets in front of each council member.

"King Beaumont Thunderdyn the Third!" The members rose as Master Brooks announced Beaumont's arrival. The king entered through the doors and looked like a fluffy lion with his mane of bushy hair and bristly beard encircling his round rosy face, his oldest son following behind. His eyes twinkled as he spotted Emrys and he gave a nod.

"And Prince Banon Thunderdyn," the master called out as the young prince bowed and took his place, standing next to the king at the head of the table. The king wore the Thunderyn colors, a plum surcoat with a lightning bolt-stamped crown, embroidered with gold and silver thread on the breast, and a massive gold belt wrapped around his paunch belly. The lush purple mantle he wore was rimmed in fine white fur and the gold crown atop his round head was lavish with shimmering gems and jewels. When Beaumont Thunderdyn did something, he did it extravagantly. Even his shoes, with pointed gold tips, bore a golden broach shaped like the royal thunder bolt crown.

Addressing the members, the king held up his royal goblet, encrusted with only the rarest of gems, in greeting.

"Welcome!" Beaumont raised his glass to the council members. "To the Kingdom, to Merenia, and to the Realm!" The king drained his mug of ale and finished with a satisfied *ahhhh*, as the others followed, sipping their drinks for the toast.

"Let us be seated." The king sat heavily in his chair and leaned back, propping an elbow on the chair arm, his other hand swirling another freshly filled cup. "We have some perilous issues to discuss this day. It is rumored that the Black Rebellion has begun to rear its ugly head again after so many years."

The king stroked his beard in thought. "Cities and towns in the kingdom are being ransacked and burned and people are being brutally murdered, without any witnesses left to stand. We are unsure of who may be leading this group or to what ends they work, and that is why we are here today."

Emrys could hear low murmurings from his fellow lords and ladies.

"Does anyone have any recent updates?" Silence rang out over the hall, only the occasional cough was to be heard.

Finally, a very dark-looking man stood, swinging back his black hooded cloak over his shoulder, revealing his green surcoat which boasted the black horned bull of House Brumble, and Emrys's eyes went wide as if seeing a ghost.

"Yes, Your Majesty," The man spoke with a husky voice like splintered oakwood, "The small town of Rivermount near my castle has been thrashed. It seems the brigands are expanding from their comfort zone of attacking the west." The dark man sat at once and acted as though he had belonged to the council for years, seemingly impervious to the astonished stares that he received.

"Thank you, Lord Brumble." The king, his eyes fixed on the man, leaned forward. "Otto, has anyone reported any survivors or had a glimpse of the attackers?"

Lord Emrys watched the long lost, dark-haired Lord with curiosity, wondering where he came from. He appeared from nowhere, as if from the Brumble family grave, with no introductions and no explanation, Emrys thought, and Beaumont treated him like a longstanding member of court.

Lord Otto Brumble gruffly replied, "Only one survivor, Your Majesty. A young maiden."

"What says she?"

"That's the problem, Your Majesty." Brumble's full dark eyebrows were flat, his face in a perpetual scowl. "She speaks naught. The House healer says she is in a state of shock. She just sits and stares, her eyes unseeing."

The king made an understanding grunt and turned to Master Brooks, "Send a pigeon to Castle Torro. See if there have been any changes to the maiden. Right now, she may be our only link." Emrys had not yet had a chance to tell the king about the clue they found near Snakewood Village.

Brooks nodded and began to scribble in a leather bound book of parchment. A low drone surrounded Emrys as people quietly exchanged their marked opinions. His eyes scanned the table and saw Lord Goldcoin, his father by marriage. The royal treasurer, with his sweaty pumpkin head, was whispering to High Justice Newton Oaktree.

Newton Oaktree, who had precided over the Snell trial years ago, was listening intently to the little treasurer, his eyes like black diamonds and skin like polished ebony.

Emrys went down the table side, mentally listing off the members he knew. There was the king and his son, of course, and then Aurous Goldcoin and the High Justice. Next to Newton, sat Norman Willoughby, his eyes drifting closed and thin face nodding asleep and then jerking awake again. Then there was Lord Brumble, with his dark hair and eyes, and his permanently scowling face sitting straight across from Brandon "Patch" MacDougal.

MacDougal was the Grand Admiral of the king's Royal Golden Fleet and wore the traditional admiral's wide-brimmed hat in the king's royal colors; plum and gold and a black cloth patch over his left eye, hence the name "Patch."

Sitting next to Patch was Grand Elder Wylie, his sunken-in, toothless mouth opening and closing in spite of himself as he leaned in to Lady Lovelyn to remark on something the king had said. She stole a glance up at Emrys and smiled, her teeth like perfectly carved pearls. Emrys smiled back.

At the entrance of the door was Sir Leof Brawnmont, Captain of the King's Goldenshields, standing guard with his hand on his sword hilt. Emrys remembered the man looking quite the same way during their battle with the Crag Trolls, like a large and appropriately hairy protective bull.

Emrys's eyes wandered to two empty chairs on the other side of him, assuming they belonged to Lady Amabel Diamond, who with no doubt had prior social engagements and Lady Maeveen Birdhill. Next to the empty chairs sat Ronald Nooney, wearing the suspect green surcoat with a black crescent moon on the breast, his short and wide stature giving him the look of a squat toad. The man smiled and nodded at him, and Emrys quickly looked away.

There were a few other members who were not in attendance, but one stood out above all; Lord Malvin Snell.

Emrys figured that Snell might not show, due to the shame on his House and his father's treason, but also hoped that he would, maybe giving them another clue to the mystery coat of arms.

Just then, the heavy wooden doors slammed wide open with a blast of swirling cold air, and Master Brooks grasped frantically at the flurry of official papers that went flying about. Emrys shielded his eyes from the setting sun that blazed into the room, pure rays of bright orange and yellow. He squinted at the figure that loomed dark in the wide doorway; Malvin Snell.

"Glad to see that you all waited for me before proceeding with your little meeting." The small-statured man came waltzing in the room and grabbing a mug of ale from a startled serving girl, sloshed it down the front of his green tunic boasting the black slithering sea snake. He then gulped the rest down in a hurry as stunned faces watched, and then took his seat next to Lord Emrys and slammed his cup down hard on the table.

"Aaah, Malvin," the king said graciously, "glad to have your presence at our *little meeting*." The king looked cautiously at Snell; the man's long and slender face was shadowed with recessed features and deep set dark eyes.

"It has been too long, my friends," Lord Snell's grimy voice was arrogant. He cast a look at Lady Lovelyn, and stood, reaching around Emrys to grip her shoulder tightly. "And what a pretty new face we have amongst the Council. Are you the sweet rosy little priss-widow of Lord Lovelyn I've heard so much about?"

Emrys could smell Malvin's breath, strong with whiskey and the stale stench of rotting teeth. Dilantha struggled from underneath his grip, obviously uncomfortable.

"What's wrong little flower?" snarled Lord Snell, his shallow cheeks widening into a grin. "Never been with a real man?" At that, Lord Emrys tore the bone-thin arm from her shoulder and Prince Banon shot from his chair saying, "You overstep your boundaries, m'lord!"

The hefty king stood as well, glaring daggers at the invited intruder. Snell sat with his hands up in mock submission. "No need to get fussy, just having a little fun."

There was a long moment of silence as tempers cooled and then King Thunderdyn sat, slowly giving a sidelong glance to Lord Malvin.

After resuming his kingly manner, Beaumont ran the rest of the meeting without incident, covering the plans for defense and collaboration of Merenian garrisons and guards, and Emrys watched the suspects, Lord Brumble, Ronald Nooney and Malvin Snell, closely while a vote of fealty to the king was held, proving unanimous. The meeting had been concluded, and lords and ladies filed out of the front entrance into the chilly twilight, stretching their stiff legs from the prolonged assembly, when Emrys felt a hand on his shoulder.

He turned to see Master Brooks's tanned face, smiling handsomely at him, "Lord Castlecray. The king wishes a word with you in the sitting room." Emrys turned to find Beaumont already gone.

Master Brooks led Emrys to a sitting room just off of the great hall, which opened to a veranda, covered in greenery and vines unlocked to the early night sky, the first stars just yawning awake with a dim twinkle.

The king was sitting in a golden-armed chair by a roaring fire, Prince Banon at his side, when he turned to see Emrys and went to him.

"Old friend!" The king chuckled heartily as he embraced his companion, thumping him on the back repeatedly. "It has been too long! How fare your children?"

"Good. They are growing so fast." Emrys patted Banon on the back, "As are yours. You've raised a fine young man here. He was quite the escort from Castlecray."

"Takes after his old man," the king chuckled. "How was Lady Aleena's feast? I trust my son, Tolan, gave you no trouble?"

"Oh, no, he was a perfect gentleman. We are happy to soon have him as family."

"And am I to have the lovely Aleena as a good-daughter." His face turned somber. "I was told of your run-in with the... trolls was it?"

"Yes. Trolls. Quite a surprise."

"I would say, a fearsome beast as that appearing as if from the past, that would be quite a shock." The king's face was frowning.

"It will please you to know that Banon fought heroically," Emrys's blue eyes locked on the young prince, "and he even saved Treasurer Goldcoin's life."

Banon blushed at the praise and reached a hand into his pocket to pull out the tattered green cloth. "We found this near Snakewood. We believe it was left behind by the ones who attacked the village."

Lord Castlecray jumped in, "It might just be the clue we need to uncover the leader of the Black Rebellion."

Banon handed it over to his father and Beaumont eyed the fabric curiously.

"We've already been through all of the records for past and present House Crests to find a match." Banon explained. Prince Thunderdyn was sounding more like a man every day, Emrys thought.

"Yes, and we found four," he interjected, "House Snell, House Birdhill, House Nooney, and House Brumble."

"Mmmhmph," the king mused, rubbing the ragged cloth between his fat fingers.

"It's got to be Brumble!" Banon spouted excitedly, Emrys now seeing the child in him again.

The king shook his head. "No. No, I don't think so."

Emrys's voice was concerned as he spoke, "The man shows up from nowhere like a ghost, wearing the House Crest of a family wiped out over a century ago. How can we be so sure that he is not apart of the rebellion? And if not, where in the deep sea did he come from?"

The king sucked in a deep gulp of air and let out a noisy sigh as though he was about to say something when a messenger appeared in the doorway hesitantly. "Your Majesty..." The king waved him in. The messenger handed him a rolled piece of parchment with a black wax seal imprinted with a spiral seashell and then left through the door bowing out awkwardly.

The king sat in his golden gilt chair and broke the seal. Emrys watched the king's eyes read the words intently, and then saw a change in his face as though turning the message over in his mind. The king looked up grimly at Emrys while handing him the paper, "Your children have been captured."

Emrys could feel his stomach cringe, his limbs go cold with a rush, and his heart began beating wildly.

The king's eyes were now filled with horror as the realization sunk in.

"I must leave now." Emrys started for the door. Beaumont grabbed him by the sleeve as he whipped his head back around.

"I will go with you." Beaumont's eyes looked as though they had begun to water when he let out a defeated-sounding sigh and hunched over, "Tolan might be with them."

"No." Emrys said firmly. "The rebellion is growing, the lands are in peril, and Merenia needs you here." Emrys pointed to the green cloth in the king's hands. "Contact Jack Piper, the bard. He is staying here in Merene and will be of great help to your search."

The king eyed Emrys and began to speak, when Banon cut in, saying, "I will go."

The two older men glanced at him, weighing his words in a moment of silence. Banon stood bolt still, his crystal blue eyes contrasting with his tanned skin, searching his father's unreadable face. And then the king broke the silence. "Courage is not the lack of fear. Courage is facing fear… "

"…like a mad man." Banon finished his father's words, and the king smiled and grabbed him in a tight bear hug.

And with that, Lord Emrys and Banon had left the comfort of the warm castle and were running down the cold wooden pier, under the dark domed sky, with only dancing golden torch light to lead the way. The water was black and calm under the sky, rippling with the silver reflection of the moon and stars, when Emrys saw something in the water.

He looked up from the watery mirror to see enormous green, red, and yellow glowing balls of light in the sky. Banon and he stopped dead in their tracks, panting, with their necks arched back and faces to the sky. The sparkling gems of colored fire grew streaming tails behind them as they began to fall towards earth and sea.

The two exchanged a wide-eyed look, as Emrys spoke quietly. "There is something I must tell you."

NOAM

And then the blazin' star will burst apart into four pieces that represent the elements o' nature, thus being scattered amongst the earth and sea, waitin' for the true savior to set the balance back right." Captain Gaderian Longship held an arm up to the invisible stars in the dusky twilight sky.

"But Captain," Noam challenged, "we saw only three pieces."

The captain began inspecting the large tangle of roped rigging, his salt and pepper beard floating up and down in the wind. "Well, aye. I've never actually read the prophecy for m'self. It's just common knowledge passed down through the generations. There are sure to be bits an' pieces amiss through the retelling."

"And who is the savior, Grandfather?" Quin's long brown hair whipped her in the face, mimicking the snapping sails of the boat as they stood on the aft deck swiftly sailing south.

Captain Longship's hazel eyes sparkled in the sunrise as he glanced at her. "Well, Quinnie-fish, that's the thing o' prophesies; they're not verra forthcoming. No one really knows who the savior is, though people have their suspicions. It's verra much like a riddle."

Quin continued questioning, "And where are these star elements supposed to be found, now that they've fallen?"

Gaderian laughed and Noam supposed it was about the myriad of questions they supplied the captain with. The husky man continued loosening and tightening certain ropes and chains and then stood back to admire his work. He stopped and sighed.

"Alright then." He pulled a wooden crate over from the cargo hold and sat down on top, waving Noam and Quin to come close. Noam plopped himself down on the timbered deck with a *thud*, and Quin joined him. "I'm gonna tell ye everything I know about the Prophecy, and that's not verra much."

Longship gazed down at his sea-tattered boots, which looked to have been black some time ago, but were now faded grey with torn strips of the leather that ruffled in the air. "A verra, verra long time ago there was a great wizard o' the sea. Pontus, I believe his name was."

"Was he a merman?" Quin asked excitedly.

"Aye, and the oldest one ever known, at that." The captain stroked his beard, wisps of fluffy grey and black hair buoyantly hovering over his head in the wind.

"Pontus was the keeper o' the stone tablet, on which the prophecy was inscribed, and kept it hidden away from any who might want it for power or harm. It is said that even the tablet itself wielded an unknown magic, invisible to the eye."

Just then a squawking chicken ran across the deck and ducked into a crevice between some crates and barrels in the hold. The captain's ship was not the most orderly one Noam had ever seen and boasted a most eclectic collection of cargo, for his trade. There were barrels and sacks filled with skins and textiles, feathers and wool, and sometimes the occasional chickens and pigs. Glass jars of roots, seeds, oils, and crushed leaves, carefully wrapped in felt, were neatly lined up and nestled in their wooden crates.

Noam, who was no stranger to spices and herbs, recognized the aroma of cinnamon and thyme, juniper and mint wafting about the deck. It reminded him of the Castlecray kitchens and of Olga's masterful stews and potions. He thought that he might actually miss the oversized cook's scowling face.

Without any sign of interruption, Captain Gaderian continued, "Now the old wizard knew that he had lived a verra long time and that his time was comin' to depart the living and, no trusting anyone but himself wi' the prophecy, broke it in two wi' magic."

Quin sucked in her breath with surprise.

"He gave one half to the Enchantress o' the sea, and one half to the king o' the sea. Recognizing that there was a longstandin' feud between the two, he knew that neither one would give up their half of the tablet to the other side, therefore keepin' the magnificent magic o' the prophecy from bein' used."

Coming out of his dreamy narration, Gaderian looked Noam straight in the eye, his "r's" rolling heavily in accent. "If the two halves o' the tablet were reunited and used by the wrong hands, its magic, the power of Mer, would be powerful enough to cause supernatural disasters of enormous proportions."

"The power of Mer... " Noam said, enchanted by the notion.

"Is it the King Nerius that has part of it?" Quin asked.

"Aye, and a sorceress named Silvana has the other. Some say she has dark plans an' dark intentions."

Noam leaned in intently as the captain continued.

"An' it is said," Longship lowered his voice as though telling a secret, "that there are clues... clues etched right into the tablet on where to find the scattered stars."

"Where?" Noam inquired. "Where might they be?"

"Up until now, the prophecy hadna' been in movement, so no one went a'lookin, but now that the stars have fallen, there's gonna' be a mighty bit of squabbling, I imagine." The captain sat up straight and made a grunting sound as he arched his back, his broad chest stretched wide, with wiry little black and silver hairs curling out of the top of his shirt. "But, I *do* know that some of the clues are on Nerius's tablet and some on Silvana's. So it might be a wee bit difficult for either one o' them to go searchin' about."

Noam imagined finding one of the glowing fallen orbs and presenting it to King Nerius in front of the applauding members of the Peace Protectors. He would be a hero as the king knighted him with his majestic staff, and even Quin might think he was brave.

Noam was brought back to the cold open sea from his thoughts by the captain's husky voice. "An' that's why it's urgent that I get back to the Invisible Island after takin' ye two home. There are important matters to see to."

"But Grandfather, I don't want to go back home," Quin pleaded, her dark lashes standing out against the pastel-colored clouds, "My place is with you and the Peace Protectors."

The captain leaned over and laid his large hand gently on her shoulder, "Quinnie-fish, ye are a young lassie of only ten name days old; yer place is back at Castlecray with yer family where ye will be safe."

"I'm a member now," Quin said as she pulled on the Protector's seashell medallion strapped around her neck, "I can help."

Noam walked to the rail, listening to their conversation, as he gazed out to the crystalline wave tips cresting the horizon, the orange sun just peeking out from the end of the world. Noam didn't want to go back to Castlecray either, but felt a sense of longing for the old stone keep and the people there he considered family. It was his home.

"Things have become more dangerous now Quinnie, and I couldna' forgive m'self if I put ye two in harm's way." Quin wrapped herself up tight in her cloak, shivering with cold and her teeth now chattering. The captain continued, "Besides, Aaric, Aleena, and yer lady stepmother will be worrit sick about ye by now."

The captain continued to mumble reassurances to his granddaughter as Noam could see South Harbor begin to materialize in the distance, the little town's lights glowing like beacons of warmth pulling them in and the tip tops of the Castlecray towers behind, reaching to the sky. As the ship came closer, the docks looked unusually peaceful in the early morning; only a few boats were at anchor with nary a soul aboard. Noam glanced past the docks up the hard-packed dirt road with the ocean side wall and noticed the stillness, very unlike the usual organized chaos of vendors and patrons who swarmed Haggler's way. Noam thought it quite peculiar.

Now reaching their destination, he heard the lookout's voice from up above shout, "Land ho!" Sounds of feet clomped busily, running about the wooden deck preparing for port. Men began climbing the roped rigging like spiders on webs and tightly furling up the sails.

Half a dozen Castlecray guards dressed in blue livery stood on the end of the fast-approaching pier with Sir Captain Swordsby at their lead, their Castle-shaped badges pinned on their chests, gleaming bright white in the now-risen sun.

Once anchored, Noam and Quin followed Gaderian down the gangway towards the straight-faced group of men, puffs of cold mist rising from their breath.

"Hello there, Sir Brently!" Longship called as they made their way down the plank. "The strangest thing happened; we found a couple o' stowaways on board. I imagine you've been missin' someone." Quin's grandfather said playfully as he tousled her brown hair, her rosy cheeks flushing with cold and possibly embarrassment.

"That is quite a relief," said the knight briefly. Brently Swordsby, a knight and the captain of Castlcray's garrison and guard, was a tall, brawny man with solid features and a closely trimmed brown beard flecked with silver. His shoulder-length golden brown hair gleamed like the mane of a freshly groomed horse as he looked from side to side, watchfully.

"Have you by chance the Lady Aleena and Lord Aaric with you?" Sir Brently's eyes searched the ship's crew that was working busily on deck. "And Prince Tolan?"

Captain Gaderian's face changed, a slight frown creasing his brow, "No... should we have?"

"They took *The Fair Maiden* shortly after you to follow you to North Harbor, looking for Lady Quinlan once they found her missing."

"Oh, no!" Quin said. "What did... father say?" Noam could tell Quin's face held a tinge of guilt. Her eyes began to water.

Sir Brently Swordsby leaned close to Quin and said consolingly, "We have sent word to your father in Merene, and not to worry." The knight's light eyes were kind as he spoke, "Lord Aaric has your father's crew, the best in South Merenia. Your brother and sister will be safe. I'm sure they will be arriving before we know it."

Captain Longship surveyed the group of guards that were now posted around the docks facing the town, their heads cautiously scanning back and forth. He addressed the knight suspiciously.

"This is quite a welcomin' party for just the three o' us, Sir Brently." He then studied the unusually quiet street and barren market leading towards the castle. "By now, Hagglers way is bustling. Where are all o' the vendors... the people? Has something happened?"

The morning sun shown bright on the knight's armor, his guards stood stockstill behind him. "There has been trouble, Captain." Sir Brently's eyes glanced at Noam and Quin. "Let us talk in private."

Quin being Quin, sternly looked the knight in the eyes, her arms straight down to her sides and her hands in fists, and her face smeared with dirt made her look a bit comical. "Anything you have to say can be said to me as well. With Aleena gone, I am the eldest lady of Castlecray, and I must be informed of any important events."

Sir Swordsby looked taken aback by her forwardness and his eyes shifted to Longship in question. Her grandfather looked amused as he smiled and nodded an approval. The knight shrugged his muscular shoulders and waved the group towards the long pier.

"Alright then, let us walk."

Noam, Quin, and Captain Gaderian were surrounded by guards and escorted through the abandoned Haggler's way to a small stable where a stray cat darted past them with a howling hiss and dodged into a rickety lean-to shack. They were led to three horses that were tethered to a wooden post running along the side of the stable, their nostrils flaring and eyes bulging. The majestic geldings were rearing and stomping anxiously, sensing strangeness in the air, as one of the guards lifted Quin atop a large brindle with a glossy brown mane. Gaderian mounted the largest black one and Noam, his foot in the stirrup, swung a leg over Quin's horse and sat directly behind her. Sir Brently took the last horse, a chestnut mare, and gesturing for the group to follow, heeled the horse's flanks and began to trot off down the roadway. Noam could smell a cool freshness of a recent rain as he watched one of the guards grab the reins of his horse and lead it, walking alongside the other four guards.

Sir Brently held his right arm across his chest, his hand firmly on his sword hilt, looking ready to draw at a moment's notice. His eyes darted through the streets as he began to speak in a guarded voice. "There was an attack last night." The hair on the back of Noam's neck stood on end. "Two people were killed."

Noam felt Quin tense in front of him as the dreadful words were spoken.

"The bodies were found last night, in that alley just up there." The knight pointed up the path and into the shadows on the left between two make-shift vendor shops. As they passed, Noam glanced into the alleyway, shadowed and empty but for a pile of timbers, and goose pimples ran up his arms.

"Were the attackers found?" Captain Longship asked, scratching at his bristly beard as he swayed in the saddle.

The knight lowered his head and ran a hand through his silky straight hair, looking as though he hadn't slept in days. "No," he raised his head and looked at the group, "and the bodies were unrecognizable. And pardon my saying but...," he quickly stole a glance at Quin, "they were ripped to shreds."

A lump rose into Noam's throat as he felt his pulse quicken. Castlecray had always been a very safe fortress, almost impregnable, being half-bordered by Mer Ocean, and now...

"There have been sightings as well. The past two nights, people have been reporting seeing something among the trees." Sir Swordsby pointed up ahead to the small forest area that lined the other side of Haggler's way. "They say that there are monsters about; large, grey, ugly, and snarling."

Quin reached back and grabbed Noam's knee tightly, her other hand on the bridle. He figured it was for comfort; his or hers, he wasn't sure.

"Master Dunley has called for a curfew for the town and for Castlecray," the knight instructed."Security has also been heightened, rounds have been doubled and expanded beyond the castle grounds."

"Good," Gaderian said quietly and then repeated to himself, "that's good." The group rode and walked in uneasy silence through the empty market street, coming to the cool green forest at its end.

"Grandfather," Quin said softly. The captain brought his horse up alongside theirs and bent close to her. She paused as if trying to find the words and then Noam heard her whisper, "Does father know about the merpeople?"

Just then, there was a rustling in the dark and shadowed trees. Sir Brently held up a hand and the group stopped, the knight standing as alert as a watch dog ready to charge. All was silent except for a nervous whinny as the horses pranced uneasily, the whites showing in their eyes. Noam's anxiety climbed, his heart racing faster. Something didn't feel right. The guards, as if by instinct, closed in around the front of the mounted riders, their hands on their sword hilts.

Suddenly, a barrage of growling grey beasts came flooding out of the trees straight towards them.

"Bloody bastards!" Sir Brently shouted as Noam heard the metallic ringing of swords leaving their scabbards, their blades shining brilliantly in the sun light. There had to be at least a dozen of them, big as bulls and as ugly as Olga, the kitchen master, sharp claws drawn and dripping fangs protruding from mouthfuls of sharp-toothed grins.

The guards took a defensive stance, holding their broadswords horizontally out across their chests, knees slightly bent, a shared look of fear in their eyes.

Noam wrapped his arms tightly around Quin, as their horse reared and jumped frantically, letting out an eerie scream while waves of monsters closed in on the men at arms. Noam involuntarily closed his eyes from the jerking motion as he heard the noises of metal whipping through the air and gruesome cracking, breaking, and wet slicing sounds.

"Gaderian!" Noam looked to see Sir Brently yell to the captain, who had dismounted his wild horse, immersed in a one-on-one fight with a large bumpy creature, another coming up on his back.

Captain Longship was a very big man, but the beasts passed him by a head, at least. He turned at the knight's warning and made a final swipe with his curved sword, taking the first beast across the gut. It whined and howled as it fell. Gaderian pulled a large rusty fish hook from a strap on his back and, while spinning around towards his other assailant, caught it through the neck, tearing out its throat. Red blood gushed out in rivulets as the beast sunk stiffly to its knees.

Noam looked to see each man swinging his sword wildly against the terrible odds of each being outnumbered by two or three of the slimy and vile attackers. Noam thought they looked almost reptilian, much like the trolls Nunny told about in their bedtime stories, but bigger and taller and a bloody lot scarier.

Sir Swordsby, still mounted on his well-trained warhorse, circled a threesome of monsters, a deranged look sweeping over his face. With a swift kick and a "*Ya!*" the knight whirled past the group of beasts, his sword flashing by in a blur. Sir Brently halted his horse before the forest trees, chest heaving, and looked back over his shoulder to see three pointy-eared, gray heads fall to the ground, one bouncing grotesquely along and landing with a *squish* beneath the hoofs of Noam and Quin's horse. Their brindled mare stood up tall on its hind legs in fright; its eyes rolled towards the back of its head.

The horse whipped its head back and forth, and landing on its front hooves, gave a great heave with its hind quarters and bucked the two children off, their bodies flying through the air.

Noam landed in the center of the ambush with an *umph* that knocked the air from his lungs. He saw little colored flashes on the backs of his closed lids, and felt his head spinning in circles. He could hear the yelling and fighting of men and the snarling and roaring of beasts melding together in an uproarious desperate fight.

Noam cracked one eye open to search for Quin, and saw that she had been thrown far to the side of the battle near a row of berry bushes, looking possibly unconscious. *At least she might be safe and out of the way.* The horse they had been mounted on was swiftly galloping up the muddy dirt road towards the tall and looming keep, its brown mane bouncing as it ran.

Noam then heard an odd sound coming from the trees to his left; an earthy heaving groan. He turned his dizzy head to see one of the troll-like creatures, not a few paces away, tightly hugging its arms around a large elm tree, and pulling mightily, veiny lines popping out over hard rock muscles under grey bumped and slimy skin. The creaking sound grew louder, and then with a timbering pop, the tall sapling, roots and all, was pulled from the ground. The monster, with sharp gray spikes running down its back, stood out amongst the green leaves and looked at a nearby guard. The beast ran at him, and with overwhelming strength began to swing the tree back and forth at its prey, saliva dripping from its mouth. The man dodged and ducked the swooping oversized weapon and, making a wrong turn, got knocked in the head and went tumbling to the ground.

Noam, his head clearing from the fall, now had a feeling that the fight looked hopeless, as he watched the captain swinging his sword in one hand and large sharp hook in the other crazily at two pressing troll creatures.

The rest of the guards were deep in fight, and Quin still lying lifelessly, as the tree-holding beast spotted Noam on the mud packed ground, its bloodshot yellow eyes glowing. Noam inched backwards scrambling to get to his feet, but before he knew it, the creature had brought back his arms and thrust the heavy sapling forward and straight at him. Noam propelled himself to the side, rolling away, and just when he thought he was clear, the tree bounced from the ground and landed atop his leg.

"Ooowwww!" Noam cried, "Bloody heck!" He wiggled and squirmed, but his leg wouldn't budge. Noam thought that the troll-thing must have been injured, as it came limping slowly towards him. The last thing Noam thought about was the people that he loved, his father…and Quin. *If there is anything good left in this world, please let Quin be spared. Please save her.*

The troll was inching closer and closer until it hovered over Noam, its stinking body heaving with hunger as a globule of saliva hung just above Noam's nose. Noam shut his eyes tight and held his breath. And then it happened: a great *crack* followed by a strange silence. No more screaming, no more growling, no more metallic slicing sounds.

Noam peeked through slanted eyes to see that the beast had retreated and was on its knees holding its hand over its eyes, a bright blue light covering its vile body. Noam sat up straight and saw Quin standing over his assailant, holding her magic stone, pulsing with icy radiance, making the waning battle look like a bloody iridescent dream. A blue sheen like liquid sapphires washed over Quin's face. Biting her lower lip in concentration, she held the stone up high, its light pouring over her hand and illuminating the forested road.

Noam glanced about to see all of the remaining trolls kneeling and clutching their faces in what appeared to be pain.

Sir Swordsby, barely showing his shock at seeing this, jumped at the advantage and one by one began to slaughter the monsters, Captain Gaderian and the other guards following suit. Just as the last beast was eliminated, Quin dropped to her knees, and as white as a ghost, fell to her side, the rock rolling from her hand and out over the ground.

"Quin!" Noam yelled. He struggled against the heavy weight of the elm trunk, but was unsuccessful. Captain Gaderian ran to Quin's limp body as two men-at-arms lifted the tree from Noam's bumped and bruised leg. He slowly moved it from side to side and, deciding that there was no major injury, got up and rapidly hobbled to Quin's side.

She lay with her eyes slightly opened, her chest rising and falling with quiet breath, cold mist rising from her lips in tiny clouds as she exhaled. She smiled up at Noam and then rolled her head to the side in exhaustion.

"Ye alright, Quinnie-fish?" The captain looked down at her with concern.

"Mmmhmm," Quin moaned.

After a few minutes of examining his granddaughter, the captain took a sigh of relief. "The poor thing's tired herself out." Gaderian cradled her small head in his large hands. "She needs to rest."

Noam grabbed the magical stone, glancing around at the tired and sweating faces of the guards, and at the bloody mess of strewn-about troll carcasses. He then looked at Quin. *What had she done? What was it about the stone that weakened the evil creatures?* Noam remembered the awe he felt the first time Quin had shown him the magical glowing rock, but they hadn't had a chance to talk about it since then. Had she found out something more about it that no one else knew? The stone did not glow for Noam as it did for her and he wondered if Quin had some sort of unique power. He gazed upon her face, her long dark lashes lying softly against her cheeks.

Sir Swordsby bent over, resting his hands on his knees and panted, "Well, I guess I'll be the one to ask. What in the bloody blue sea was that?" He pointed to the hunk of stone in Noam's hand that was now dark ebony since the blue light had faded. "Not that I'm complaining."

Noam studied it as the captain spoke. "I'm no quite sure, but I could make a pretty darn good guess."

Noam held the stone up to a sunbeam that came streaming out of the trees, its shiny jet black facets sparkled. He spoke as if finishing the captain's thoughts, "The Prophecy… "

Gaderian glanced up at him and pointedly said, "Exactly."

KALAYA

Kalaya's mouth was gagged with a strip of cloth that had been knotted tightly behind her head, and her wrists were raw and achy from the rough rope that held her hands behind her back. If that wasn't enough, her captors had chained her tail to a rock; the rusty metal links chafed and scraped at her scales. The tide was rising and she could feel the cold water slowly climbing up her stomach in the shallow bay of Shadow Rock where she had been brought just a few moments before.

She looked in towards the jagged spire mountain that reached towards the wispy sunrise clouds from the depths of the water, and could see the two young humans sitting on the rock shelf in their prison cave in the side of the craggy cliff. They had their knees pulled up away from the sea water that was filling the floor, reaching as high as their seat, faces drawn and weary.

The sun just began to pull itself above the edge of the world, the twilight being brushed with reds, pinks, and oranges, as King Nerius arrived with his brother, Ormon, and a small regime of Mer guards, their heads emerging from the ocean as they swam inland to the shallow cove to meet the Enchantress. Kalaya could feel the point of the shadow's knife at her back as her father stole a glance at her, and keeping the distance required, quickly resumed his royal disposition. As Nerius shifted, revealing Captain Cade to his side, the merman's face was wrought with tension and determination. To his other side was his brother, Ormon, looking like a mirror image of the king, if less tall and muscular, silver hair flowing down his back.

Although the king had brought a dozen Mer guards with him, they were greatly outnumbered by the mob of shadows looming about, their tattooed skin glowing like etched charcoal in the dawn light. Kalaya knew it was a trap, and that no matter what her father did, he would more than likely be taken and killed. There was nothing she could do, and she felt utterly helpless.

"Oh, Nerius," the sea witch began to giggle in a childlike manner. "I'm so glad to see you've made the right decision and brought the stone tablet." Her jet black hair was glossy in the sunrise as she shook it off her shoulders.

"I've brought what you want, Silvana. Now, give me my daughter and let this be over with." Nerius's voice was deep and edgy, like the calm before the storm, betraying the fear and anger that Kalaya saw in his eyes.

"A little harsh, aren't we?" Silvana's sly voice was tinged with sarcasm. "I thought we could have a friendly and civil exchange." Silvana ran her fingers playfully across the water, small trenches following behind.

"You lost any chance of that when you took my daughter captive." The king held his staff tightly, his knuckles turning white. "Let her go and you will have what you asked for." With his other hand he held up his half of the broken slab of stone, his eyes blazing like wild fire.

Silvana laughed maniacally. "The tablet first… and then the princess."

Kalaya could see her father's sun-tanned face turning a deep shade of red. "How am I to know that you will hold up your end of the deal?"

Silvana's eyes, like black diamonds, studied him. "There's only one way to find out." Silvana waved one of her shadow guards towards the king. "Bring the tablet by yourself, no guards, and you will have back your precious Wavekeeper."

Kalaya tried to yell out, tried to warn him, but nothing more than a muffled *mmmph* came from her mouth.

"That is unfair!" Cade yelled, but was silenced with a halting motion of Nerius's hand.

Kalaya's father, with the white coral crown of twisting waves cresting his head, glanced between her and the shadow guard who held out his hand. Nerius gave a deep, chest-heaving sigh. Everyone watched intently in complete silence, only the soothing sound of water lapping at the beach could be heard. After what seemed to be a deep inner struggle, he began to stream towards the waiting merman and reluctantly handed the tablet to him.

Suddenly three shadows popped from the dim water and grabbed the king in a splashing struggle. To their surprise, Nerius's staff began to glow bright, and the ground beneath them began to grumble and shake as he summoned his power to fight back: the power of the waves.

Kalaya began to fight against her captor, but stopped when she felt the knife blade at her throat. And then it all happened at once, in a foggy blur of screams and motion.

The Mer guards came for their king, their cloaks of green seagrass, flowing out behind them, grazing the water. They were suddenly stopped by an invisible wall, like clear glass, and waves of vibrations radiated from the points of contact of their pounding fists. Silvana held one hand out, her palm flexed as if holding up the invisible wall, and then looking at the king and his struggling captors with the other hand, shot out green icy beams of light, knocking the king's glowing staff from his hands.

Kalaya could hear the humans screaming and looked to see that the tide how now raised even farther, filling half of the cave; the young ones stood on the rock shelf, their hands pressed to the rocky ceiling.

She was brought back to the fight in front of her by a yell. "I've got it!" Gibson, Silvana's small redheaded merman, had the staff of waves in his hands, raising it up high in triumph.

Kalaya could see her father's assailants struggling with the powerful king. Even without the connection to his staff, Nerius was a mighty force with the strength of ten mermen.

Silvana's slight assistant, holding the staff high above his head, brought it down atop her father's skull with a sickening, bone-snapping *crack!* The king's head dropped and his body fell limp in the arms of the three dark-eyed shadows.

"You said you would return the princess unharmed!" Ormon shouted to Silvana as he pounded his fists on the crystal clear wall, his long silver hair stuck out in every direction. "You have no honor. You will never get away with this!"

"There are only two souls in all of Merenia who can conquer my magic." Silvana looked at Kalaya and then her father. "And I have them both!"

Cade, standing next to Kalaya's uncle, shouted angrily, "Aren't you forgetting someone? Nerius has a son, and he will come to avenge you!"

Silvana laughed at that, her smooth skin glistened with droplets of water. "You silly merboy," Silvana sneered, "don't you suppose I've already thought of that?"

One of the shadows materialized out of the water, with Kalaya's brother Kai, his skin red and inflamed with the newly tattooed black scrolls running up his shoulders and neck. Kalaya's body went numb at seeing him, and tears welled up in her eyes.

"You can't do this!" Ormon shouted.

Silvana's voice was cold and thin as she spoke, "I did nothing. Your nephew, the prince, came to me willingly." She patted Kai on the back.

The Mer guards were quiet and still, their mouths hanging open in astonishment.

With a shaky and uncertain voice, Kai spoke to the guards, his uncle, and his sister. "It's better this way. We have to protect our own, and uniting the prophecy is the only way."

"Smart one, he is." Silvana smiled at Kai and then dismissed him with an impatient wave; his accompanying shadow grabbed him roughly and swam off.

Cade pleaded with the Enchantress. "You can still right this, Silvana." He clenched his fists in fury. "You have what you wanted. Let the king and the princess go."

"I've always been known for being very smart," Silvana giggled. "And that wouldn't be very smart of me, would it?" Silvana gestured to the shadow guard who held the tablet and he passed it to her. "You didn't think they would just hand me the stone tablet and let me swim away to do as I wish, did you?"

Cade hung his head.

"No. I didn't think so."

Despite the razor sharp blade at Kalaya's throat, she began to labor against the shadow's large arms, wishing she could scream or fight or flee.

Silvana took notice of this, as Kalaya's captor held her tight despite her thrashing. "Don't worry, Kalaya, I may let you live and then breed you. I will need more Wavekeepers who will work for me once this is all over." Kalaya could feel warm blood trickling down the hollow of her neck, where the knife had nicked her skin during her struggle.

Silvana looked down at the entablature, captivated, and hugged it to her body. Her voice rang out over the water, magnified as if by the ocean itself. "The stone tablet will finally be united! The prophecy will be fulfilled!" Kalaya's stomach churned as she heard the shadows roar and cheer with delight. It was obvious that Silvana thought *she* was a main part of the prophecy.

"Now, Gibson," Silvana looked to her spindly, redheaded assistant. "Bring me the staff of waves!" The enchantress looked at Kalaya and smiled. "Now that I have the king Wavekeeper and his heirs, I am unstoppable!" She laughed and then looked to her helper.

"Gibson?"

The merman's skin turned pale and an expression of wide-eyed shock spread over his face as he looked down to see a sword blade emerging from his chest. Time seemed to stop as a drop of blood ran from Gibson's lips and dripped down his chest, his body rigid and stiff. The merman's bony hand released the royal staff and let it fall, in slow motion, towards the water.

Just before the staff was engulfed by the sea, a different hand, (this one strong and built with muscle), swooped up from below and grabbed it. Gibson's lifeless form gave a heave, and the sword blade that was embedded in his chest was jerked out and replaced by surges of streaming blood, the body sinking slowly below the sea-green waves.

A man... no... a *hu*man emerged from behind the fallen shadow, chest deep in water, his waves of brown hair touching his shoulders and his blue eyes shining in the sunlight. He kept his balance surprisingly well against the pitching current for having legs. Kalaya thought he looked familiar but couldn't place where she'd seen him before.

Silvana was speechless, her mouth twitched nervously at the surprise visitor. With her distraction, the invisible barrier weakened and shattered like glass as the Mer guards broke through and made a mad dash towards their enemies.

The stranger held out her father's staff, his chiseled jaw clenched tight in concentration, and pointed it in Silvana's direction, with the same sea grumbling sound and blinding glow emanating from the miniature coral carved waves on top. Immediately, Silvana's palm came up to meet the threat and shot out hundreds of icy green and silver bolts, creating a large shock of energy, her black eyes sparkling with amusement.

Blue light and warm air began to bellow out from the staff in pulsating surges, like the vibrations that come off of a large metal bell after being struck. The warm azure billows stopped Silvana's razor-thin bolts halfway between the two fighters, and the magic stayed, held in mid-air, fluctuating back and forth like an inconclusive match of strength.

Kalaya couldn't believe her eyes as she watched this man summon magic from her father's weapon. *What in Merenia is going on? That is the staff of waves! No one else should be able to use it!* It was well known that the staff of waves could only be used by the king of Mer Ocean, or the heirs to the crown. It had even been made a yearly event. At the annual solstice festival, merpeople would travel from all over to see if they could wield the power of the staff, and after a ten-year tradition, no one had proven successful.

Kalaya jumped as she felt the shadow's body behind her go stiff and suddenly drop away. A hand ripped the cloth from her mouth and she took a deep desperate pull of air, trying to look behind her at whoever was untying her hands.

"Ssshhh." The male voice said. "Everything's going to be alright."

Kalaya's head spun amongst the chaos, everything around her seemed to be moving at super speed now. The battle raged between shadows and Mer guards, sounds of metal meeting metal in a blur of splashing water, flipping tails sparkling in flashes, and screams of the wounded resonated over the ocean waves. She watched the struggle between

Silvana and the mystery man, their faces strained with effort and concentration, as she felt hands fumbling with the chain links that bound her fin.

Kalaya fell exhausted against the large rock after being released from her chains and, laying her head back in the hollow, finally saw her savior. His face came close to hers, crystal blue eyes sparkling like sapphires. She studied the handsome face, his smooth tan skin held a dimple on either side of his bright smile and his short cropped brown hair was moist with water and sweat. *Another human*, Kalaya thought dizzily. He wore a plum tunic embroidered with a silver bolt stamped golden crown.

"Are you alright?" he asked.

She began to nod her head when an angry hand suddenly grabbed her and began to pull her under the water. Her young hero drew his sword, and with ease, chopped the limb from the body of a shadow. Kalaya screamed when she saw the tattooed and severed hand still gripped on to her. The young man pulled it off and flung it far into the ocean, a small *splash* following momentarily. She could feel her savior's strong arms wrap around her protectively. "You're safe now," he said. And it was true, she had never felt safer.

Being that she was enveloped in her own little bubble of warmth and safety, sounds of a raging battle could still be heard, perhaps less intense than before. The ground shook, the water quivered, and a vibrating hollow sound rose and fell as Kalaya watched Silvana and the strange man struggle against each other's power.

The Enchantress's face was dubious at the fact that a mere human could hold her off, and spoke her feelings as she held steady the shooting stream of beaming green and silver shards. "Who... are... you?"

The man chuckled, his rugged and brawny form held strong against the blast of his foe. "It would appear that I've come back from the dead." The man's smile flashed white from within a stubbled face. "And just in time it seems."

The sea witch looked at him with disbelief.

"It couldn't be... "

"It is." He said frankly. "And I am."

The Enchantress had a moment of uncertainty and the man, sensing this, took advantage of her wavering magic. The flow of turbulence from his staff grew stronger and louder, pushing back the shocks of icy green shards closer and closer to their maker.

Sweat began to bead on Silvana's brow as she struggled to hold her position, and not doing well by it, collapsed under the pressure. An explosion of green fire and icy sparks burst out over the ocean from her hands, the water mirroring their bright glittering image.

"The humans!" Kalaya yelled involuntarily as she looked to see Aaric and Aleena screaming for help, submerged in water up to their necks, hands pressed flat against the cave ceiling.

Captain Cade, glanced up from the fleeing shadow he had been fighting, and dismissing the retreating savage, bolted as fast as a sea snake to the prison, his green tail flashing in the sun.

As he dove beneath the water and began to strike the metal lock with his sword, her savior laid her down gently and half-swam, half-sloshed through the shallow but rising water of the inlet. In the lead was the strange warrior human, looking frantically worried, as he watched Cade through the surface of the sea hack at the sturdy lock again and again with no luck.

Kalaya surveyed the water, her head still spinning and body weak from lack of food, and struggle. Her father was coming to, but was still weak, clasping onto two Mer guards who held him upright, his crown tilted and blood crusted on his scalp. The shadows were now fleeing into the vast expanse of the sun-gleaming ocean and Silvana and the stone tablet were nowhere to be found.

“Stand back!” The stranger yelled as he pulled himself onto a grouping of rocks near the prison bars. The young human’s arms and legs flailed frantically under water, trying to stay afloat. Their faces were now shoved against the ceiling, only their mouths and noses were above the surface of the fast climbing tide, desperately gulping at the cool air.

The princess watched eagerly as the man held the rod out towards the submerged bars and, again with a concentrated look, began to wield the power of the staff of waves. The earth groaned and the water shivered, as blue waves of air pounded from the staff.

Kalaya clasped her hands to her ears as she heard and felt the familiar *waow waow waow* of the king's staff, vibrating in tremulous pulses. A loud metallic *crack* was heard and her brave human, his sapphire eyes intent, swung the door open against the push of water as Cade swam in and pulled the two humans through the underwater entrance and up to the surface. Aaric and Aleena's heads crested the white foam swells and, spluttering and coughing, they gasped for precious air.

The stranger jumped off of his perch into the water and grabbed the two younger ones and held them tight.

"Father!" Aleena cried.

So he would be Lord Castlecray, Kalaya thought as she watched the small group make their way to the narrow sandy beach and lie down, exhausted and panting. *He's their father.*

Dark clouds began to boil and tumble in from the south; another icy cold rain storm. As Kalaya watched the sky turn from a mid-morning sun-shiny blue, to a muddled slate grey mid-day, she turned over the recent events in her mind. The princess breathed deeply of the cool salt air as she watched the odd humans glugging fresh water from a type of cylindrical holder. Well, that answered the question of who the stranger was. Now for the most important question, how could someone other than a Wavekeeper summon the magic of the staff of waves; and being a *human* for that matter?

Kalaya, feeling her head clearing a bit, quickly swam to her father. They wrapped their arms around each other in a long embrace, tears of relief, joy, anger, sadness and every other possible emotion began to flow from her eyes.

"Oh father... Kai... " Her voice was trembling and she lowered her head in sorrow. "My brother... "

Nerius patted her on the back, and with a wave of his hand, dismissed her uncle and the nearby guards. He spoke softly to her, his voice deep and comforting. "I know, my child. I know."

Kalaya let the warmth of her father's arms comfort her, as he brushed her long chestnut brown hair from her face. She looked up into his eyes.

"What is going to happen? Silvana has both pieces of the tablet now."

Her father smiled. "A small price to pay for your life." He brought up his arms and held her face. "And not to worry, the tablet is only words carved on stone, and the prophecy is nothing without the star elements."

Kalaya's mind began to flood with questions. "Who are these humans; the Castlecrays? Are they Peace Protectors?"

The king sighed, "No. No they are not."

"Who are they? And how could that man possibly summon the power of the waves?" She studied her father's face inquisitively.

Nerius's dark brows furrowed in thought as he gently laid a hand on her shoulder, "There's something I should have told you a long time ago."

QUIN

The fire crackled merrily from the large hearth in the common room as Quin snuggled in tight to the warm blanket that Nunny Ana had brought earlier. She had been trying to immerse herself in a book to wipe away the images of nasty slime-ridden trolls from her head, but the effort was failing. Noam was quietly playing a game of chess with Master Dunley in the corner, and her grandfather had gone to see about something with Captain Swordsby in the library.

Quin got up from her comfy pallet on the floor and walked to the window; she could see guards making their rounds through the rain-streaked window. Defense had been doubled since the attack in Hagglers way, just that morning, and Quin had heard Brently Swordsby saying that the Castlecray army was recruiting more and more guards, some boys as young as Noam. Her grandfather had said that they were preparing for what's to come, and what that was, Quin wasn't sure. The new recruits were already starting their training in the practice yard using wooden swords and shields, clumsily attempting defensive techniques, many of them coming away black and blue with bruises and bumps. In fact, Noam had volunteered himself and was told he could start his training with the younger boys on the morrow. No doubt, Olga the kitchen master, wouldn't be happy about that.

"Checkmate!" Noam cried out, startling Quin, as she spun around at the shout.

"Good game, young Noam. You're getting better," Master Dunley said, the skin of his cheeks hanging like that of an old hound dog.

Quin paced to the next window over and looked out over the practice yard, watching the trainees unsurely attack each other, most of them green boys, farmers, and men usually deemed too old to fight. She pressed her face close to the cold glass, and her breath made foggy spots, as she pondered her current situation.

Grandfather had told her there was something important that they needed to discuss, after he saw to his duties, and for her to just rest. But she couldn't rest, she couldn't think straight, she couldn't do anything, for being so anxious and her mind churning like a tidal wave.

Why had the magical stone weakened the trolls, and what had possessed her to pull it out and try it in the midst of the battle? She remembered the feeling she had gotten. Being pulled from unconsciousness and drawn to it, like unspoken words filling her mind, causing her to take her hands and place them on the lifeless black rock, making it to glow and pulse brightly with blue light. And there had been a sound, like a *pop* or a *click*, as though something had been activated within her, bonding her to the stone, allowing her to be one with it and use its unknown power. And why was it that Aaric and she were the only ones who could make it glow? If it were a link between siblings, would Aleena have control over it as well?

Quin stopped and looked to the fire in remembrance. It was so lonely here without her brother and sister, and without father. It was not that long ago that they all sat cuddled up together on a stormy night, very much like this one, and listened to Nunny Ana's bedtime stories. And that's what they had thought; that they were just stories and nothing else. Well, they had been proven wrong, hadn't they? Mermaids and trolls, giants and faeries; what other "stories" were not fabled but true? What other mystical creatures were out there just waiting for the right time to reveal themselves?

Quin shivered. Whether it was from her thoughts or from the cold night air, she couldn't tell. Quin turned as she heard the heavy door creak open and saw Nunny shuffle in holding a platter filled with goblets and a serving girl behind her with one of steaming bowls.

"A bit of cider and hot soup will do you two some good," Nunny said, her voice like gritty old sand, as she eyed Quin and Noam. "What with all that you've been through. You'll need to rebuild your strength." The brittle old nursemaid set the dishes down on the table as Master Dunley moved the chess board aside.

"Nunny," Quin said impulsively, "You know the stories you tell about the mermaids?"

The older woman nodded as she busied herself tidying the room. "Mmhmm."

"They're real, aren't they?" Quin paused. "I've seen them."

Nunny stopped suddenly and the young serving girl's eyes went wide as she stared at Quin. After some thought she said, "Well, I suppose some would believe they are… but… "

Master Dunley stood abruptly, making a groaning sound, his knees cracking and popping. "Ana," he spoke quietly, "if you will leave us alone for a moment?"

"Of course, Master Dunley." She gave a slight nod and left the room, urging on the ogling serving girl to follow.

Dunley gestured for Quin to have a seat at the table next to Noam, who was busily slurping from a bowl of steaming broth, oblivious to the recent exchange.

"You children must listen to me carefully." Noam lifted his head and the old master looked back and forth between their eyes. "There are certain things that must be kept secret and to stay as they are, tales and stories."

Noam's sunshine blonde hair was hanging in his eyes. "Master Dunley, you know about the... ?"

The master's long pointed nose stuck out prominently on his long hollow face. "I know a few things, but it is none of my duties to be putting my nose where it does not belong."

"Quin is magic!" Noam spouted, unable to control himself, now that the cat was out of the bag.

Quin shot him an icy glare, her face flushing with heat. "No, I'm not! It's just...just that... " She seemed unable to finish her own sentence. *Do I have magic?*

Dunley handed Noam a candle and waved him towards the blazing fire, insinuating that he should go and light the wick. As the boy regretfully got up and walked to the hearth, Dunley leaned close to Quin, his foggy half-blind eyes reflecting the red and orange flames. "Don't you go worrying yourself, little one," he reassured her softly. "You shall have your answers soon enough and all will be well."

Noam brought back the lit candle and placed it in the iron holder on the table, two fingerholds curved up on the side like a number eight.

"Noam," the master looked at him, "I understand you are to start your training tomorrow?"

Her friend nodded.

"I have something else in mind for you." Dunley said and Noam stared inquisitively at the wrinkled old hound. The master slid a piece of parchment out from under the chess board and handed it to Noam. Quin leaned over the boy's shoulder to see what it was.

Noam's face lit up, like the candle. "Apprentice?" He said with disbelief, "You want me to be your apprentice?"

"That's right. Not only that, but a squire."

Noam still looked suspicious as he spoke, his voice a little higher than usual. "But I've always been in the kitchens... and... and never had any training."

"Oh, you will still be training with Sir Captain Swordsby , but will report back to me for your duties."

Noam let a small smile creep across his face.

"You're a strong boy," Dunley reached across and patted his arm, "and quite a bit braver than most boys your age. And, although it is something not usually looked upon highly, running off and stowing away, I mean, I was told that you had Lady Quinlan's best interests in mind when you followed her on to the boat to protect her."

Quin could sense Noam's embarrassment, as he fixed his eyes on the paper, his cheeks turning rosy.

"And besides," Master Dunley continued, "I'm not a spring chicken anymore, and *someone* will need to take over as Castlecray House Master when I am physically... unable, someday."

Quin had a sense of overwhelming joy for her friend. Wow, *House Master.* That was a title not taken lightly. Noam seemed to be feeling the same way as he got up and rushed at the old man, squeezing him tight.

"Er...oh..." Dunley's words came out in a choking stammer. "Well, alright then." He patted the young man and pried his arms from around his neck.

As Quin watched the heartwarming display she could hear a noise outside the door, a squawking of some sort, echoing down the hall. She exchanged glances with her friend as the noise drew nearer and *louder*.

Just then the door slammed open and Lady Odelyn came bursting in. "No, you may *not* take Quinlan away." The wide and squat woman rushed at Quin and grabbed her painfully by the ear, causing Quin to drop the blanket that was warming her. "She's just returned; the poor thing."

And appearing from behind another one of Odelyn's many flamboyantly tall wigs, (this one with a tinge of pink,) was Quin's grandfather, looking flustered, as he stroked his salt and pepper beard.

"But m'lady," he said, "It is o' the utmost importance."

The crazy-eyed woman, oddly enough, was crooning small reassurances to Quin, like you would a baby, making Quin feel queasy. Odelyn looked up and glared daggers at Gaderian's husky form in the doorway. "And what reason could you possibly have to rip away a young lady such as Quinlan from her home?"

Her grandfather frowned. "Well, I canna' tell ye exactly..."

Quin squirmed as Lady Odelyn made cooing sounds and pinched her cheeks until they burned. Without looking his way, she addressed Quin's grandfather. "It is *out* of the question, Gaderian!"

Gaderian's unkempt and dark bushy brows came together in frustration as he took a step closer to Quin. "But if Lord Emrys was here… "

"Lord Emrys is *not* here and *I* will be making the decisions! Quin…stays…here!" Odelyn's face was turning a bright shade of red, almost purple, making her look like a fat plum wearing a wig.

"You must let him take the girl," Master Dunley said flatly as he slowly stood.

"I *will not!*" Lady Odelyn wrapped her arms around Quin. She smelled sickeningly of potent perfumed roses and strong lavender, as if she had just come in from rolling in the garden.

"I am the Master of House Castlecray," Dunley said sternly, his voice dry and brittle. "And while Lord Emrys is away, *I* will be making the decisions."

Quin watched Noam cowering in his seat, as Gaderian pried her mother-by-marriage's arms off of her. Yes, Noam was brave, but there was not a knight in armor that wouldn't cower from that furious and screaming over-painted face.

"But… " Odelyn protested.

Dunley all but barked, his hanging jowls flapped as he spoke. "She will go with Captain Longship and that is final!"

Lady Odelyn fell to her knees and looked pleadingly up at Quin. "You…you wouldn't leave your mother all alone would you?"

At first, Odelyn wanted nothing to do with the Quin and *now* she didn't want to let her go.

Quin stood, straight as a board, her hands in fists and arms tight at her sides. "You…are *not* my mother."

Odelyn gasped.

And at that, Quin's grandfather had her by the arm, flying down the great stone halls of Castlecray. Noam had tried to follow behind them, but with a stern look from both Dunley and Gaderian, he reluctantly abided and shrunk back into the common room.

"I've already had a servant pack yer things and taken 'em to the boat." Gaderian said hastily.

Quin's heart pounded in her chest at the flurry of activity, her long brown hair flew out behind her as she ran her to keep up with her grandfather's wide gate. "Where are you taking me?"

"I've some questions of me own first, Quinnie-fish." Her grandfather, dressed in his captain's garb as usual and his battered boots that clomped heavily on the marble floor, looked warily behind them at the empty corridor. And then turning back forward asked, "Where did ye find that…er…blue rock thingy?"

Quin hesitated. "I… I… " She then thought about Nimbus Nooney and his warning to tell no one of the stone but dismissed it. This was her own grandfather she was talking to after all. "I found it in a locked chest... well, it was locked... but then." Quin stumbled over her words as they passed through the dining hall doors and under the tall barreled ceilings. She took a breath and started over. "I found it in the underground tunnels, here, at Castlecray."

The bear of a man looked down at her with a pondering expression.

"And at Haggler's Way," Gaderian began, "when the trolls... well... there was a loud *crack* an' a blinding light." Gaderian navigated them through another corridor and through a set of doors with a blast of spraying cold rain and wind. "Ye didn't even flinch, or cover yer eyes like everyone else. What happened? How did ye... do what ye did?"

Quin tensed under the shock of the icy pelting sheets of rain as they hustled out to a stable boy who was holding the reins of two horses, under the sanctuary of a large umbrella-shaped tree.

"I... I don't know, something just came over me... a feeling." Quin swiped away a wet strand of hair that was plastered to her face.

Her grandfather dismissed his own barrage of unanswerable questions with a wave of his hand. "No matter. The important thing is to get ye to the Mystic Forest. And fast."

"What is the Mystic Forest?" Quin looked up at her grandfather's towering figure; his mane of fluffy hair encircled his wide face and his hazel eyes gleamed. "Where are we going?"

Dismissing the stable hand, Gaderian hoisted Quin to the saddle of a big black mare and spoke directly to her. "Quinnie-fish, now I'm no scholar, but I think you've gotten yerself a verra rare and wanted item." Quin looked at her Grandfather with bewilderment.

The Captain scanned their surroundings suspiciously, and when he was sure they were absolutely safe from listening ears, he looked back to Quin. "I think that magic stone that ye found is the water star."

"The water star?" Quin's eyes became as wide as fish ponds. "Do you mean the fallen elements from the prophecy? But —"

Gaderian cut off her words, saying "I'm sure ye are quite a bit confused, as is to be expected, but all ye need to know is that ye have a verra special and a verra *dangerous* power. I'm gonna take ye to a safe place where there's a group that will know how to help ye with that power, something I know a verra wee bit about. And if indeed you do have the water star, as I suspect, we are in a trifle bit o' danger. Whoever holds an element will be hunted down like a wild hog on Beltane."

Anxiety began to build in the pit of Quin's stomach. She would be leaving Castlecray again after being back for such a short time, and under normal circumstances she would be dancing with joy, but just now she felt scared and sad. *Hunted like a wild boar?* And when would she ever see her father again… and Aaric and Aleena?

"Who are these people you are taking me too?" Quin asked tentatively.

Her grandfather paused for a moment. "Well, they're no exactly human."

Quin's face went numb. "If they aren't human, what are they?"

"They are the Oracles."

BANON

The slate gray sky was cold and black clouds cooked a promise of ice and rain, hanging idly in the late morning, adding to Banon's urgency to find out more about his brother's disappearance.

Banon felt cold goose bumps sweep his arms, as he looked at the mermaid princess, her face seemingly familiar. "Are you sure you didn't see him?"

"I'm not *exactly* sure; there were many who did not survive." Kalaya said. He could see sadness in her eyes, the color of acorns and fall leaves.

Banon sat at the edge of the water on the side of the bay, running his fingers through the soft sand. If anyone knew anything, it would be her, for she was the ones who found Aaric and Aleena after the wreck. Immediately proceding the battle, he had questioned Aaric and his brother's soon-to-be wife about the situation or any possible clues, but they'd had no recollection of what had happened after the wave hit their boat until Kalaya and Cade rescued them.

"Tolan is younger than I. Tall and lanky with dark hair and eyes, and his teeth are a little larger than normal. Looks a bit like a baby chipmunk." Banon sucked in his lower lip and stuck out his top teeth in a bad imitation of his brother.

Kalaya giggled at him and then thought for a moment. Looking down at him from her perch on the smooth rock she said, "No, I'm sorry. The only... bodies we found from the wreckage were old sailors, none of which fit that description."

Banon's head was spinning. Just since last night, the prince had learned that merpeople really did exist, fought a battle with them, and was now carrying on a conversation with one; which, despite the circumstances, was strangely mesmerizing, with her large chestnut eyes and rich brown hair.

Not only that, he had come to find out that his brother was attacked by a black rebellion war galley, shot with an arrow, and then lost at sea when the boat had capsized from an unnaturally big tidal wave, more than likely never to be seen again, but Banon would not rest until he found him, alive or dead.

"Well, he's always been quite the swimmer, maybe he'd been carried away by the current and made it to land," Banon said hopefully as he glanced towards the beach at the king merman, who was talking quietly with Lord Emrys, Aaric, and Aleena.

"Yes, maybe." Kalaya said kindly. She then lowered her eyes and began to play with a fringe of sea grass that hung loose from her chemise. "In a way, I also lost my brother."

"Really? I'm sorry," Banon said sincerely. "What happened?"

"He has joined the shadows." Kalaya got a sudden burst of anger and spouted out, "Why would he do this? To father and the kingdom?!" her voice softened, "...and to me"

Banon watched the sadness in her eyes and wanted to go to her and comfort her, but his body wouldn't move. He took a second look at the merking, and noticed his white coral crown, a crown of waves. It hit Banon like a sudden summer storm.

That's it! Banon realized that that was the crown he had seen in the book of crests at the Golden Library back in Merene. *Custos de Fluctus*.

And then it came to him with a heart-stopping bang. That was also the crown that the beautiful girl wore in his dreams! His eyes looked to Kalaya.

With the battle against the sea witch and the shadows coming on so suddenly...and everything had been in such shambles...he couldn't believe he hadn't noticed! His heart skipped a beat as he looked up at the mermaid, who was haloed by a beam of golden light that shot from a temporary break in the clouds and glowed around her as she smiled at him. *Could it be?*

A thunderclap rang across the uneasy sea waves as Banon tried to recall the girl from his dreams, but she was hazy, like a dense fog. While he was awake the strange dreams would fade from his memory like the ghost of a time long past, but during sleep they appeared as vividly as the colors of spring flowers.

Banon's palms began to sweat, and his body filled with a superficial heat as he looked at the princess; she was lounging comfortably, looking down at him, her tail glistening like blue gems.

"Goodness Landie, you're injured!" She shouted and Banon looked down to see a rosette of red blood slowly leaking through the leg of his breeches, wet and warm.

"Oh, that," the prince spoke nonchalantly. "Just a bit of a scratch."

"A scratch, is it?" Kalaya said sarcastically as she slid off the rock into the water. "Come here, let me see."

Banon gingerly limped into the shallow water. "Really, it's nothing." Kalaya ignored his refusals and rolled up the leg of his breaches to reveal a deep gash in his shin, readily oozing blood. She gasped at the sight.

"Wait here." The mermaid dove into the water and while Banon waited he heard masculine hooting and shouts of agreement. He looked out into the deeper water of the bay and saw the merman named Cade, the captain of the Mer guard, giving the battle-worn Mer guards a speech of encouragement; they patted each other on the back and shook their fists in the air. *They really aren't that different from humans*, Banon thought warmly.

Just then Kalaya resurfaced with a leafy green plant in one hand and a small fist-sized rock in the other. She placed the plant in a hollow of the boulder and began to crush the roots into a mushy green paste.

Banon watched her working and smiled in amusement. “Did you call me Landie?”

Kalaya cupped her hand and scooped up a handful of seawater and trickled it onto the concoction. “What?” She looked up at him. “Oh, yes.” She laughed.

“What’s a Landie?”

Kalaya continued to crush and mix the goopy matter. “A human. One that walks the land.”

“Well, then I guess I should call you scales?”

Kalaya playfully shot him a look of offense. “No, thank you. Kalaya will do just fine.”

They both laughed when Banon suddenly jerked and loudly sucked in his breath as she began to dab the balm onto his wound. “It will only sting for a bit.”

Banon’s face relaxed after the initial shock and he curiously watched the princess tend to his leg. “How did you learn how to do that?”

Kalaya was wrapping the cut with the large flat leaves of the strange plant, like a bandage, the sticky plant roots acting as a paste. She glanced up. “This? Oh. My mother was very friendly with the Jengu kith. They are well known healers of Mer Ocean, and I would go with her to visit them often. They taught me well.” She looked far off to the murky sky, cradled by the glassy waves of the horizon, seeming to be in a distant memory. "My mother was killed when I was just a young mergirl."

Banon looked down, "I'm so sorry for your loss."

"It's alright." The mermaid princess patted his thigh and, rolling down the leg of his breeches, spoke cheerfully. "There we are. Just leave it on until it falls off by itself and it will be as good as new in no time."

"Thank you." Banon said as he watched most of the Mer guard swim off in formation, only to disappear under the storm-colored sea, flashes of far off lightning bouncing off the water. To his surprise, Captain Cade was shooting him a sidelong glance, and from this distance it didn't look too friendly.

Banon inconspicuously gestured at the Mer guard captain. "Is he your…?"

"Mate?" Kalaya burst out laughing at Banon's, obviously ridiculous, assumption. "Goodness, no! We grew up together and used to play sharks in the fisheries when we were just merlings. As captain of the Mer guard, he's taken it upon himself to be my personal guard. Cade's just like an overprotective swordfish; there's nothing between us."

You should tell him that, Banon thought as he watched the merman's jealous glare.

"It is a bit draining sometimes, though," Kalaya confided, "having someone looking over you, watching everything you do."

Kalaya's words struck a note with Banon. He related completely.

"I know how it feels being the heir to a king," he said as he bent and straightened his leg, testing its flexibility. "It seemed that someone was always there telling me what to do, like I had no mind of my own. Sometimes it made me just want to run far away and never look back."

Kalaya giggled, "Exactly!"

The lightning was getting closer, purple bolts zigzagging electrically across the sky, and the thunder's booms echoed over the vast expanse of frigid water.

King Nerius shouted to his daughter, his voice sounding very much like the rolling thunder, "The sea grows angry, Kalaya, we must leave now!"

Banon bent down to her, the cold water soaking his pants. "Will you help me?" he whispered softly. "Find Tolan, I mean." Banon couldn't just leave his brother's body to the fish. He would find him and take him back to Merene for a proper royal burial.

She looked to her father across the bay and then back to Banon, the wind beginning to whip her hair with vigor. She spoke to him in low tones, as if she wanted no one else to hear. "There is a small rowing boat on the other side of Shadow rock." She pointed to the west side of the island. "It was used for transporting human slaves. Silvana will have no further use for the boat, seeing as it doesn't look like the shadows will be returning here anytime soon, and we could use it to search for Tolan."

Banon flinched at the words *human slaves* but also felt a sense of relief at knowing he just might be able to find his brother, and most of all for the fact that he might see Kalaya again. "So you'll help me?"

Kalaya again glanced at her father and then back to Banon. "Yes, but I do not think my father would be too happy about me getting involved." The wind started to pick up speed and fat drops of rain began to fall, loud and wet.

Kalaya spoke as she swam away slowly. "Stay here at Shadow Rock. Don't worry, it will be safe for now. Guards will be posted, and there should be plenty of provisions inside. I will come back to meet you before dawn tomorrow."

And with a flicker of her cobalt blue tail, she was gone.

"Banon!" Lord Emrys called to him. The prince knew that they would be getting on their boat and heading back to Castlecray and wondered how he would tell them that he would not be going.

Banon ran a hand back through his salty, sand-matted hair as he played out the recent series of strange events in his head, hobbling towards his group. *What are the odds,* he thought as a smile crept onto his face, *me, the prince of Merenia meeting her, the mermaid princess of Mer Ocean.* This was going to be a very interesting adventure.

THE CLOAKED MAN

The view of the river from the dock was breathtaking, surrounded by lush greenery, whispering reeds, and brown cattails that emerged from the shallow bank of water, swaying and tickling the air. The sun had just begun to set and cast a dreamlike, sheer pink blanket over the picturesque scenery.

The air was icy cold, and the cloaked man could smell the promise of rain on the breeze and feel it in his bones. He looked to his side at Sir Theodore Tornbuckle, the has-been knight, his tall and slumped figure stood still, dirty blonde hair ruffling in the wind.

Since Tornbuckle was in fact the person who had captured the princess mermaid, his cover as a Peace Protector had been blown and he was unable to return to the Invisible Isle, much less his own castle.

For whatever reason, the man had reluctantly offered him an invitation to stay at his castle, and to his dismay, Theodore had accepted eagerly. The cloaked man mentally dismissed the inconvenience. It was no matter, for he was already housing a number of rebels and black knights, what was one more mouth to feed or one more guest for a good cause. Tornbuckle looked his way, flashing a golden-tooth smile. The man grimaced.

He then looked to his left, at Lord Aurous Goldcoin, face red and beaded with sweat despite the cold temperature, and wondered how he had been able keep up his cover as the Royal Treasurer, what with all the secret meetings and rendezvous. The little man, dressed at the top of fashion as usual, was wearing a golden velvet gown over woolen hose, cinched around his waist with a glittering jeweled belt, soft cream ruffles spilling from his neck and wrists. From his leather pointed shoes to his chaperon hat that sat on his melon-shaped head, pinned with a golden pendant with velvety tails hanging down past his shoulders, the man thought Lord Aurous looked a vain fool.

The man, cloaked in a hooded black cape, looked down at himself, and smoothed out his green tunic with his black house crest, seeing the image upside down from his angle, wanting to look presentable for Silvana, upon her arrival.

The three men stood together, outlined by the sunset-colored clouds, at their meeting place on the end of the pier. They stood between the wooden dock pilings, quietly awaiting the Enchantress of Mer Ocean, surrounded by silence and serenity. They knew that if she did not show up that the plan had failed, and the man became nervous at the thought of it. *She should be here by now.*

As if reading his thoughts, the surface of the river began to pop and froth in front of them with a gurgling sound. The three watched intently as the water churned and fizzled, spraying out wisps of frosted smoke that rose thick in the air. Just then, the crown of a head crested the surface, black glossy hair slicked down with water as the entire river began to slowly bubble and foam with increasing intensity like a large cauldron of boiling stew.

The man couldn't believe his eyes, as hundreds of forms rose from the water, wading chest deep in an orderly formation, Silvana at their lead rising higher than the others. Her palms were flexed and facing upwards towards the darkening water-colored sky, as if she were holding an invisible platter. The man had never seen her before, nor any merperson for that matter, only working through a web of spies and secret messages that were passed down through the ranks, and had thought himself better prepared for this than what he felt; knees shaking and weak.

The mermaid pushed her palms up higher, as if calling the life-like river by magic. It swirled and shimmered as a column of water rose up beneath her, lifting Silvana high above the surface, the man's eyes in direct line with her sparkling jet black fin. His heart beat loudly in his chest at the magnificent display of her power.

The water began to glow an eerie jade green, as it curled and morphed into different shapes, forming itself to the Enchantress's body. It crawled up her back and under her arms, and then settled on a final form, what looked to be a perch made of water, crystal green spikes cupped around behind her. The pure liquid started to solidify, clicking and crackling into place, creating a throne of glowing green ice.

The man glanced to his side to see Sir Theodore Tornbuckle smiling wickedly, his eyes like deep pools, reflecting the looming emerald statue and his stubbled beard catching sparks of green light. And to his left, the short lord looked as if he was ready to run, scrunching his beady eyes and shrinking away behind the other two. The cloaked man felt a surge of emotions; a mixture of fear, cowardice, delight, and awe, as he reached up and slowly pulled back his hood to see more clearly, letting it rest on his back.

Silvana held herself like a queen, her posture like a prancing stallion, made of primacy and utter control. Her flawless skin shown in the waning light, as white and as soft as a dove's feathers, and her eyes gleamed like black cut jewels. The sinuous curves of her body were contoured by her long flowing dark hair, reaching around her shoulders and touching her stomach.

The mermaids and mermen who were surrounding her, their moistened skin bearing scrawling designs of ink, had barely caught his notice, because he only had eyes for her with her braided and woven top, sheer and sparkling, covered in emeralds and moonstones, chains of gold and silver. She was spellbinding.

"My humans," she said lovingly as she opened her arms and tilted her head, the three men dropped to their knees and bowed down. "Today will be a day marked in history." The enchantress theatrically held her arms out wide and looked up towards the first twinkling stars of night.

"Today we will secure our place amongst the greatest names of all time and tonight… " The man's body went numb as she looked him directly in the eyes, "we will unite the stone tablet; we will activate the prophecy!" Shouts of agreement and affirmation arose from her shadows in the water, as if in a bethel on worshiping day.

The Enchantress continued, the moonlight casting her and the surrounding river in a silver lining. "The Lord of Shadows has come to me in my dreams, and is pleased with our progress and also your part in the rebellion. Things are almost as they should be. But there is more… "

Theodore's voice startled the cloaked man. "That is pleasing to hear, Enchantress. How may we be of greater service to you and the Shadow Lord?"

"You Sir Tornbuckle, stand." She commanded Tornbuckle. "The Dark Lord has been very pleased with you." Her mouth twitched with pleasure.

The cloaked man frowned. *How could he be pleased with that paunch-bellied slob who calls himself a knight?*

Silvana continued, "He asks that you be my new assistant, a messenger of sorts between me and him, as well as corresponding with our army, and relaying orders."

Tornbuckle bowed his head in submission, his rusted armor peeking out from beneath a sun-faded red tunic. "Yes, your eminence."

"You, Lord Goldcoin," she looked at Goldcoin. "Stand." On shaky knees, the treasurer stood and hesitantly looked at her. "You will continue with matters of dispersing payment, and seeing our black knights and army of bush-fighters have sufficient food and supplies. I will see that you have all the gold and silver you may need."

Aurous Goldcoin bent his sweaty melon head in submission.

"And you, Lord Snell," she said to the cloaked man, "you will continue to meet with secret messengers and relay information pertaining to the goings-on at the king's royal court, smoothing out any suspicions... by whatever means necessary." She paused. "How fares your relationship with Beaumont Thunderdyn?" She all but spit out the land king's name.

Malvin Snell hesitated, not knowing exactly what to say. "He... I... it had been a long time... we... we are... cordial."

Silvana's mouth twitched as she pointed to the waving river below her. She twisted her finger as if spinning thread, and a rope of water came twirling from the surface like a coiled iridescent snake. She thrust her hand towards Snell, commanding the glassy snake, it shot out at him and wrapped around his neck.

"That will not do." Silvana's voice carried a tinge of anger and her eyes flashed, as he groped at the watery serpent, unable to pry it from his blocked airway, his fingers slipping through the cold liquid. "You will earn the land king's trust, and become one of his most loyal companions." Malvin felt his lungs burning with the need for air, as he raked his fingers desperately at his choking throat.

The powerful mermaid smiled at him. "Do you understand?"

Strangled muffling sounds came from his throat; his eyes began to bulge and his heart pounded with panic.

Silvana repeated herself. "Do you *understand*?"

With all of his might he managed a slight nod of his head and then gasped at the release of the binding water, it splashing down around his boots.

Lord Snell fell to his knees, coughing and gasping. His head hung to his chest as he unseeingly stared at the slithering green sea snake on his black surcoat, the crest of his father's treacherous legacy; the House Snell coat of arms. "Yes... yes... Enchantress." The lord's chest was heaving as he sucked in gulps of delicious air.

The Enchantress let out a light-hearted sigh, abruptly changing her mood. “Now that all of that is settled, we must move on to more important matters.”

“I have designated certain black knights, human shadows and mershadows, and trusted merpeople to begin the search for the elements. Now that the tablet has been united and we have all of the clues, it should not take long, and then I… ” Silvana brushed backed a curtain of her dark-tressed hair behind her shoulders, revealing more of her gem-encrusted corset, and corrected herself, “*We* will possess the greatest power known; the power to control all bodies of water everywhere, the power of MER.” She giggled like a small child. “And the Lord of Shadows will reward us for our hard work, and the balance shall be right again.”

Malvin tentatively peered up from his hunched position, watching the witch carefully.

“But not all of our news is good. Yes, we were successful today in bringing home the tablet, but unfortunately there was a chink in our plan.”

“What happened?” Sir Tornbuckle was being dangerously bold, the man thought.

The Enchantress snapped her head in his direction, and lighting her eyes on him, sat back calmly. “I was to kill king Nerius and hold the princess Kalaya captive, but… ”

Tornbuckle had an odd look upon his dirt smudged face. “Yes?” He prodded her on.

Not seeming to mind, Silvana continued. "A *human* showed up; a very powerful human with the ability to control the power of the waves. He... " Lord Snell couldn't quite tell for the darkness, but the sorceress's features seemed doubtful and insecure. "He was supposed to be dead."

"And who might this human be?" Theodore spoke again, now seemingly friendly with the sea witch.

"*Custos de Fluctus.*" She spoke the old tongue. "His name is Eros. He now goes by the name of Lord Emrys Castlecray."

AARIC

"Oh father! We were sure to have drowned, how did you know we were here?" Aleena cried out as she hugged their father, her long golden brown hair curling down her back over her ragged and damp dress.

"I have my ways." He hugged her tight.

"So you knew about the merpeople?"

Aaric watched his father's chiseled face parse in thought, his blue eyes looking to the activity of the Mer guards out in the water. "Yes."

Aaric could see the far-off lightning crackle across the dark and cloudy sky; as his mind drifted into thought, the rumble of thunder rolled across the ocean. He was sure his father was happy to see his sister and him safe but felt that all of this was his fault. After all, he was the one to take his father's boat, putting Aleena and Prince Tolan in danger, not to mention his father's captain and crew, who had perished during the boat crash. Now Tolan was also dead and they hadn't even found Quin, which was the whole reason for their journey.

Aaric hung his head, the wind whipping and tugging at his hair. "I'm sorry, father."

"You did what you thought was best, son," Emrys grabbed his son and embraced him. "You were very brave." Aaric felt that he was twelve name days old again in his father's arms, not a man grown at sixteen.

Reading Aaric's thoughts, Emrys added, "Don't you worry. We will find Quinnie."

Just then the merman king materialized big and looming out of the water before them, his tanned skin gleaming.

"Lady Quinlan is safe with her grandfather, the Captain Gaderian Longship. They should be back at Castlecray any time now." King Nerius's white hair and beard gleamed with water beads as he smiled warmly at Aaric. He then looked at Emrys and chuckled. "Quite a ball of fire, she is."

Aleena let out a noisy breath of relief at hearing that their sister was safe and Aaric's tense body relaxed.

His father's face was always stern-looking, but Aaric caught a glimpse of relaxation in his blue eyes. "We will all finally be together again," Emrys stated, looking at Aaric and his sister, "and safe behind the walls of the castle."

Aaric's father looked down at the object in his hand. "This belongs to you," he said as he handed King Nerius the wooden staff, the top intricately carved with curved and twisted waves, matching the king's crown.

The staff began to glow in the sea king's hand and the blue-green water around him began to sway. A small whitecap wave surged beneath Nerius and pushed him up and out of the water, suspending him in mid-air, the motion of the water continuing, but confined in one place, looking like a living painting.

Nerius bowed his head to Emrys as he held the staff upright; his voice was deep and heartfelt as he spoke. "Thank you... Lord Emrys, I owe you my life."

His father bowed his head back to the king, "And you mine."

Aaric watched the confusing exchange and thought that things could not possibly get any stranger. Just in the span of a couple of days, he had been attacked by the black rebellion, almost drowned, been saved by a mermaid princess, then captured by a sea witch, witnessed a battle, almost drowned *again*, and then saved by his father, who, come to find out, knew of the merpeople's existence all along. But oddly enough, Aaric felt at ease with the merpeople, as though he was connecting with a long lost memory, an unknown past.

Just on the other side of the bay, Prince Banon was talking with the mermaid princess, Kalaya, Aaric's former cell mate, and Captain Cade of the Mer guard swam towards the king, leaving his band behind in formation.

"Your Majesty," Cade bowed and then looked up to his king, who hovered on the airborne water. "We lost Silvana's trail, but I've sent Ormon out with the scouts to see if we can recover it."

King Nerius nodded. "Good. Set up a post here and double the Tidebreak Tower's watch. Also send back word to ready the garrison. We will need more guards."

"Right away, Your Majesty." And with that, Cade swam off to relay orders to his mermen out in the bay, Nerius's eyes following and then lit on his daughter, who was nursing Banon's leg on the other side of the cove.

"Do you see the way she looks at him?" Nerius spoke to no one in particular, as he sat atop the streaming current of water, seemingly detached and lost in thought. "I've seen that look before."

Aaric glanced to his side at his sister, a lost look settled upon her face.

Nerius, coming out of his daze, looked at Aleena, and a tear ran down her cold flushed cheek. "You grieve for your lost prince?"

Aleena nodded, "He... he... sacrificed himself to save me, and now... he's gone." Aleena wiped her wet eyes on the backs of her hands as their father laid a comforting hand on her arm.

"I know how the sting of a great love lost feels, as does your father," the king said understandingly.

Emrys looked to his daughter and cupped her face in his hands, and whispered. "Time heals all wounds. Just give it time."

Aaric looked at Emrys and realized just how hard it must have been losing his wife Llewlynn, Aaric's mother, many years ago. They all sat in silence, their thoughts speaking a connection of wordless emotion as the broiling clouds grew thicker and bolts of bright lightning began to strike the sea not so far away.

King Nerius suddenly shouted across the bay to his daughter. "The sea grows angry, Kalaya, we must leave now!"

"Yes, we must be on our way as well," Emrys stated.

The wind grew stronger and the time lapse between electric bolts and clapping strikes of thunder grew shorter and closer together as the storm closed in on top of them. Aaric watched a boat slowly come around the side of the rock island and curve inwards toward the narrow beach inlet, heading straight for them. He looked closely, but saw no one aboard.

"Banon!" Emrys waved and shouted across the beach at the prince, who now stood alone, longingly watching Kalaya hover weightlessly out in the water by the Mer guards. The prince looked their way and began to half-walk and half-hop across the smooth sand, favoring what looked to be a badly injured leg.

Banon finally stopped in front of their little group, hunched over with his hands on his knees.

"M'lord," Banon puffed, catching his breath. He then stood up straight. "I'm not going with you."

Emrys studied the young prince without a hint of emotion on his face, Aleena holding onto his arm tightly with anticipation as if knowing what Banon would say.

"I will stay and search for my brother," the prince said matter-of-factly as Aleena made a small cry of joy. "Kalaya said she would help me and my father will send assistance before long."

Aaric's father looked at Banon with a straight face. "I imagine that urging you to do otherwise would be a waste of my breath?"

Banon's crystal blue eyes shown like lights in the storm. "Yes, m'lord."

Emrys sighed. "I thought so."

Just then the unmanned boat came to a stop in front of them like magic, casting a long shadow over the sand, its sails rippling loudly in the ferocious wind.

"Once I return to Castlecray I will send out one of my crews to help with the search." Emrys looked at the prince kindly and then bowed. "Fare thee well, Your Highness." Aaric followed suit along with Aleena, who curtsied awkwardly in her sodden skirts, streams of happy tears flowing down her face. "Please take care," she added.

"Fare thee well, my friends," Banon nodded his head to them and then bowed to the sea king. "Your Majesty." The prince hobbled off towards the dark craggy rock mountain, flurries of rain beginning to fall behind him.

Aaric clenched his teeth as sheets of icy rain began to sweep over them in waves as they boarded the strange ghost boat. Once aboard, Aaric and Aleena peered over the bow, and saw a group of brightly colored heads lining the bottom of the boat urging the galley on out of the stormy bay. Aaric chuckled at the thought of riding a boat that was solely powered by mermaids.

The king swam a little ways out into the sparkling water that was flashing between a dark grey and a bright blue-white, mirroring the blazes of fire bolts in the sky. He stopped and floated there, looking directly up at Aaric's father, who was leaning out over the bow.

"I always knew I'd see you again." Nerius's voice was strong but quivering. Aaric sensed a sadness coming from the king and then looked at his father, his eyes also glazed over and wet.

As they exited the cove Aaric heard his father shout out to Nerius, who was almost invisible through the curtains of rain. "May the power of the waves be with you!"

And so King Nerius of the Wavekeepers , of Mer Ocean waved and replied, "And with you my son!"

TOLAN

Tolan blinked. Feathers of sunlight peaked through the thatched roof of heather and rush fluttering with motion. *Where am I?* The small wattle and daub room rocked and swayed as if on a boat, but there were no sounds of water and no salt in the air. As a matter of fact, the air was fragrant with fresh pine and the sounds were not of the ocean, but of the rustling of trees, creaking and groaning in the clean breeze.

Tolan shot straight up (or rather, that is what he intended to do), but pulled slowly to a half-slumped and half-sitting position, leaning on the arm of his uninjured side. Pain shot down his back and straight throught the marrow of his left leg, taking his breath away in electrical shocks. His body shook with fever. Looking down, Tolan realized that he was not wearing his shirt, but had been bandaged in white gauzy linen which was tightly wrapped around his midsection and coming up and around his left shoulder, covering his wound.

Coming to the realization of what had happened he cried out the name of his beloved.

"Aleena!"

He flinched with pain.

"Aleena," he said more softly, feeling his insides turn with not only pain, but heartache.

His head was heavy and his vision a trifle dizzy as he felt a soft long fingered hand rest upon his arm. His gaze drifted to the figure looming over his shoulder and stopped abruptly. The stranger's white eyes, slashed with a dark vertical pupil, studied him thoughtfully.

Tolan jumped in shock. The tall willowy stranger was green like the trees, its lanky long arms touched him gently as if for comfort and its deep colorless eyes, almost tilted like a cat's, shown brightly in the filtered sunlight.

"Who... wh... wh... what are you?" the young prince's voice cracked as he tripped over his own words, anxiety building through his sore body.

The creature stared at him intently but made no effort to verbally communicate.

"Wh... where's Aleena? Wh... wh... where am I?" The lengthy stranger stood straight. Its head almost touching the tall heather ceiling as it brushed strands of, what could only be described as, green grass-like hair from its face. Its chalky eyes glanced away from Tolan as it crossed the circular wooden room to a table made from the stump of a tree, which there upon sat a brown lacquered bowl, laces of steam rising from its contents.

Tolan inched backwards on his itchy pallet; a blanket stuffed with pine needles, and clunked his head on the beamed wall behind him. Tolan watched the creature, who he assumed was a female due to her delicate features and curves draped with sewn together leaves, carefully lift the bowl and gracefully come to the bedside and kneel. Her eyes, as though speaking unspoken words, squinted in a smile and it nodded its green head, urging Tolan to take the bowl.

Not having much of an escape plan, for he sensed that they were high off of the ground, and not wanting to offend his foliate host he took the bowl and nodded back. Tolan considered the hot soupy mixture, which was a clear broth that gave off the aroma, of what was seemingly a lot like chicken broth. His stomach grumbled at the thought of food as he hesitantly brought the mixture to his lips, but was stopped when the creature touched his wrist, suggesting that he wait. The green giant reached in a small leather pouch strapped to her side and brought out a pinch of a powdery substance. Tolan felt a random shock of throbbing pain going down his back and slowly lowered the bowl. The stranger flicked her fingers over the soup, dropping the powder inside.

Whoosh! In a flash of light and smoke, the concoction created a small explosion, making Tolan jerk suddenly, flowery aromatic spices wafted through the air accompanied by a white fog. The prince scrunched up his face, coughed, and waved away the pungeant vapors.

Then his wordless companion pushed the bowl back to his lips, urging him to drink. *What else am I going to do?* he thought. He sipped the strange tangy liquid and felt its hot contents crawl though his insides like soothing warm snakes, making him shiver.

Tolan sensed someone watching him and glanced to the small window overhead to see two pairs of ivory eyes with black slited pupils staring in at him. He tensed and looked to a movement in the doorway, which was hung with straw. Green figures, all draped in foliage, begun to filter into the circular room, one by one, until there were at least half a dozen blank eyes pondering him.

Tolan grabbed the linen blanket at his feet and brought it up to his neck, feeling like a naked freak being watched in a traveling gypsy show. A small creature, 'small' being the figurative word, for it was almost as tall as Tolan, emerged from behind another green skinned figure and came to his side. It reached out and slightly carressed the prince's cheek, in a manner that seemed normal for them, and smiled.

"Th…th…thank you?" Tolan said dubiously.

He wanted to yell at these…things, ask them where he was and where his Aleena was. Tolan couldn't believe that he himself was alive and he had a gut-wreching fear for his future bride's safety. His head shifted back and forth studying his surroundings more closely. And then he saw a bloody arrow leaning against the wall near the door. *That's the arrow that nearly killed me.* Or it would have, had it not been for the massive wave that probably pushed him to shore near this strange place.

"N... n... none of you speak?" The prince opened and closed his right hand in a puppeting motion, mimicking someone talking.

The creatures just stood and stared in silence.

"W... well that's just great." His patience began to wear thin. "If only father could see me now.The stuttering Prince Thunderdyn, Prince of the trees," Tolan made an overexagerated motion with his hand as though he was declaring a royal decree, "stuck high above the ground wi... with giant shrub people." Tolan spoke sarcastically as he hung his head and covered his face with his hands, exhaling a long and hard breath.

"He claims to be a prince," a lazy voice spoke mundanely.

Tolan's head jerked up as he lowered his hands, revealing another strange being, this one a bit different; his grassy hair withered and brown, where the others were lush and green.

"I am the one called Bice." The stranger spoke again.

Startled, Tolan addressed the newcomer. "You can sp... speak?"

"And dance, and sing, and think too." The stranger's voice was slow, as if just awaking from sleep, its syllables long and drawn out.

"Where are we?" Tolan questioned.

White glassy eyes contemplated the young prince. "'Where are we not?' is the question."

Tolan frowned at the riddled answer. "The last thing I remember was being struck by an arrow on the b…boat…and Aleena…and then the w…wave. Have you seen a young woman with curling brown hair and a fair smile?"

"Yaya," Bice gestured to the one who had earlier fed Tolan the broth, "found you washed up alone on the beaches of saltstone." He wove his way through the others to get to Tolan's side. "She had to pry this from your hand." Bice, whom Tolan assumed to be their leader and much older than the rest, brought up a small golden dagger; encrusted with rubies and moonstones.

The prince's eyes went wide and a lump rose into his throat as he reached for the dagger, a present he had given to his love. The stranger swiped his hand away holding the knife just out of Tolan's reach.

"Give it here B…Bice," stretching his arm out for the weapon, Tolan continued, "It belongs to me…to Aleena."

The old one stepped back. "I cannot let you have it back, Prince."

"And why is that, may I ask?"

"It is dangerous."

"I'm P... Prince Thunderdyn, second heir to the Gold Crown. I think I may know a thing or t... two of handling a weapon."

"That is not of which I speak." The old tree creature's white eyes gleamed from within its sage skin as he stepped into a beam of sunlight rushing in through the window. "It is dark and holds dark powers. We will find a suitable place for it."

A sudden gust of wind made the tree house shift in the air. Tolan winced in pain as he grabbed the timbered wall to steady himself. The willowy people just swayed naturally with the motion, seemingly undisturbed.

Tolan became a bit irritated. "I thank you for your h... hospitality, but I must be on my way." He clumsily rose to his knees, bracing himself on the wall. "There will be p... people looking for me. And dark powers or not, I will be taking my dagger as well." He reached his arm out, palm facing up, ready to receive his weapon.

Bice laughed a slow and cumbersome laugh. "No, Prince. You will not be leaving."

Tolan, getting flustered with his situation, spouted out, "*Who* are you? No, better yet, *what* are you?" He gestured to the green creature and its companions. "You surely are not human."

"We are what you see. We live in the trees." The old (and very frustrating) stranger rhymed nonchalantly.

"You cannot hold me hostage. I am royalty, and my father, the king, will be searching for me." The prince got to his feet and wobbled unsteadily.

"It is not safe to leave now. Crag trolls flood the surrounding areas."

"Crag Trolls?!" Tolan said in disbelief, "Like in the bedtime stories?" Tolan remembered being a young boy and curling up by the roaring hearth, Master Brooks telling him and his brother Banon stories of Trolls and hobgoblins, faeries and merpeople. But they were not real. *Or were they?* Tolan mused as he studied the very unreal creatures in front of him.

"Yes, Prince of the trees. Times have turned dark and evil beasts in all shapes and sizes roam the lands. Our magic is waning and our barrier's are breaking down."

Tolan then remembered the rumors. Great beasts accompanied by an army of risen black knights. *Could it be?*

The prince stood up straight, making his decision. "Crag Trolls or no, I am leaving on the morrow. If what you say is true, I will be needed."

Tolan glanced at the one called Yaya, her white eyes looked sad. He shifted his gaze to the elder, who spoke slowly. "Yaya is a seer. She has seen the future. You must remain here with us."

"Will she not speak for herself? Will she not tell me how long I'm to be held captive?" Tolan became angry and his knees were shaking from the fever and injury.

Bice spoke for the seer. "Our kind takes a vow of silence, for nature speaks in and of itself. Only may they speak every seventh day. I am the oldest of their kind, and I speak for all."

Yaya stood in silence, staring at the Prince, her green grassy hair blew with a breeze that whistled through the straw doorway.

The withered old tree man looked at Tolan as he spoke. "A captive you are not. A guest you shall be."

The prince shook his head, wishing he could just get a straight answer. "Can *you* not tell me just how long I must remain? And what will happen if I don't?"

"If you leave, destroyed we will be." The slow moving voice gradually eased out his words. "The stars have fallen and activated has been the prophecy. Yaya says that you must not leave until the balance is aligned. Yaya has seen."

"And when, might I ask, will the balance be aligned?" Tolan was becoming tired of playing word games. He turned his head to Yaya. "What did you see, Seer?"

The older creature continued, "You must stay until the realm is ruled by a brideless king. Yaya has seen."

Tolan flinched. "But that would mean... even so that could be many many years! How am I to believe you? You haven't even told me who you are!"

"The prophecy will come to be. And we are the Oracles that see. For years you must not leave. Yaya has seen."

APPENDIX

MERENIAN COURTS AND HOUSES

THE GOLD CROWN KING
HOUSE THUNDERDYN

KING BEAUMONT THUNDERDYN III, King of Merenia, The Gold Crown.

—his wife, QUEEN WILONA THUNDERDYN, Queen of Merenia.

—their children:

—PRINCE BANON THUNDERDYN, first born son of Beaumont Thunderdyn and heir to the Gold Crown. Seventeen name days old.

—PRINCE TOLAN THUNDERDYN, second born son of Beaumont Thunderdyn. Fournteen name days old.

—King's Court:

—MASTER BROOKS, the King's right-hand man, has overriding responsibility to domestic and royal affairs of House Thunderdyn.

—HIGH JUSTICE NEWTON OAKTREE, Royal Judge and Master of Laws.

—LORD AUROUS GOLDCOIN, Royal Treasurer, Chief of Currency.

—ADMIRAL BRANDON "PATCH" MACDOUGAL, Grand Admiral of the Golden Fleet, Master of ships.

—SIR CAPTAIN LEOF BRAWNMONT, Captain and Knight of the Goldenshields.

—GRAND ELDER WYLIE, Holy man, bethel keeper, scribe, library keeper, Master of the Acolytes.

—ACOLYTES, Dedicate their lives to the service of the light. Men of the cloth.

—The Golden Council:

—HIGH JUSTICE NEWTON OAKTREE, Royal Judge and Master of Laws.

—LORD AUROUS GOLDCOIN, Royal Treasurer, Chief of Currency.

—ADMIRAL BRANDON "PATCH" MACDOUGAL, Grand Admiral of the Golden Fleet, Master of ships.

—GRAND ELDER WYLIE, Holy man, bethel keeper, scribe, library keeper, Master of the Acolytes.

—LORD EMRYS CASTLECRAY of Castlecray Keep.

—LADY AMABEL DIAMOND, richest widow in North Merenia of Goldbridge Castle.

—LORD RONALD NOONEY, Lord of Castle Nooney, Brother to Nimbus Nooney.

—LADY DILANTHA LOVELYN, recent widow to Lord Willis Lovelyn of Northshore Castle.

—LORD OTTO BRUMBLE, A descendant lord of House Brumble who mysteriously reappears a hundred years of after all members were thought to have been completely vanquished in the bloody battle of Songstone River.

—LADY MAEVEEN BIRDHILL, wife to Lord Randolph Birdhill of Songstone.
—LORD NORMAN WILLOUGHBY, a very old Lord of Highcastle.
—LORD MALVIN SNELL, son of Lord Lavoy Snell, who was beheaded for treason against the Gold Crown. The remaining members of House Snell were forced to give up their keep to the Castlecrays and moved into Tumbledown Tower.

HOUSE CASTLECRAY

LORD EMRYS CASTLECRAY, Lord of House.
—his new wife, LADY ODELYN CASTLECRAY of House Goldcoin, mother-by-marriage to Aaric, Aleena, and Quinlan. Daughter of royal treasurer, Lord Aurous Goldcoin.
—his deceased wife, LADY LLEWYLYNN CASTLECRAY, mother of Lord Emrys's children. The late daughter of Captain Gaderian Longship.

—their children:

—LORD AARIC CASTLECRAY, eldest son and heir to Lord Emrys and the late Lady Llewylynn. Sixteen name days old.

—LADY ALEENA CASTLECRAY, eldest daughter to Lord Emrys and the late Lady Llewylynn. Fourteen name days old.

—LADY QUINLAN CASTLECRAY, youngest daughter to Lord Emrys and the late Lady Llewylynn. Ten name days old.

—his council:

—CAPTAIN GADERIAN LONGSHIP, father of the Late Lady Llewylynn, Grandfather to Aaric, Aleena, and Quinlan. Captain of a Merchant Vessel.

—MASTER DUNLEY, overriding responsibility to domestic affairs of household and official business. Well known herbalist and healer.
—NUNNY ANA, assists Master Dunley in matters of house, nursemaid and teller of bed-time stories.
—SIR CAPTAIN BRENTLEY SWORDSBY, knight and captain of the Castlecray garrison and guard.
—PAGE DUNCAN EADMORE, page boy of eight name days old, being fostered at Castlecray for page training until squire training.
—OLGA, Master of kitchens.
—NOAM FINBAR, boy of eleven name days old, works in the Castlecray kitchens.
—JACK PIPER, traveling bard, singer, storyteller, keeper of the past, drinker of whiskey.

THE PEACE PROTECTORS (HUMANS HALF)

—NIMBUS NOONEY, Keeper of the Invisible Island, head of the Merenian District of the Whisper Web.

—CAPTAIN GADERIAN LONGSHIP of South Harbor, captain of a merchant vessel.

—LADY AMABEL DIAMOND, richest widow in North Merenia of Goldbridge Castle.

—LADY DILANTHA LOVELYN, recent widow to Lord Willis Lovelyn of Northshore Castle.

—SIR THEODORE TORNBUCKLE, a washed-up knight from Tornbuckle Castle, has a gold tooth.

—LADY MAEVEEN BIRDHILL, wife to Lord Randolph Birdhill of Castlebridge.

—LORD NORMAN WILLOUGHBY, a very old Lord of Highcastle.

—SIR WINCHELL TALLHART, retired knight and tourney champion from Songstone Castle.

—BARDOLPH AND BETHA BELECOAT, successful wine merchants from Belecoat Keep in Knos.

MER OCEAN KITHS AND OTHER SALTBLOODS

THE CORAL CROWN KING
WAVEKEEPERS OF TIDEBREAK TOWER

KING NERIUS, King of Mer Ocean, The Coral Crown, first born son of Pearl of the Wavekeepers, of Tidebreak Tower.

—his mother: MOTHER PEARL of the Wavekeepers, Coral Crown Regent, Daughter of Thallasa, Mother of Nerius. The oldest living Merperson.

—his brother, ORMON, second born son of Pearl of the Wavekeepers, Brother to Nerius.

—his children:

—KALAYA, heiress to The Coral Crown, firstborn Daughter of Nerius. Blood Twin to Kai, son of Nerius.

—KAI, First born Son of Nerius. Blood Twin to Kalaya, daughter of Nerius.

—merguard

CAPTAIN CADE, Captain of the Merguard of Mer Ocean. Protects Kalaya, heiress to the Coral Crown.

THE SHADOWS OF SHADOW ROCK

ENCHANTRESS SILVANA, Sea witch and enchantress. Sovereign of the Shadows of Shadow Rock. Separate entity and exempt of rule from the Mer Kingdom and King Nerius. Only takes orders from the faceless Lord of Shadows.

—her councelor, GIBSON.

—her minions, THE SHADOWS, or the TATTOOED ONES. Merpeople of all kiths who are orphaned or for whatever reason, leave the kingdom.

THE SHAPESHIFTERS OF SHADOW ROCK

AMIAS, one of the most powerful shapeshifters, lover to Silvana, harpooned and killed by fishermen.

—his predecessor, LAR of The Shapeshifters who took Amias's seat in the Peace Protectors after his death.

THE ZEBRATA (TINKERS)

—MOSELLE, leader of the Zebrata, works with the Whisper Web.

ACKNOWLEDGEMENTS

The author's grateful thanks to:

First and foremost, my partner in crime, Ryan Phillips, who has listened to me ramble on and on about characters, plot spins, grammar, and all other things book-related for countless upon countless hours. And also for having a brilliantly twisted mind full of suggestions, making me say, "Really? Wow! I would have never thought of that!" You have been so supportive; I couldn't have done any of this without you. I love you forever.

My dad, Frank Felciano, for diligently reading every chapter as I wrote them, and always coming back for the next—and who will always be my hero.

My daughter Abigail who says, "Women work too. I wanna' be like my mommy when I grow up and stare at my computer."

My son Brandon, who is constantly coming up with new ways to crack me up and always leaving a trail of dirt and rocks behind.

All of my wonderful family and friends who, with their praise and support (and proofreading), kept me going when I thought I couldn't.

Christy, may you rest in peace and paint the clouds of heaven in beautiful colors.

And lastly to my mother, who not only told me I can do whatever my heart desires, but helped mold me into the person I am, a little excessive, but always a dreamer.

Tome 2 of

MER

Coming December 2013

Made in the USA
San Bernardino, CA
24 January 2013